Look what people are saying about the Lady Priscilla Flanders Mysteries . . .

"Jo Ann Ferguson leads readers on a wild adventure of murder and mystery, and while the only hint at romance comes in the very last pages, readers can't help but fall in love with the characters."
—*Romantic Times of* A Rather Necessary End

"With this book, she proves that she can plot a mystery novel with enough twists and turns to capture and retain the mystery novel reader's interest. And for the romance novel reader, the relationship between Neville and Priscilla is beginning to simmer nicely."
—*Rakehell.com of* Grave Intentions

"Ferguson keeps the delightful duo's antics as fresh and invigorating as ever. Clever use of secondary characters helps carry the tale forward while keeping the blossoming love between the main characters a lightly trod path of sweet desire."
—*Romantic Times Top Pick 4 ½ stars on* The Greatest Possible Mischief

"Fast-paced and full of twists and turns, Digging Up Trouble will keep readers until the very end. Jo Ann Ferguson is a storyteller full of surprises!"
—*Affaire de Coeur*

". . . a pleasurable read as Priscilla makes the search for her friend's killer a priority. Hopefully, there will be another book in this series soon."
—*Romantic Times of* The Wedding Caper

"The adventure that begins is one of sheer mystery and fun, as the highwaymen abduct Priscilla in order to force Neville to come back into the fold and help them figure out who is killing the members of the Order."
—*Romantic Times 4 Stars of* Gentleman's Master

Lady Priscilla Flanders Mysteries

Gentleman's Master

Fool's Paradise

Short Regency Fiction
Lord of Misrule
(A Regency Yuletide Collection 1)

Yule Be Mine
(One Winter's Night: A Regency Yuletide Collection 2)

Fool's Paradise

by

Jo Ann Ferguson

IMAJINN

ImaJinn Books

This is a work of fiction. Names, characters, places and incidents are either the products of the author's imagination or are used fictitiously. Any resemblance to actual persons (living or dead), events or locations is entirely coincidental.

ImaJinn Books
PO BOX 300921
Memphis, TN 38130
Print ISBN: 978-1-61194-584-3

ImaJinn Books is an Imprint of BelleBooks, Inc.

ImaJinn Books was founded by Linda Kichline.

We at ImaJinn Books enjoy hearing from readers. Visit our websites
ImaJinnBooks.com
BelleBooks.com
BellBridgeBooks.com

10 9 8 7 6 5 4 3 2 1

Cover design: Debra Dixon
Interior design: Hank Smith
Photo/Art credits:
Landscape (manipulated) © Kevin Eaves | Dreamstime.com
Woman (manipulated) © HotDamn Stock Designs
Fountain wall (manipulated) ©GueSphere | Dreamstime.com

:Lpft:01:

Dedication

For Echo

Who keeps me looking good and loves
Aunt Cordelia as much as I do

Chapter One

AS SHE WALKED along the sun-splashed shore road on a warm spring afternoon, Lady Priscilla Flanders Hathaway had no idea she was being stalked. Her usually observant mind was focused on the errands she had to complete before she returned to her home on the cliffs overlooking the sea. She paid no attention to the birds singing in the hedgerows or the cat slinking along the ground in pursuit of them. Lost in her thoughts, she never guessed she was being as steadily hunted.

And why should she? The seaside village of Stonehall-on-Sea had been quiet after the disturbing deeds of more than three years ago. Since that fateful evening when she had discovered a dead man in her garden, her life had changed. In most ways for the better.

Priscilla was pleased at how her children had welcomed her husband, Neville Hathaway, who had recently been raised to a baronage, into their lives. Perhaps it was no surprise because he had known them since birth. More than a few people were shocked that a parson's widow had married a man with a less than pristine reputation, but those same people had been horrified when she, as an earl's daughter, had previously married a man whose only title was vicar.

Foremost among those disapproving was her aunt, who would be arriving on the morrow. Nothing stayed tranquil when Aunt Cordelia called. The terse note that had preceded her informed Priscilla that her aunt intended to air her opinions about Pricilla's behavior and that of her children after their recent visit to the country home she shared with her most recent husband. It had mentioned nothing about Neville, which was no surprise because Aunt Cordelia seemed to harbor the hope that if she ignored him enough—or insulted him enough—he would vanish. Priscilla wondered how her aunt could cling to that expectation when Aunt Cordelia was married to one of Neville's best friends, Duncan McAndrews.

As Priscilla chuckled at her thoughts, she imagined someone thinking she had taken a knock in the head. One should not stroll along a country lane laughing to oneself. She could imagine what Aunt Cordelia would make of that.

The truth was that she missed Neville. He had gone up to London several days ago, and she knew he would not be back for at least another fortnight. He had been summoned there by someone so highly placed in the government that Neville had not been able to reveal his name, even to Priscilla. As high as the Prince Regent? Neville had handled difficult matters quietly for him in the past, but he refused to discuss the details of those situations. She suspected the prince's name was the sole one Neville would keep from her.

A glint close to the hedgerow on the path's right side caught her eye. What was that?

"Who's there?" she called, then felt even sillier when she received no reply.

A low grumble came from her right. A grumble or a growl?

Suddenly she was aware of how far she was from the village. Her shrillest scream would not reach even the closest outlying cottage. If she ran . . .

No, she was not going to flee from what might be only her imagination. Not now. Even though she had not yet shared the tidings with anyone but Neville, she was in a delicate condition. It was a most unexpected situation for a woman who had recently announced the betrothal of her older daughter. The children would be as thrilled as Neville was, but she had no interest in having everyone keep her from doing the slightest thing simply because she would have a baby in five months. She had worked side-by-side with her late husband, Lazarus, during her previous three pregnancies, and she saw no reason not to keep to her regular schedule now.

As regular as it could be with Daphne asking her endless questions about various minutiae for the upcoming November wedding. Daphne wished it to be perfect, even after Priscilla had warned her no event could be without small mistakes. Daphne refused to listen. She thought . . .

The leaves in the hedgerows rustled. Was something trying to thrust its way through the thick tangle? The growl came again.

Closer.

Priscilla's steps quickened. Her heart thudded. It faltered when she stared at the break in the hedgerow ten feet in front of her. Mr. Atkins drove his sheep from field to field through that narrow gate. The beast following her could come through there as well. But what could it be? No great predators prowled the southern coast of England, though occasionally a beast escaped from a traveling show and killed farm animals until it could be trapped or slain.

She searched her mind. Had she heard of a circus nearby? Surely if a beast had gotten out, word of it would have spread.

She was letting her imagination get the better of her.

"Silly," she said under her breath. A terse laugh battered at her lips.

Something leaped at the hedgerow to her left, rattling it wildly.

She grasped her skirt, raising it so she could walk faster. Not quite a run. She needed to save a burst of speed for when she reached the gap in the hedgerow. Her breath was loud in her ears, echoing beneath her simple straw bonnet.

She drew in a deep breath and held it as she neared the gate. Something jumped at her from the shadows. She gasped and fled.

Then she heard laughter behind her.

Laughter?

From a fearsome beast?

Slowing, she steadied her breathing. More laughter rang along the lane. Familiar laughter.

Priscilla turned and saw her husband and young son leaning against each other, weakened by guffaws. She shook her head as she walked back to them. Even though she was pleased to see Neville standing beside her son, she was going to let him know she was not amused by his behavior. But first, she wanted to know when he had arrived from London and why he had returned so soon.

"Neville, you are going to prove my aunt right," she said, scanning his face and seeing the tension he was trying to hide behind a smile. "You *are* a bad influence on Isaac."

He grinned at her, and her heart began to pound anew. Not with fear, but with the resounding love she had never expected to find with her late husband's friend. With his dark hair and sparkling eyes, Neville Hathaway was the most dashing man she had ever met. As well as the most vexing. *On dits* whispered he had lived a criminal life before his family's tarnished title had come to him, but she knew him as the man who cared deeply for her and her family, a man loyal to his friends and dangerous to his enemies, a man who was not ashamed of his past as he shared his present and his future with her.

If only he could put aside his pleasure with such pranks . . .

"Quite to the contrary," Neville said in his warm, deep voice that never failed to send a pulse of joy careening through her. "This time, young Isaac was the bad influence on me." He put his hand on her twelve-year-old son's shoulder. "It was his idea."

"I see, and while it may have been his idea . . ." Priscilla tried to don a fearsome frown when she looked at her youngest, but failed when she saw the bright twinkle in his eyes. Every day, she could see more of his father's features on his young face. His hair had darkened over the winter, but with summer, it would lighten again to the golden-brown it had been when he was an infant. "No matter whose idea it was, Neville, it is clear you heartily embraced it."

"I do believe you have said, more than once, that it is important to listen to the children."

"And heed them?" She began to smile then froze when she heard a strange, sharp sound.

"Mama, look!" cried Isaac as he tugged on a rope she had not taken note of before.

A lanky puppy, yipping wildly, exploded from behind him. Only Neville grasping her around the waist and gently lifting her out of the pup's reach saved her gown from large, muddy paw prints. For a moment, she thought the whole creature was mud-colored. Russet patches appeared along its matted fur.

"This is Bay-o the wolf," Isaac announced, his cheeks barely able to contain his smile.

"Beowulf," Neville corrected with an indulgent smile.

"What is a Beowulf?" Priscilla asked, sidestepping again to avoid the pup's muddy coat.

Neville chuckled. "Beowulf is a who. The hero of a great epic poem from a few centuries before the Conquest. Parts of it were translated a few years ago from an ancient manuscript. One night, when I was having dinner with a Scottish poet named Walter Scott, he told me about Beowulf between fish and dessert."

"Beowulf fights a troll, Mama!" Isaac bounced from one foot to the other.

"Very brave," she said.

"Like my new dog."

"*Your* new dog?" She looked from him to Neville who had the decency to wear a sheepish expression. "You do know being near dogs makes your great-aunt sneeze."

"He can stay in the garden when Aunt Cordelia visits."

"Or at least what will be left of my garden after he digs it up."

"Mama, Beowulf needs us. He has no other home."

Before she could answer, Neville said, "Isaac, take Beowulf home and await us in the garden. Your mother and I need to speak of this matter. We will let you know our decision."

"You will let me keep him, won't you, Mama?" Isaac clearly wanted to be reassured before he obeyed.

"Do as Neville asks, please."

Isaac nodded and gave a tug on the rope. The boy and the dog went along the road, each one trying to pull the other.

As soon as her son was out of earshot, Priscilla asked, "Neville, how could you agree to let him have a dog without consulting with me?"

"Atkins caught the pup chasing his sheep and was ready to dispatch him when we chanced upon them. Young Isaac, ever the champion of justice, was determined the pup be given a lesser punishment than death when no damage had been done to the herd. Atkins condemned the pup to a life sentence with Isaac as his warden." He took her hands between his. "A task your son accepted, exactly as his mother would have wished."

"That is true." She could not help being proud of her son. "But really, Neville . . . a dog?"

He laughed and drew her closer. "You have taken one cur into your home and heart and tamed him, Pris."

"If you refer to yourself, then you speak in error. I daresay the day you are tamed, Neville, is the day the sun sets and does not rise again."

"Ah, Pris, you give no quarter when it comes to the sport of words."

"Would you wish me to?"

He released her hands and put a finger beneath her chin. "No." He kissed her right cheek, and she put her hand against the buttons on his embroidered waistcoat. "Never." His lips brushed her left cheek. Her other hand settled on his shoulder. "I would not change you an iota, Pris." His mouth found hers.

No matter how many times she enjoyed her husband's kisses, she relished each one as if it were the first. When he offered his arm, she slipped her own within its crook and continued with him toward the village.

"How are you feeling today, Pris?" he asked.

"Fine." She laughed. "Though you might have considered my state before you and Isaac tried to frighten me half to death."

His smile vanished. "Pris, forgive me! I never imagined we would frighten you. Are you certain we did you and the baby no harm?"

"I am certain." She slapped him playfully on the arm. "Stop fretting like a hen with a single chick, Neville."

"I will, but you must own that I am about to become a rooster with a house filled with chicks." He leaned his head against hers. "I think Isaac is ready to give up his place as baby of the family."

"Why do you say that?"

"He was asking some mature questions. It seems there is a young lady in the village who has caught his eye."

Priscilla rolled her own. "Heaven above save us! It has been hectic enough with Daphne and now Leah suffering calf-love for boy after boy."

"Are you sure you want to go through this again?"

"Very sure, if for no other reason than to see you go through it for the first time."

He laughed and tweaked the straw rim of her bonnet. "You can be a cruel woman, Priscilla Hathaway."

"And you are a mysterious man, Neville Hathaway. I did not expect you home so soon."

"Need I wait here while you rush to warn a lover to flee?"

She slapped his arm. "Be serious, Neville."

"I am." He shook his head. "No, I am not. If I discovered some bounder trying to woo you, I would not give him a chance to escape."

"You are worrying needlessly."

"Better me than you. That would not be good for our baby."

She paused in the middle of the lane. "I agree, so tell me what has you really worried."

All humor fell from his face. "Not here, Pris. When we are at the house and alone. I promised that I would keep this information to myself, save that I can share it with you. The one I promised comprehended, albeit reluctantly, that my best solutions always come when we work together."

Before she could reply, the day was shattered by a distant scream. It rose, then quickly vanished. Sharp words, distorted by the breeze, rushed toward them.

"Where is that shouting coming from?" Neville asked.

"Need you ask?" She took a deep breath and stepped away from him. "After all, it was *your* idea to let Isaac have a dog." She hurried toward her home, hoping the damage would be minimal so that nothing would postpone her hearing what Neville had to tell her.

THE HOUSEHOLD was in a complete uproar when Priscilla entered the stone house, and she knew she would need to be very patient while she waited for an opportunity for her and Neville to be alone. The fact that one of the footmen was not at the door, ready to open it, warned her the situation might be more out of hand than she had despaired.

From the direction of the kitchen came shouts and the crash of pots and pans and bowls. Mrs. Dunham, the cook, shouted, "Catch 'im!"

Priscilla rushed into the room. Mud was splattered on usually pristine walls and the hearth. Around the table in the main room, Isaac chased the pup. Beowulf—what an absurd name!—clearly believed it was a game because he barked and nipped at anyone who tried to halt him.

Wading into the chaos, Neville grasped both the puppy and Isaac by their napes. He easily lifted the pup off the floor as he brought the boy to a quick stop.

Priscilla turned to calm Mrs. Dunham and the kitchen maids, then paused as Neville asked, "What do you want me to do with these two troublesome pups?"

"Take them out to the garden," she replied.

"But Mama, he is my responsibility," Isaac argued. "That is what Mr. Atkins said."

"And Mr. Atkins is right. Take the puppy outside and make sure he does not run away."

He gazed up at her with pleading eyes she always found difficult to resist.

"I can keep him, can't I?"

"Isaac." She did not need to add another word. They would not have this discussion in the kitchen where he and the pup had added to Mrs. Dunham's work.

"Yes, Mama." He hung his head as Neville released him. Bending, he scooped the filthy puppy up into his arms. His coat received another layer of mud as the puppy squirmed against him and tried to lick his face. "Let's go, Beowulf."

"Beowulf?" repeated the cook as Neville moved to open the back door. "What's a Beowulf?"

Priscilla started to explain, but her words were drowned by a drawn-out, "Nooooooooooo!"

Neville arched a brow, and Priscilla hurried from the kitchen. No one other than her oldest could make such a sound. Because the breeze had been coming off the sea, distorting the sound, she had failed to identify the voice before. She returned to the entry hall where her older daughter was storming away from the direction of the informal sitting room.

"Daphne Flanders," she chided in her sternest voice, "unless you are signaling the end of the world, stop that caterwauling."

"Mama! Thank heavens you are here." Daphne flung her arms around her mother. "I am *so* glad to see you."

Putting her hands on her daughter's shoulders and stepping back, Priscilla was glad to see her daughter showed no physical signs of distress that would provoke such a cacophony. With her blond hair swept up in flattering curls and her cheeks bright with color, she resembled Priscilla, though she had inherited her father's stubborn chin.

"Maybe you can instill some good sense into him, Mama," her daughter continued, her voice quivering with strong passion.

"Him?" Priscilla asked, though she knew the answer.

Seeing her younger daughter Leah peeking around the stairs with a wide grin, Priscilla could not help wondering what was happening. She hoped it would not be as disruptive as the addition of a puppy to the household, but somehow already knew that wish was doomed.

"Burke is in the sitting room, Mama!" Daphne cried, flinging out her hands in a wild gesture. "He is spouting nonsense, and he will not heed a word I say. Do you think he will listen to you?"

"About what?"

"Where we have our wedding. I don't know why we are discussing it. *I* am the bride. The wedding should be held where *I* want it, and I want to have it at Papa's church. But will he listen? No! He says it must be—"

"Yes, I know. I know. We have gone through this before. I thought it was settled."

"So did I!" Daphne glowered in the direction of the sitting room. "But no! Now he is saying it cannot be here because his mother is insisting it be held at their family's estate."

Priscilla sighed inwardly. Burke, Lord Witherspoon, adored her daughter, and the affection was wholly returned. When the young marquess asked Daphne to be his bride, her daughter had been beside herself with joy. Then the wedding preparations began. Priscilla wanted her daughter to have the wedding she had dreamed of, but her sympathy was utterly with Burke, caught between his stubborn betrothed and his equally obstinate mother, the widowed Lady Witherspoon. The wedding venue had not been the only bone of contention, but it was the most insolvable one. The soon-to-be dowager marchioness had not been reticent with her opinion that it was a mistake for her son to marry a girl too young and inexperienced in the ways of the *ton*, a girl who had given her heart irrevocably to the first man who touched it.

No, Priscilla reminded herself with a silent laugh. *Lord Witherspoon had been the second, for Daphne first had decided she would wed Neville before I did.* What would Burke's mother think if Priscilla told her of that difficult time?

Priscilla could not ease the situation with silly thoughts. "This is a matter you and Burke must resolve."

"But he will not listen to me, Mama!"

"By listening, do you mean he will not agree with you?"

Daphne did not answer as she lowered her gaze.

"She means that exactly," said Burke from the sitting room doorway. He was a well-favored young man whose tawny curls could not soften his strong jaw. His wide shoulders seemed to dwarf Daphne, but there was a gentleness in him Priscilla admired. The young man reminded her of her first husband . . . and Neville. Not that she would ever say that because Neville would find it more an insult than a compliment.

Almost as an afterthought, Burke added, "Good day, Lady Hathaway."

"I thought you were going to address me as Priscilla."

"As you wish." He bowed his head toward her with a smile, but his lips straightened into a frown when he focused on Daphne. "See? It is not difficult to compromise."

"Don't be churlish!" Daphne snapped back. "*You* are the one refusing to compromise."

"Every marquess in our family has been married at the church on the estate. I am asking that we comply with a longstanding tradition."

"And doing so will make your mother happy."

"Certainly."

With a wordless cry, Daphne pushed past him to the stairs. She paused with her foot set on the lowest one. "Is making your mother happy more important than having some part of my father there for our wedding?"

"Daphne, please listen. If—"

"*That*, Lord Witherspoon, is the wrong answer!" She gathered her skirt in her trembling fingers and ran up the stairs. Moments later, the sound of a door slamming reverberated through the house.

Priscilla said nothing as emotions flashed across Burke's face. Anger, frustration, dismay, even fear he was hurting the one he loved.

Putting a consoling hand on his arm, she said, "Don't take her words to heart. Once she has a chance to think more clearly, I am sure you two can work something out that will please both of you."

"If only it were just the two of us." His eyes widened. "Oh, I should not have said that."

"Then I shall forget I heard it. Burke, every bride is frantic about her wedding."

"You were not."

Priscilla smiled. "If you are referring to my second wedding, no, I was not, but I daresay while planning my first, I was as much of an air-dreamer as Daphne. I drove everyone around me quite out of their minds."

"Are you suggesting Witherspoon reconsider and become Daphne's *second* husband?" asked Neville as he stepped into the entry hall. "That seems a high price to pay simply to avoid a bit of distress."

"A bit?" Burke's tone lightened at Neville's teasing, and Priscilla wondered if the young marquess would feel more comfortable discussing the plans for the wedding with another man.

The very idea of the two very masculine men sitting with samples of fabric and menus and deciding on which flowers to use and where to seat each guest was ridiculous. She laughed. They looked at her, and she shook her head.

"A bizarre thought. Nothing more," she explained.

"I hate to ask," Burke said, glancing up the stairs, "but do you think you could speak with her? Holding the wedding in the family church is important to my mother. I thought Daphne would understand and want to make me happy."

"She does," Priscilla said. "Making you happy makes her happy, but she has come to believe, for some reason, that the only way her father can be a part of the wedding is if it is held in the church here where he was vicar for most of her life."

Neville cleared his throat and asked, "Could it be, Witherspoon, your mother does not want to remind the *ton* you are marrying the daughter of a vicar?"

Color washed from Burke's face. "No . . . I don't know. I never considered it from that angle. Mother was less resistant to me proposing to Daphne after you were made a baron, Hathaway."

"Who would have guessed *I* would become the respectable one?" Neville chuckled.

Another shout rang through the house. Beowulf careened into the entry hall, eluding both Burke and Neville who tried to grab him and failed. In his wake followed Isaac and Leah, her hair ribbons askew and the hem of her dress green with grass stains.

"Sorry, Mama!" yelled Isaac as he jumped in front of the excited puppy to keep him from heading toward the kitchen.

"I have him!" Leah leaped forward to throw her arms around the puppy but grasped nothing but air. "No, I don't."

"Beowulf," Priscilla said in the same calm but stern tone she used with her mischievous children.

The puppy halted and looked up at her. His tail wagged like the baton of an insane orchestra conductor. Panting, he loped over to her.

"Here please," she said, pointing to the floor by her feet.

No one spoke as the puppy collapsed in front of her, his nose on his paws and his tongue lolling out one side of his mouth.

Squatting down, she ran her fingers lightly along the top of his head, one of the few spots not covered with drying mud. His fur was as smooth as smuggled French silk. She murmured to the puppy, who slowly closed his eyes, showing he was exhausted. She wondered when he last had a home with someone to make sure he was fed.

"Good boy," she whispered.

She watched as he fell asleep. Poor little beast! The puppy began to snore, a sound almost as loud as his barking.

Priscilla smiled as she stood. "Another good reason for him to sleep out in the back garden. Why don't we let him rest, then—?"

The door opened, and Beowulf was instantly on his feet, making a sound halfway between a bark and a howl. He raced toward the door and the two people entering.

"Priscilla, why is nobody at your door to greet your guests?" Cordelia Emberley Smith Gray Dexter McAndrews looked down her nose at her niece. The disdainful expression did not annoy Priscilla because she had seen it too many times before. Priscilla could be crowned the queen of England, and her aunt would still find fault with her.

Oh, bother! The dog's arrival was nothing compared to the up-heaval Aunt Cordelia's early arrival would create.

Priscilla shouted a warning before the pup could put his oversized feet on Aunt Cordelia who was dressed, as always, in the very pink of fashion. Neville grabbed the pup, holding him back. The pup escaped again, and Burke leaped forward to grasp it by the rear legs. He fell to the floor as he locked the pup between his knees. Isaac ran to help while Leah shouted for them to be careful and not hurt Beowulf.

Looking past them to her aunt's shock, Priscilla shrugged. What could she say? The situation was self-explanatory.

"It would appear, dearest, your niece has her hands full with other matters." Aunt Cordelia's newest husband, Duncan, stepped into the already crowded entry hall. He gave Priscilla a warm smile. "I trust you and Neville have the situation under control."

Edging around the wrestling match as Neville, Burke, and Isaac tried to keep the pup from escaping, Priscilla said, "We did not expect you until tomorrow."

"So I see." Aunt Cordelia sniffed. Her black hair was beautifully styled, without a single silver hair evident. Priscilla had no idea if her aunt did not get gray hairs, but she certainly could give them. In fact, Priscilla was surprised her own hair was not completely gray.

"But we are glad you are here." She gave her aunt a kiss on the cheek, then did the same to Duncan. Looking over her shoulder as Isaac yelled a warning, she stepped aside as the pup rushed up to sniff at their guests before racing away.

Neville came to stand beside her, wiping dried mud from his coat. He held out his hand to Duncan and offered Aunt Cordelia a smile she did not return. Before he could say a single word, the door reopened, knocking Aunt Cordelia toward him. He caught her before she stumbled, then pulled her and Priscilla aside as a pudgy man burst into the house.

Maurice Beamish! What was the miserly baron doing in Stonehall-on-Sea? He disdained the village, preferring his estate to the north of its boundaries or London. The last time he had spoken to her, all he had offered was a sniff of contempt when she asked him to donate to the parish fair.

His face was full beneath his thinning brown hair, and he wore a waistcoat as bright a yellow as the summer sun. It was cut in a style popular more than a decade ago, but the man had a reputation for wearing his clothes until they were threadbare.

Before Priscilla could ask the reason for his unannounced call, the baron seized her hands and dropped to his knees.

His eyes were wide and frenzy filled his words when he cried, "Lady Priscilla, I need your help. You must aid me in saving my daughter's soul, mayhap her very life. Please, Lady Priscilla. I beg you. Help me!"

Chapter Two

NEVILLE HAD NO idea how Priscilla managed it without raising her voice or allowing a whit of distress to slip into her words. In moments, Witherspoon and Isaac had retreated with Beowulf to the back garden to set up a place for the pup to stay until he could be cleaned. Aunt Cordelia and Leah had gone upstairs to Daphne's bedroom where they could console her after her tiff with Witherspoon. Neville, Duncan, and Maurice Beamish were herded into the formal sitting room where Priscilla was soon serving tea as if nothing out of the ordinary had happened.

"Astounding," Duncan murmured as he pulled a silver flask from beneath his coat and poured what Neville guessed was his favorite whisky into his tea. He concealed the flask when Priscilla turned to offer him his choice of the iced cakes. Taking a pink one, he added in the same whisper, "How does she do it?"

Not having an answer because he was in awe of her special talent to persuade people to do as she wished and let them think it was their idea, Neville looked at Beamish who sat on Pris's far side and dabbed at the sweat beading on his forehead. He must be close to Duncan's age but looked much older. Thick jowls gave Beamish a bulldog appearance, as did his small brown eyes.

Neville hoped the others grasped that underestimating Maurice Beamish would be foolish. He was a powerful force in Whitehall. He held no official post, but it was said several of the ministers in the current government danced to his tune. Rumor suggested he had found them in compromising situations. Neville doubted it was anything simple because powerful men often were found in embarrassing circumstances. Everyone would forget their *faux pas* as soon as the next member of the Beau Monde was found where he should not have been. Therefore, Beamish must have some other hold on them.

Keeping his face bland, Neville wondered if Beamish had any idea of the bumble-bath going on up north near the lakes. Impossible! His royal highness had said that Neville was the only one beyond his network of spies and the military commander in that area to be privy to the Regent's concerns about an odd settlement that was being built there by Sir Thomas Hodge St. John.

There were rumors that the baronet was gathering soldiers and training them. To fight whom? And why? No one seemed to have been able to get close enough to the village, which apparently was surrounded by a wall, to answer that. What did that crazy man need with a private army? Neville was eager to leave Stonehall-on-Sea and get north so he could see the situation with his own eyes.

As if Beamish was privy to Neville's thoughts, the heavy-set man said, "I didn't expect to see you here, Hathaway."

"Why not?" he asked, honestly astonished.

"Because Lady Priscilla is a woman of the finest breeding and class. You are—"

"My husband." Pris offered him a plate of sweetmeats and continued to smile, though her eyes sparked at the insult Beamish had almost spoken.

"Your . . . husband?" He stared from her to Neville and back in disbelief, then recalled himself. "I may have heard something about those glad tidings," he continued in a tone that suggested he had thought it was gossip. "You must excuse me. Matters of society don't matter to me."

"What does matter to you, Lord Beamish?" Priscilla asked in the matter-of-fact tone that warned she found Beamish bothersome but would not request him to leave as she clearly wished.

"My daughter. My dearest Bella." He moaned and covered his face with his hands. Shudders rippled along him. The man was distraught.

Or was he?

Neville had seen plenty of overacting players, both on the boards and off. Beamish's entrance had struck him as more than a little melodramatic.

Pris glanced at Neville before asking, "Why do you feel your daughter is in danger?"

Only a groan came from the baron.

Neville held out his hand to Duncan. His friend had the decency to shoot Pris an apologetic grin before pulling out his flask. Taking it, Neville opened the top and poured a generous serving into an empty teacup. He offered it to the moaning man.

"Beamish, this may help," he said.

"Nothing can help."

"If that is so, why did you come to throw yourself on Lady Priscilla's mercy?"

"Neville," chided Pris under her breath.

Maybe Beamish heard her, or maybe he heard only Neville. Either way, he raised his head and seized the cup, splattering whisky on the saucer. Duncan mumbled something about the waste of fine whisky, but Neville ignored him.

Beamish wiped his mouth, ungraciously, with the back of his hand. "Lady Priscilla, I apologize for my outrageous behavior, but you are my final hope. No one else will heed me." His mouth tightened, and Neville guessed the baron was deciding how to repay those who, in his estimation, had failed him in his time of need.

"Tell us what brought you to our door," Pris said in a tone Neville had come to think of as her "parson's wife" voice. It was calm and kind and aimed at convincing people to set aside their emotions long enough to explain what was wrong. It also worked to hide her own opinions of the person. She used it only when she disliked someone.

"My daughter is in trouble," Beamish said, taking another hasty gulp of the whisky.

"Can you be more specific?"

"It began with that cur Sherman."

"Which one?" Neville asked, sitting beside Pris again.

Beamish scowled. "The viscount's heir, Clarence Sherman. He started sniffing around my daughter's skirts last Season, but I kept a close eye on Bella. I have high hopes for her, and I don't wish to have her wed a penniless gamester."

"That is wise," Neville said as he translated the baron's words in his head. Beamish intended to wed his daughter to a fortune.

"It certainly was, but Bella failed to see my wisdom. She spent time with him whenever we chanced to be at the same event. She said she enjoyed talking about northwest England with him."

"Northwest?" It had to be a coincidence. The Prince Regent might be witless around women, but he usually had a clear head when judging men. Everyone knew that trusting Beamish was want-witted because Beamish would quickly trade information for money or power or better yet, both.

"I was astonished, too." He shook his head. "Why would a young woman care about that desolate place? She gets her wayward ways from her mother, which is no surprise, considering how she was raised for the first ten years of her life in the wilds of Scotland. There, they only think of the past instead of the future."

"The past?"

"Those Highlanders still complain about the loss they suffered at Culloden and act as if the plaid is still outlawed. My daughter needed to be retaught the truth after I insisted she come to live with me. I had hoped time in Town would teach her the importance of an established future, but she chose poorly."

"If her heart led her elsewhere," Pris said, "it is sometimes impossible for a young woman not to heed it."

"A woman of any age." Beamish harrumped. Draining his cup, he set it on the tray, but took time to aim a glare at Neville. "That is why it is vital for a father to make sure his daughter does not do anything that might ruin her."

Pris arched her brows at Neville. When Duncan tried to stifle his laugh, Beamish scowled and asked why Duncan was part of the conversation. When Pris reminded him that Duncan was married to her aunt, Beamish acquiesced, albeit reluctantly.

"Do you think they eloped?" Pris asked with the candor that endeared her to Neville.

"It is possible." Clearing his throat, Beamish added, "But their carriage has been found in the fells of Lakeland. At an inn. The Rose and Thistle Inn near Windermere. It had been abandoned."

Neville stood and refilled the baron's glass. "I know something of the area." He did not add that, when the title of baron had been granted to him by the Prince Regent in exchange for Neville's fixing of an embarrassing matter that could not be spoken of in polite company, he also had been given a generous portion of land not far from that northern lake. He suspected that was why his royal highness had contacted him to investigate the odd activities going on there.

"A vast wilderness and lawless place," muttered Beamish.

"Quite to the contrary. It is peaceful for the most part."

"So you say, but my daughter and her companions have vanished."

"Someone could have met them there with another vehicle," Pris said with her cool logic.

Her suggestion seemed to deflate Beamish whose face became a sickly shade of gray that no actor would be able to achieve without cosmetics. Was the man truly so devastated by his daughter's elopement? Maybe Beamish's finances were in worse shape than anyone had guessed.

"I wish that were so," Beamish whispered. "But I have proof Bella has been abducted."

"Proof?" asked Duncan at the same time Neville did.

"This was found." Beamish pulled a crumpled piece of paper from under his coat and held it out.

When Pris took it and smoothed it on her lap, Neville shifted so he could read the few words written on it in block letters.

> *To whomever finds this message,*
>
> *Please let my father, Maurice, Lord Beamish, know as of the writing of this note, I am alive. We have been halted on the road, and I have no idea what may happen next. But I have been told they intend me no harm. As for the others, I have not seen them in more than an hour.*
>
> *I am told my father will be notified of what he must do in order for my release to be arranged.*

It was signed with a scrawl that might have been Miss Beamish's signature. Raising his gaze to Beamish, Neville asked, "This is her handwriting?"

"Yes. Bella never had much interest in penmanship. Nor in other subjects that a young miss should study. Rather she preferred when her classes were about history. That girl can spout off more facts about English history than a Cambridge don."

"What did her abductors demand when they contacted you?"

"That is just it, Hathaway. Nobody has tried to get in touch with me. More than a fortnight has passed since this note was delivered. And Bella ran away to be with that cur more than a month before that."

"She has been missing six weeks?" gasped Pris. "Why haven't you hired a Bow Street Runner?"

"I tried. None of them is willing to travel from London. That is why I was hoping you might help me, my lady. I know you have handled other—shall we say, other unsavory situations?"

Pris held the note out to Beamish as she shook her head. "I am sorry, Lord Beamish. I am not the right person to help you, even if I had the time which I do not with planning my daughter's wedding."

"Your daughter's wedding is more important than my daughter's life? How dare you suggest that, Lady Priscilla!" Beamish jumped to his feet, his hands curling into fists as he aimed a furious stare at Pris. He started to raise his fist in her direction.

Neville stood without saying a word and stepped between Pris and the overwrought fool. Duncan got up, too, but did not move farther. When Beamish saw them, he lowered his fist. He might be willing to intimidate a woman, but he would not stand against one man, let alone two, who could knock him senseless with a single blow.

"I am sorry," Pris said as if they still all sat and sipped tea. Her taut expression warned that Beamish had crossed a line with his question and his actions. Neville suspected only her own excellent manners kept her from ordering Beamish from the house. She might sympathize with the man who was frantic to find his daughter, but she would not knuckle under to a bully. "It is not a matter of which is more important. I simply would not know where to begin, my lord. Perhaps Bow Street could suggest someone closer to Lakeland who might assist you."

"I told you! I have asked everyone I know. Nobody wants to go that distance from London." His eyes narrowed as he refocused on Neville. "You have dirty acres up there, don't you?"

"Yes." He did not want to prolong the conversation. Not only did he know that Beamish was likely to do something else that would make Neville forget *his* manners, but he wanted to talk to Pris about what had been discussed in London. Her insight was always valuable. So he only added, "Lady Priscilla has said she cannot help you at this time. Perhaps you should take this opportunity to find someone who will."

"Who?" Beamish turned from her to him and on to Duncan like a desperate child demanding someone give him his way. "I do not know anyone up there except that Sir Thomas Hodge St. John. I cannot count on him for help because, from what I hear, he is involved in another of his crazy schemes."

Neville exerted all his self-will to hold back his gasp of astonishment. He had not thought Beamish would mention *that* name. What did Beamish know of St. John's activities in Lakeland? "As you said," he drawled, "you know I have part of my estate there at Tarn's Edge, so you know someone other than St. John."

Beamish scowled. "Are you saying that *you* will find my daughter?" He laughed tersely. "Your family's reputation precedes you, Hathaway. None of them has ever done anything unless there is some reward in it for them."

"I never said I would find your daughter, but I can ask some questions about her whereabouts when I visit there next week." He saw Pris's surprise, which she quickly masked. He knew he could trust her not to reveal that, until moments ago, he had had no plans to go north until after Daphne's wedding. "I am a father of daughters now, Beamish, and not knowing if they were alive or dead would drive me quite insane as well."

Duncan made some sound that might have been a squelched laugh, but Beamish either did not catch the barely veiled insult or chose to ignore it.

"I would appreciate that." He took Neville's hand and pumped it vigorously. Releasing it, he reached under his coat and drew out a miniature portrait. He handed it to Neville. "This is an excellent likeness of my darling Bella."

Neville glanced at it and saw the painting had been done by a barely competent artist. The dark-haired woman was distinct only because her long neck gave her an arrogant pose. Or perhaps, the haughtiness might be simply a trait she had inherited from her father.

"It will help you find her," Beamish added.

"Whoa there." Neville gave Pris the portrait. "I did not say I would find her. I said that I would ask about her."

"One and the same. You might want to start with St. John."

"Why?" Any information he could garner on the eccentric baronet might be the very clue he needed to discover the truth, even before he took the long drive north.

"He always spoiled Bella when she was a child. He may have assisted her in her foolish plan to elope." Beamish picked up his cup, drained the last of the whisky from it, and walked toward the door with a jaunty step. Turning, he added, "I will expect a report from you by the end of next week. You can send it to me in Town, where I have vital business." Strong emotions glittered in his eyes. "Very vital."

Neville did not caution the baron not to burn his bridges in front of him. A fool could see that no matter how sweet Beamish believed the vengeance would be against those who had turned from his pleas, he needed to keep open every possible avenue to find his daughter, until she was safe.

He left without another word.

"Do you want to explain that about-face?" asked Pris in a tone that held an undercurrent of exasperation.

"As I told Beamish, now that I am the father of two daughters, I—"

"Balderdash." She looked past him to Duncan. "Don't you agree, Duncan?"

"I agree," his so-called friend said with a grin. "Balderdash of the first order."

"Listen to you!" Neville frowned at them. "You know me. You know I would do anything for a friend."

"True, but Beamish is not," Pris said quietly, "your friend. Not by any definition of the word. He is a despicable miser who cares only for the weight of his pockets. But suddenly you are acting as if you cannot wait to help him. What is going on, Neville?"

"You need to trust me, Pris. Just as you did when I had to go up to London."

Her eyes widened, and again he knew she had understood what he could not say with Duncan listening. His tie-mate would never spill the truth, but Neville had been sworn to secrecy by England's next king. Only now did he wonder how many others might be privy to what was happening in Lakeland. Others that even the Prince Regent was unaware of.

But Neville needed to find out . . . fast.

Chapter Three

PRISCILLA SET THE last of the used dishes on the tea tray, replaying the bizarre conversation through her mind. No matter how often she went over it, she could not guess why Neville had changed his mind about helping Lord Beamish. She did believe he understood a father's anguish at having a child missing, but Neville could have found some-one else to assist Lord Beamish. She doubted there was a corner of England or beyond where he did not have a crony he had worked with in the past.

So what was he thinking? She had assumed he would tell her in the wake of Lord Beamish's departure, but he had agreed to go with Duncan to see his friend's newest team of carriage horses. They had left ten minutes ago, and she had no intention of waiting in the parlor any longer. Her house was filled to overflowing with guests, and she must make sure that each of them had a comfortable bed for the night.

She looked up as Neville came back into the sitting room.

Alone.

When he closed the door behind him, she sat again. She waited for him to do the same, but he began to pace back and forth across the room. She had learned this was his way of sorting through information. The questions roiling through her refused to wait for him to reach a conclusion.

"Tell me," she said.

"I was asked by an important friend to discover what St. John is do-ing at the village he apparently is building in Lakeland."

"Why?"

"St. John is insane."

"That is a strong accusation, Neville."

He did not slow his pacing. "And a true one. I have met him at least two or three times, though unlike Beamish, who once counted him as a friend, I never have had a conversation with him. He is like a hummingbird hawk-moth, flitting here and there and never settling. He believes in the most peculiar things."

"Such as?"

"Breeding a herd of sheep with wool that peels off with a single tug."

She laughed. "I assume he didn't succeed."

"No, nor did he find a way to build a bridge from Dover to Calais."

"How convenient that would be for Napoleon to march his troops across!"

"I doubt he considered that." He chuckled then grew serious again. "St. John dreams the impossible without having any idea of how to make it possible. If ideas were gold, he would be the richest man on earth. As it is, he should be a scholar stashed away in Oxford where he would bother no one but his students with his half-baked ideas. Instead, he holds an ancient title and makes ducks and drakes of his money by tossing it away trying to change the world."

"Or a small piece of it."

Again he nodded, this time rubbing his chin with his thumb and fingers. His gaze turned inward as he said, "You have, as always, cut to the quick of the matter, Pris. He may have finally realized he cannot change the whole world, so he has decided to make a small portion of it into his image of perfection."

"But why is your *friend* concerned about an eccentric man? Or specifically this eccentric one because Sir Thomas is not the only quiz in England."

He paused and smiled. "Listen to you, Pris. Throwing around London slang with such ease."

"Quiz does mean eccentric, right?"

"Quite right."

"Then please answer my question. Why is your *friend* curious about Sir Thomas?"

Sitting next to her, he folded her hands in his. He leaned his forehead against hers so he could speak without his voice reaching the door and the hallway beyond it. He outlined his contact's anxiety about the bizarre project St. John had created. She gasped when he mentioned how St. John seemed to be gathering an army, which he was training out of view of the rest of the world. Why would anyone build a towering wall if they did not want to keep everyone from discovering what they were doing?

"We cannot be sure if his army will support England or turn against it." Neville's voice grew grimmer with every word. "Without knowing the army's size and its capabilities, it is impossible to guess at what his intentions might be. That is why I was asked to investigate. Dismissing the old widgeon as harmless might be a huge mistake for a country at war with both France and the Americans."

"That makes good sense."

"And you think you can get closer to the community than anyone else has been able to?"

His smile was feral. "After all this time, you need to ask that question, Pris?"

"Not really, but I am curious what your plan is."

"That detail is one I have not hammered out quite yet, but I will have resources available up north."

As she listened, she realized the person who had given him the task could be the Prime Minister or even a member of the royal family. The inherent respect in his voice, along with the information he shared, could have been gathered only on the orders of someone with that much authority.

She stood and went to look out the window at where the sunlight was glittering on the sea. "Now I see that it was the mention of Sir Thomas's name that convinced you to help Lord Beamish."

He shook his head. "There is no help for that skinflint, but, yes, it was the baronet's name that compelled me to use Beamish as an excuse to go north to do what I promised I would. As far as Miss Beamish, I am sure she has done as she planned—escaped his pinch-penny ways—and is now happily wed." His brows lowered. "Beamish seems to think St. John might have some insight into where she is."

"So why didn't he ask the baronet himself, if they once were friendly enough that Sir Thomas spoiled Miss Beamish?"

"A very good question, Pris. I wish I could give you as good an answer."

"I am missing something important."

"Me, too."

She smiled at him, always amused when he acted with a touch of humility. It was a sure sign that he was devising, examining, and tossing aside theories as he searched for the one that solved the puzzle.

Becoming serious again, she said, "My guess is that Miss Beamish continued on to Scotland where she married and took her new husband to live with her mother's family."

"A logical conclusion."

"And a happy ever after one." She sighed. "But we cannot assume that Lord Beamish's daughter is not at Sir Thomas's settlement."

"True." He gave her a rakish grin. "After all, how can you have the community without a future population?"

Her eyes widened. "Neville! What you are suggesting . . . !" She could not bring herself to speak the words burning on her tongue.

"He *was* interested in breeding sheep."

"Do not be crude. No one would confuse sheep and human beings."

"You have not met St. John. He is also deeply interested in gambling, especially when he is cup-shot. I have heard him say more than once that any man who is unwilling to risk everything is a fool."

"Keeping a baron's daughter and her servants hidden is an incredible risk."

"My thoughts exactly." He clasped his hands behind his back as he faced her. "However, since I agreed to ask questions about Beamish's daughter, I need to consider every possibility."

"Including the fact that she might be at the new settlement."

"And that what St. John is doing may very well endanger anyone who is too curious."

She stepped around the table and put her hand on his arm. She was not surprised to discover his muscles taut with tension. Her dear husband never did anything by halves. "Neville, you can protest all you want that you are going to do nothing more than ask questions about Miss Beamish, but I know you will not be satisfied until you are assured that she is safe."

He gave her a warm smile. "You would never turn a deaf ear to such a need. That I think him disagreeably high in the instep does not bear on the decision to help him. I could think only of how I would feel if it was Daphne or Leah who was missing."

"First of all, my daughters are not silly."

"I sometimes wonder when Leah calls me 'Papa Neville.'"

"She is teasing, and you love it."

"I do, but I will never admit it to her. Who knows what she would come up with next? Your daughters are too smart."

"Do not be certain. If Burke asked Daphne to elope, I daresay she would agree." She chuckled. "Or, knowing my daughter, it is more likely that the whole of it would be her idea."

"She does have her mother's wit as well as her beauty."

"Save your nothing-sayings, Neville."

He slipped an arm around her shoulders. "Why? Then you would not flush prettily when I compliment you."

She longed to spend the rest of the day in his arms, but that could not be. "I assume the place to start looking for Miss Beamish is where the carriage was found with nothing but the note inside."

"Not far from Windermere." He gave her a smile. "I was wondering if you wanted to announce our happy tidings tonight? It might make it easier when you have your aunt under your roof for who knows how long."

"Neville, are you being intentionally obtuse? What are you talking about?"

His eyes widened, and she realized frustration had tainted her voice. "I thought I was offering a suggestion to make your life simpler while I am gone. If I leave in the morning, at top speed, I can get to Windermere in three to four days."

"I will not be able to travel at top speed. Not now."

"Pris, you cannot be thinking of accompanying me."

Folding her arms, she gave him the same frown she had when Isaac mentioned he was adopting the puppy. "You cannot be thinking of going alone."

"No, I planned to ask Duncan to go with me."

"You two are welcome to take your leave in the morning, but I am going with you."

"No."

She was as shocked as if he had told her the English Channel was filled with treacle. Neville was never autocratic with her.

Her astonishment must have been visible because he stroked her arms gently. "Pris, how effective do you think I shall be in chasing down the rumors of St. John's army if I have to worry about you every minute? Didn't you tell Daphne compromise was a good thing?"

"Actually Burke did. It is a lesson you should learn, too."

He shook his head as he took her hand and drew her closer to him. "I know there are times to compromise and times to stand one's ground. If you think I am going to allow you to travel in your delicate condition—"

"Allow me?" She tugged away from him.

"Bad choice of words, but you must agree my plan to go alone is for your own good and for our child's."

"I am as healthy as a horse, and it is well-proven that we work best as a team."

He drew in a deep breath and released it slowly. "You are not going to give an inch on this, are you?"

"No."

"I could have you imprisoned in the cellar until I get back."

She laughed, knowing his jesting was a sure sign he had already relented. "Now *that* would unquestionably be in the best interests of my health and the baby's." She brushed her lips against his in unspoken gratitude. "To own the truth, Neville, it would be more difficult for me to remain here, never sure how you were, than if I were to go with you."

He wrapped his arms around her, holding her close. His voice rumbled through his chest beneath her ear. "That is the sole reason I have yielded. It could be dangerous for you, but at least, if you are with me, I can make sure you do not over-do."

"I will not. I know confronting an army would not be wise at any time. I am well aware of what I should and should not do."

"Yes, I know. It is your fourth child but only my first. Allow me to be a worried father."

"Fretting will gain you nothing and add to my stress. I—"

The door burst open, and Aunt Cordelia stormed in with Duncan. Her gown was covered with paw prints. "Priscilla, you must do something about that unruly cur without delay! It was his—" She scowled fiercely at Neville. "It was his ridiculous idea to bring home a muddy, flea-ridden dog."

Priscilla was not surprised when Neville did not retort. He had protected her from highwaymen and traitors and murderers, but Aunt Cordelia overmastered even his courage. How many times had he said only a fool—and Neville Hathaway prided himself on not being a fool—would confront her aunt without full armor and an enchanted sword worthy of slaying a fire-breathing dragon?

She kept her smile to herself. Aunt Cordelia would not appreciate being compared to a flaming lizard. On the other hand, it was, Priscilla had to admit, probably the best analogy he had ever devised for Aunt Cordelia.

Instead of arguing, she used the tactic that always worked best for her with her contentious aunt: make her feel important and needed. "I must ask a favor, Aunt Cordelia."

"Ask what you wish. I would do anything for *you* and the children." She fired another frown at Neville.

Priscilla ignored what sounded like a muffled snort from beside her. One of these days, her aunt and Neville would come to their senses and behave like adults, but it appeared it would not be today.

"Will you take the children to your estate for a fortnight or two?"

she asked. "You will have a lovely time helping Daphne plan her wedding."

"Yes," her aunt said in a warmer tone, "I have some ideas I want to discuss with her. That girl needs to learn her husband is the head of the household."

Priscilla almost laughed when Duncan rolled his eyes. He truly loved her aunt, but like everyone else, he accepted the fact that Cordelia seldom practiced what she preached.

"Thank you, Aunt Cordelia. You will provide her with the perfect example of what she should consider for her future."

Her aunt preened, and Duncan pressed his hand over his mouth to keep his laugh from escaping.

"But where are you going, Priscilla?" her aunt asked.

"Why isn't it obvious, Aunt Cordelia? Duncan, Neville, and I are traveling to Lakeland to look for Lord Beamish's missing daughter." Without a qualm, she used the excuse that Neville had created.

"Have you lost your mind?"

"Undoubtedly, but," she added, not hesitating on stretching the truth, "we made a promise, and we intend to keep it."

Chapter Four

WHEN NEVILLE handed her out of the carriage on the gray after-noon, Priscilla wondered if every bone in her body ached. The journey north to his estate of Tarn's Edge had taken longer than she had guessed, and she could not fault Duncan for riding ahead to see what he could discover before they arrived. Neville had been correct to insist they halt their journey early every day. He was worried how the jostling and long hours would affect their child. It had taken them almost a week to reach the center of Lakeland and a small lake south of the much bigger Windermere.

They had stopped by a small grove of evergreen trees. A path wandered into it. Soon the lane would need to be cleared because brambles stretched into it.

Mist curled around her feet and hung like a gray cloud over in nearby fields. The last of the day's sunlight glistened on it, turning it into a blanket of silver and diamonds. Ancient ruins could be seen through the trees. If it had once been a small castle or a fortified house, there were no signs.

The ground sloped gently down to a lakeside where water lapped beneath the overhanging branches of a tree. Sheep baa'ed in the dis-tance, but were invisible in mist that was the same color as their wool.

"I thought we would reach Tarn's Edge today," Priscilla said as she drew her shawl around her shoulders. Rain was driven by the breeze that made the fog contort on the lake. The weather had grown colder and damper as they drove north, leaving spring behind them. She gazed across the small lake toward the black trees on the other side. With the mist wafting like a living creature across the water, she half-expected to see a fairy peeping out from behind the tightly rolled ferns.

"This *is* Tarn's Edge." He gestured toward the lake. "That is Tarn Laal, which is a north country name meaning small lake." He pointed at the ruins. "And what you see through the trees is Tarn's Edge. Or more accurately, what is left of it."

She peered at the piles of stone again. "Oh my! It is in worse condition than Shadows Fall was before you began repairs. At least the house in Cornwall had four walls and a roof, though they leaked and some were ready to cave in."

"That is the curtain wall for the inner courtyard. The house is beyond that. It has been closed for almost fifty years and is uninhabitable." He put his arm around her. "It would be like the Prince Regent, with his bizarre sense of humor, to saddle me with one estate that will consume the income from the other."

Priscilla smiled. "You will not get much sympathy from anyone when you were granted three hundred acres, a house, two ponds, a lake, and the remnants of several mines along with your title." She shivered as a stronger gust of wind came off the lake, driving the rain harder. "Is there somewhere to get warm?"

"An excellent idea." He laughed. "Why didn't I think of that? The gatehouse still has a roof and walls."

"Gatehouse?"

He pointed toward the thorn-edged lane. "It is that way along with a small stable, the only two buildings with secure roofs on the whole estate." He gave quick instructions to the coachman on how to reach the stable as well as the kitchen, where supper should be ready.

"How can supper be waiting?" Priscilla asked.

"Before we left Stonehall-on-Sea, I sent word ahead to the groundskeeper and his wife that we would be arriving. Last night, I confirmed we would be arriving today by having a lad from the inn where we stayed deliver a message here. I hope the meal will start with a hearty soup."

"What are we waiting for?" She nestled closer to him when the thorns tore at her woolen cloak.

Once they discovered what Sir Thomas was planning, it was time to turn their attention to Tarn's Edge. The first thing she would arrange for was to make a wider path to the gatehouse, though she did enjoy any chance to be next to Neville. He smiled down at her, and the dank chill seemed to vanish.

As they stepped into the shadows cast by the evergreen trees, she could see the hidden building. It was two stories high but could not be more than two or three rooms deep. A section curving back away from it to the left probably held the kitchen. Small arched windows were set in what might once have been arrow slits, and the roof was crenellated.

"Tarn's Edge was an abbey originally, wasn't it?" she asked.

"Right up until King Henry VIII dissolved the monasteries, claimed the lands for himself, and sold the properties to his lackeys and political allies." He looked up as she did. "Parapets? I wonder if they were added for decoration or for protection."

"I did not realize you were such an English history expert, Neville."

"Only if Shakespeare wrote a play about it." He chuckled. "A lot of my education was in the theater."

Priscilla looked past him as a simple oak door opened and welcoming candlelight flowed out. A young woman stepped back as they entered. She bobbed in a quick curtsy. Her simple black gown was covered by an apron splattered with a variety of foods. Surprisingly bright red hair peeped from beneath her cap, and her freckled face was stretched wide in a broad smile.

"Welcome, m'lord, m'lady," she said, curtsying again.

The entry hall was as simple as the exterior but more than five times the size of the one in the house in Stonewall-on-Sea. Through a grand arched door, Priscilla saw an ancient carved oak staircase wide enough for four people to walk abreast. A trio of stone steps led up in the other direction to a room where a fire roared on the hearth.

"That be enough, Lizzie." A grizzled man came into view as Priscilla moved closer to a small fireplace beside the door. "Off to the kitchen with ye. Yer ma will be lookin' for ye."

"Yes, Papa." The young woman nodded, gave another curtsy, and hurried out as the man came forward.

"George Oldfield, m'lord." He gave a generous smile to Pris, and she saw much of his daughter in his face, including the freckles. His hair might once have been as fiery a red, but now it was the color of the mist curling at the edge of the door, trying to sneak in. "M'lady, welcome to Tarn's Edge."

"Thank you," she said as she drew off her shawl.

When Oldfield held out his hand for it, she gave it to him. He folded it over his arm with the precision and grace of a Mayfair butler. She was curious where he had worked before coming to the isolated estate in the Lakeland fells. She would have to ask Neville later.

As Neville handed his greatcoat to Oldfield, he said, "You have been overseeing the estate, I understand."

"Aye, m'lord. I 'ave made sure the buildings, the ones that could be saved, 'ave been shored up and the fields leased out for hay or grazing. I can give ye a full report whenever ye wish, Lord 'Athaway."

"Let's leave that until tomorrow. We have had a long journey."

"Certainly. The missus 'as made up rooms for ye, as Mr. McAndrews requested."

"Duncan is here?" Priscilla asked.

"Aye, m'lady. Been 'ere for nigh on a week."

"Excellent." Neville smiled at her.

He hoped as she did that Duncan had already uncovered the truth behind the disappearance of Miss Beamish and her servants. It would be nice to have that quickly resolved, so they could focus on the true reason they had come north. Though she had to own, she would like to take a few days to explore Tarn's Edge and see what could be salvaged. She would not say that to Neville because he would tease her about becoming domestic now that she was in a delicate condition.

"The missus 'as a sturdy tea ready for ye at yer convenience," Oldfield said.

"That sounds wonderful," Pris replied with a grateful smile.

"Shall I have it brought to the old hall?" He pointed to the room with the blazing fire. "It is the warmest part of the house."

When Priscilla nodded and thanked him, Oldfield dipped his head. He walked away with a slight limp, taking their outerwear with him.

Neville put his arm around her shoulders as they went up the trio of steps to the old hall. It was a long, narrow room with chairs scattered around it. Leaded glass in the huge window revealed how closely the trees had grown to the building. Branches pressed against the panes. At the far end of the room, the fire danced merrily on the hearth set below a magnificent chimneypiece. Stuffed animal heads, most decorated with antlers or horns, covered almost the whole surface to the peaked ceiling.

"Welcome to Tarn's Edge," said Duncan, getting up from a chair in front of the hearth.

"I believe that is my line." Neville shook his friend's hand, then guided Priscilla to another chair and urged her to sit.

She considered demurring because she had been in the carriage for hours. But when she lowered herself to the chair upholstered in worn blue linen, she sighed. The seat cushioned her like an embrace. She listened to the men and watched rain trickle down the uneven windows edged with dark blue velvet draperies. The flames danced, and her eyelids grew heavy.

A hand on her shoulder roused her enough to realize she had fallen asleep. Neville squatted by the chair and whispered, "Why don't you rest?"

"We need to make plans for finding Bella Beamish," she argued, though there was nothing she wanted more than to close her eyes and sleep. She and Neville had agreed on the ride north to use Miss Beamish's name as a code word for learning more about the baronet's plans and if he truly intended to amass an army. Alone, they would speak plainly, but when they were with others, they would pretend their sole reason for their journey was to uncover the truth about Miss Beamish's location.

"There is time later. Rest now, and I will have a tray sent up to you. It will be best for everyone."

She nodded, knowing he could not say more when Duncan stood within earshot. "I think that would be wise, Neville."

After he drew her to her feet, she kissed his cheek, bid Duncan a good evening, and took her leave. She hoped she had enough stamina to climb the stairs to the room that had been made ready for them. This baby business was going to slow her down more than she had planned.

NEVILLE WATCHED Pris go up the stairs at a painfully slow pace. He did not realize he had sighed until Duncan asked him what was amiss.

"Nothing. Tired."

"You?" His friend chuckled. "The Neville Hathaway who cut a wide swath through the *ton* and was welcomed at every door and every assembly, no matter the hour?"

"I think you are confusing the man I am now for an earlier version." He was glad Duncan had misunderstood.

He was not tired, but Priscilla looked exhausted. Convincing her to rest was usually a thankless chore, but he had to find some way to get her not to push herself too hard. The only way to persuade her to listen to him would be reaching St. John's community and learning the truth as quickly as possible. If they could find Miss Beamish and her servants and return them to Lord Beamish posthaste, that would be a bonus, but he needed to concentrate on the task the Prince Regent had given him.

Lizzie, Oldfield's daughter, arrived with a large oval tray holding the largest tea Neville had ever seen. In addition to sandwiches and cheese, pieces of roasted meat were piled high at one end. Small cakes and sweets claimed another section of the tray. She placed it on a chest that was dark with age. With another curtsy, she hurried away after asking them to ring if they wished more.

"More?" Neville asked in amazement. "There is enough for a dozen men."

"Speak for yourself." Duncan picked up a plate and placed a generous serving on it. "Mrs. Oldfield is a cook of rare talent. I may try to steal her away from you."

"I doubt Lady Cordelia's cook would be happy to hear that." He winked as he selected a roast beef sandwich. "Or Lady Cordelia."

Instead of agreeing with the obvious, Duncan asked, "Do you wish to hear what I have learned about the goings-on around here? Or has the man you are now changed to the point he no longer cares?"

Neville chuckled. "I doubt I could ever change that much. You have had plenty of time to meet people and get them to tell you what is on their minds. So what are they talking about?"

"St. John's latest insanity."

"More than about a missing heiress and her servants?"

"It might have been a nine day's wonder, and there *is* curiosity about what happened to Miss Beamish. That is, however, nothing compared to curiosity about what St. John is doing. I visited a variety of public houses, inns, and other gathering places. At every one, without fail, the conversation turned to St. John."

"What are they saying?"

Duncan went to stand by the largest window where the wild wind battered rain against it. "From what I was able to discover, St. John and his fellows have settled somewhere up there in a high pass. He has been purchasing land west of here for almost a decade. No one took note of it until he started bringing people there, settling them in, and building a wall around the place to keep the curious out."

"Who does he think he is? Some great feudal lord?"

"Don't laugh, Neville. He is up to something, but no one knows what."

"Really? *You* don't know what is going on?"

Duncan sat back down in his chair. "I saw no reason to tramp through the wet gorse to pay a call when I was informed that no strangers were welcome past his wall. After all, we are not here to see what that loose screw is up to." With a shrug, he began to eat.

"True," Neville replied, though he hated to wait to satisfy his own curiosity. "We are here to find Miss Beamish. Any news on her?"

"Apparently her carriage is now at an inn on the west side of Windermere. A place called The Rose and Thistle." He raised his hands that held a sandwich in one and a sweetmeat in the other. "Before you ask, my boy, I have not been there either. The mists and rain and wind settled in for the past two days, so I decided to enjoy the comforts of Tarn's Edge. You could use a better stocked cellar."

"I did not know there was anything in the cellar."

"Nothing worth drinking, and *that* I did check. Fortunately, I never travel without a couple bottles of whisky. I had your man decant it and put it on the sideboard in the dining room next door."

"I should have guessed you would make yourself at home." Neville picked up a piece of cheese. Taking a bite, he added, "To own the truth, I agree with your sentiment about leaving St. John to his insanity. Focusing on what we came here to do is the best idea."

"I am glad to hear that. Wandering through the fells is a worthless way to spend our time. I speak from experience. We Scots have known these fells for longer than history has been written. Some of the bravest or most stupid, your choice, of the border reivers dared to come this far south, though I cannot imagine how they could have driven a herd of cattle back over the border. And before that, the Scots stopped the Romans here and never let them conquer us." He grinned. "They saw our faces painted blue, and Hadrian decided to build his wall to denote the edge of civilization at that very spot. Beyond it lay chaos and barbarians."

"Did you ever stop to think they built the wall because the legionaries saw your faces *without* the paint on them?"

Duncan wagged a finger at him. "Such insults will keep my whisky unshared."

"We cannot have that, can we?" Neville chuckled with his friend.

An hour later, filled with good food and fine whisky, Neville asked Duncan how long he intended to stay at Tarn's Edge.

"How long do you need me?" his friend asked.

"If you could stay another day or two that would be good." A day or two would allow him time to examine the carriage that had been abandoned at the inn near Windermere and ask questions about St. John's community which was in the fells beyond the town.

"I can do that."

"I appreciate it. I know you would prefer to be with your wife after a fortnight apart."

"Cordelia is having her rose garden replanted, and I do not intend to return until the task is finished." Duncan added more whisky to his glass. "She frets about where every plant is placed. I made the mistake of being there when she redid her white garden, and she drove me out of my mind."

"I can understand." He did not add that Pris's aunt annoyed him at the best of times.

"So why do you need me here for a day or two? Though I hardly need to ask."

"No doubt, he has some tasks that he needs done while we go to The Rose and Thistle Inn." Pris's soft voice came from behind him.

Neville turned, glad her eyes were no longer heavy with exhaustion and more color warmed her face. "Pris, I thought you were resting." He was not surprised that she had guessed the first step in his plan to find out what St. John was up to. By adhering to the façade of searching for Miss Beamish, they could keep anyone else from learning the real reason for coming north.

"I did rest, but I am still hungry. I hope you left something for me."

Neville looked at the decimated tea tray where only a few pieces of cheese and meat, both dried from the heat on the hearth, remained. He exchanged a guilty glance with Duncan. "I can ring for more."

"Thank you."

Mrs. Oldfield answered the bell this time. She was a neat woman without a black hair out of place or a spot on her white apron or dark gown. Welcoming them as warmly as her husband and daughter had, she nodded when Neville asked Mrs. Oldfield for additional sandwiches.

"For Lady Priscilla," he added, though he did not need to explain himself. There was something about the housekeeper that made him feel like a naughty lad who had been caught trying to steal a pie cooling in a doorway. Surprising heat climbed up the back of his neck when the housekeeper's expression became chiding before she looked at Pris. He was relieved when she said only, "Of course, I will bring more food for her ladyship."

"Thank you, Mrs. Oldfield," Pris said, gracious as always.

"Whatever I can do for you, say the word. I know how it can be at times like this."

Pris's golden brows shot up, and she put a finger to her lips before glancing toward Duncan who was picking through the tray for something that caught his fancy. Mrs. Oldfield nodded with a smile before hurrying away.

Neville marveled at the unspoken communication shared by two mothers. If he had not been privy to Pris's condition, he doubted he would have guessed what they were *not* talking about.

Duncan excused himself to seek his own bed. "Country hours," he said. "To bed with the birds and up with them again." He winked at them before adding, "Guess I have changed, too." He paused long enough to kiss Pris's cheek before bidding them a good night.

"What was that about? Changing?" she asked as Duncan disappeared upstairs.

"Two old men regretting their youthful mistakes." He took her slender hand and led her to where he and Duncan had been sitting. He sat her on the upholstered chair and took the wooden one for himself.

"You are hardly old, Neville."

"Older than you."

Her eyes widened. "Oh, that *is* ancient."

He laughed, but grew serious as he asked, "Pris, will you be ready to travel again tomorrow?"

"Of course."

"Are you sure? You could stay here with Duncan."

She got to her feet. "I have come all this way, and you want me to stop now?"

"What I want is for you to be safe." He looked up at her, so beautiful, so brave . . . so stubborn. "The roads have gotten rougher as we have come north."

She drew aside the draperies and looked out to where a few stars had poked through the clouds to admire their reflection in the lake. He wondered when the rain had stopped. "You need to stop worrying so much and let me help while I can. In a few months, I shall be as big as a barn."

"I can't envision that."

"You shall see soon enough." She laughed as she let the velvet draperies fall back into place. She waved away the brownish cloud that burst from them. Sneezing, she crossed the room to where he held out his handkerchief. She smiled her thanks as she took it before she sneezed again.

He was surprised when she knelt by his chair, but he withheld his protest that she should sit comfortably while in her delicate condition. She had made it more than clear that she did not appreciate him questioning every action she took.

When she put her hands on his arm, she gazed up at him. "Do say that you will not protest me going to Windermere with you tomorrow, Neville. You know as well as I that there are people who find you intimidating to talk to, especially when you are firing one question after another at them."

"True." He nodded, knowing this was a battle he could not win. She was correct in her reasoning, and she would never do anything to endanger their unborn child. "But you must promise me one thing, Pris."

"What is that?"

He lowered his voice so only she could hear him. "When I sneak close to St. John's settlement to discern exactly what they are doing, you will remain here at Tarn's Edge."

"Yes. I promise, Neville." She rose and slid onto his lap, putting her arms around his shoulders. "And I always keep my promises."

As her soft lips found his, he made himself a pledge as well. He would keep her safe . . . no matter what he had to do.

Chapter Five

BY THE TIME THE carriage had reached the inn the next day, it was raining. Neville held his cloak over Pris as they hurried toward the door beneath the creaking sign. The faded letters on it spelled out the inn's name: *The Rose and Thistle*. Remnants of paint stuck to the wood, but Neville could make out the faded image of a red Lancastrian rose crossed by a Scottish thistle. Once, when the Lancastrians and the Yorks fought their War of Roses and when the borders were a constant battlefield, such symbols would have been dangerous. Now they looked old and tired.

He did a quick scan of the dooryard and smiled when he saw a barn behind the inn. Once he had Pris inside and out of the storm, he would get the horse to shelter. He hoped the morrow would have better weather so local residents would be out on the streets. That would allow him and Pris to ask casual questions to garner any information they could about St. John's activities before his first scouting mission.

He threw open the door and ushered Pris into the small entryway. He had to push an inner door closed, but it refused to latch, swinging back to reveal a staircase beyond it. Pulling off his cloak, he shook it out on the stone floor before following Pris into a narrow room with a long bar, a few tables, and a hearth where the blazing fire was a welcome sight.

The only occupant was a woman standing behind the ancient oak bar. She watched him and Pris with curiosity. Her skin was almost the same shade as the top board, and like the wood's grain, her face showed every year she had lived in the unforgiving region. The kerchief covering her brown hair was the same unbleached linen as her apron. Her cleaning cloth made ever smaller circles as Neville escorted Pris to a settle beside the fireplace that took up the whole wall on the opposite side of the room. A gray-striped cat looked through half-closed lids then continued its nap as near as it could get to the leaping flames.

Neville returned to the bar. Water fell from his greatcoat to puddle between the stones.

"Ale?" the woman asked.

Instead of answering her question, he asked, "Are you the land-lady?"

"Aye. Are ye and the lady plannin' t'stay the night?"

"If you have a private room."

She glanced around the deserted bar. "I 'ave a room ye can use, but I cannot say it will be private. There be a lot of traffic near the lake."

Neville kept his innocuous smile from slipping. Did she expect she could gain a few more pence from him with such tactics? "What is the price for a private room and a place for my horse?"

She gave him a number that was probably outrageous for the area but far less than he would have paid closer to London. He negotiated a bit as any innkeeper would expect him to do, then pulled out a handful of coins. Tossing them on the bar, he watched her scoop them up with the ease of practice.

"Sup be extra," she said as she stashed the coins beneath her apron.

He placed a few more coins on the counter, got instructions for where to take the horse and their bags, then walked back to where Pris was holding her hands out to fire. It would have been more comfortable driving in the closed carriage, but she had suggested it might be easier to get answers if they were not seen as nobility. So they had borrowed Duncan's small carriage, left their coachee back at Tarn's Edge, and made sure the vehicle was liberally covered with mud by the time they arrived at the inn.

Even in a plain gown and a rain-battered bonnet, Pris was beautiful. She smiled, and his heart did a somersault as it had the first time she had given him that special smile which was as intimate as a kiss. When she held out her hand to him, he took it and let her draw him down to sit beside her.

"We have a place to stay for the night," Neville said. "I doubt it will be much."

"As long as it is clean and dry."

"I cannot promise either."

She chuckled. "It is one night. Tomorrow, we will be back where we belong." She did not speak Tarn's Edge's name. As always, she was the perfect co-conspirator. "What now?"

"I need to look around."

"You?" She arched her eyebrows.

"With your help, Pris. Can you speak with yon landlady while I tend to the horse? That will give me an excuse to ask questions of anyone I chance to see outside. Anything that happens in the area will be repeated at an inn when the ale is flowing freely."

She rose gracefully and walked over to the landlady. At the same time, he headed for the door. He yanked up the collar on his greatcoat and tilted the broad-brimmed hat he had borrowed from his coachman. He hoped more cold raindrops would not fall down his nape.

When he reached the doorway, he paused and smiled. Already Pris had drawn the landlady into conversation, talking as if they were longstanding friends. That was Pris's way. No one could resist her genuine charm. He wondered if she had always been that way or if it was a skill she had to learn as a vicar's wife. Either way, it served them well now.

The rain seemed to be coming down harder, if possible. Ducking his head, Neville led the horse around the back of the inn. It needed paint, but otherwise was intact. It would keep the horse and carriage dry.

"Need 'elp, mister?" called a young voice as Neville began to unharness the horse.

He looked at the stable. A lad, who looked to be close to Isaac's age, stood inside, just out of the rain. The boy's face was thin, and his wrists protruding far below his cuffs suggested he had had a recent spurt in growth. Neville could have tended his horse on his own, but he motioned for the boy to assist him.

The boy, who said his name was Jocko, rushed out. The name seemed too big for such a scrawny lad, but he was good with horses. Instead of shying away from a stranger, the horse relaxed under Jocko's attentions. His ears twitched to catch every word the boy spoke as Jocko led him into the stable.

Once his eyes had adjusted to the darkness inside, Neville was astonished to see how long and narrow the stable was. Maybe the landlady had been honest when she said rooms would be at a premium. Several teamsters could get their wagons and horses under the roof in this stable.

His eyes narrowed. What was at the rear of the stable? The shadow was large and bulky.

"Is that a carriage?" Neville asked.

Jocko put a handful of oats in a bucket and offered it to the horse. "Aye. Wish 'is lordship would take it away." The boy began to towel down the wet horse. "Takes up too much room 'ere." He looked toward Neville, and his eyes lit up. "Did 'e send ye t'take it back to 'im?"

"Why do you ask?"

"Ye talk like them from down south where 'is lordship lives."

Neville would have to watch his step with this boy who took note of every detail. Though it was a worthy skill for a lad living by his wits, the wrong word or action could give away information Neville wanted to keep to himself. So he accepted the excuse the lad had given him.

Resting an elbow on a low wall, he nodded. "He asked me to check it and make sure it could make the journey back south."

"Ain't nothin' wrong with it." The boy ran to the back, gesturing for Neville to follow. "Stinks 'cause it was left out in the rain, and the leather got soaked. Seats will 'ave t'be taken out, but otherwise 'tis in fine shape."

"I need to check myself."

"Go ahead!" He waved a magnanimous hand like a grand king offering a boon to his lowest subject. "Ye won't see anything different from what I told ye."

"I am sure I won't, but you know how bosses are."

That was the right thing to say because the boy launched into a soliloquy about how shortsighted the tavern-keeper could be. While the boy listed his litany of woes, real and imagined, Neville opened the carriage's door and peered inside. The stench of mildew was strong as he ran his hand along the cushions and behind them. He found two mismatched buttons, something that might once have been a piece of bread, and a tuppence. Commonplace items which told him nothing.

"Anything in the boot?" he asked as he closed the door.

"Nothin'."

"Mind if I look?"

"'Tis yer time, mister." The boy pulled out a piece of straw and twirled it in his fingers. Though he was trying to look nonchalant, he was watching every motion Neville made as closely as a constable eyed a felon.

Neville discovered Jocko had been honest about the empty boot. He could see where items had been slid in and out, but nothing remained. Whether Miss Beamish's bags had been taken by her or by thieves, there was no clue.

"Told ye." The boy leaned one shoulder against a post. "Rich folks are dicked in the nob, if ye ask me." He pointed to his temple.

"They can act crazy." Here was the opening Neville had hoped for. As he squatted to look under the carriage, he asked, "Have you heard about that fool who is building a new village out in the fells?"

Jocko snorted. "Everyone 'as. 'Tis the talk of the shire. Old m'lord comes up 'ere with more money than good sense. First, 'e pays men t'build 'im a big wall." He stretched out his arms as far as they could go. "Big! Like some old castle, but instead of a castle, 'e says 'e is buildin' a new town. The first in a whole new world."

"New world?"

"Told ye 'e was crazy. This world is good enough for the rest of us. Dicked in the nob."

Neville looked under the carriage to keep the boy from guessing how puzzling his words were. St. John intended to create a new world? What in the blazes did that mean? One thing was for sure. To have a new world, the old one must be destroyed. The Prince Regent and his advisors were right to be worried about what St. John was doing in Lakeland.

As soon as he could return Pris to Tarn's Edge, he must reconnoiter St. John's walled settlement. The builders would know its exact location. When he asked the boy if he knew any of the men hired by St. John, Jocko could give him only a single name and it was a man who lived several miles outside the village. First thing in the morning, Neville would pay the man a call. He hoped to get more information from him.

Neville frowned as he stared at the underside of the carriage. The vehicle had been used hard because the suspension showed cracks along it. Where had it been before it came to the inn? The roads north from Chester, Miss Beamish's most likely route, were rough, but not bad enough to cause such damage. The carriage underpinnings looked as if the carriage had been driven up the side of a mountain at top speed.

He plucked pieces of a plant from high up in the suspension. Had the carriage been driven through a field? He could not imagine why anyone eloping to Gretna Green would do that. Not only would it damage the carriage but it could ruin the horses pulling it. Someone would have to be desperate to drive at such a speed off the road.

Someone who was on the run.

Could Beamish's fears be legitimate? He swallowed his groan. He could not afford to be distracted from his task, but neither could he forget how desperate he would be to find Daphne or Leah if they went missing as Miss Beamish had.

He had planned to ask about Miss Beamish and her companions anyhow, but now he would have to consider any answers he received as closely as he did any about St. John. From the moment his royal highness had asked for his help, he had known that the task would not be a simple one.

Neville stood and brushed his hands on his damp breeches. The dirt would add to his disguise. Letting his sigh sift past his clenched teeth, he climbed up to the box. Scuff marks showed there had been a struggle, further confirming Beamish's worst fears.

He jumped down and walked around the carriage, examining the walls. He saw no signs of holes from shot fired at it. That was the first bit of good news.

"Are ye takin' it with ye?" asked Jocko. "'Tis been here nearly a month."

"A month? Do you know where it was before then?'

"'Twas found out by the lake. Empty and without anyone 'round. But word came that the carriage belonged to a m'lord. Time for 'im t'come after it if 'e wants it." He grimaced. "Takes up too much room."

"I will tell him that." He tossed a silver half-crown to the boy who snatched it out of midair and made it vanish before Neville could change his mind. It was probably as much as the boy earned in a year. "Thanks for your help."

"Any time, mister." His grin grew wide and a bit cocky.

Ducking his head, Neville walked out in the rain. He was feeling more than a bit cocky himself. Tomorrow should be a very interesting day.

SUPPER WAS DELICIOUS and plentiful at The Rose and Thistle. It was also rowdy. A half dozen drays, carrying goods, had stopped at the inn shortly after Neville came in from the stable.

Priscilla sat at one end of the long table in the common room beyond the bar and listened to the loud, boisterous voices. She was the only woman other than Mrs. White, the inn's landlady, and the men had tipped their caps politely to her as they arrived. After that, they ignored her as they discussed road conditions and markets. As he pretended to be one of them, they spoke with Neville openly. Again she was grateful for the skills he had garnered during his years in various playhouses.

"I 'ear there is good money t'be made," a younger man was saying as the men pushed back their empty trenchers and reached for mugs of ale, "takin' goods up into the 'ighest passes west of 'ere, but 'tis tough on 'orses. Maybe I should get me some donkeys and see if they can make the journey."

"The 'igh passes to the west?" asked a grizzled man who was missing two fingers on his right hand. "Why go that way?"

"'Aven't ye 'eard? Some m'lord is building a new settlement up there," Neville said. "A new place needs supplies t'build it."

The drayman looked around the table, then said, "If ye 'ave any sense in yer 'ead, take yer cart and go in any direction save toward St. John's lands."

"Why?" asked Priscilla.

The men stared at her in disbelief. Did they think her incapable of speech because she had remained silent while they groused about their jobs?

Neville tensed but said nothing while waiting for an answer to her question. The youngest driver, the one who had brought up the subject, repeated her question.

"No one goes there. Not 'less they be invited." A balding man waved his mug to emphasize his words. He ignored the splatter of ale that flew farther with each motion. "If ye be asking, ye 'ave not been invited. Don't go there, if ye want t'live a long life."

The draymen nodded in agreement.

"Long life?" asked Neville as if musing over the words. "Are you saying folks have been killed going up there?"

The man with the missing fingers aimed a fierce glance around the table, but a slight tremble in his voice betrayed his fright. "Ye are not the coroner, mate, so ye would be wise to stop askin' questions." He took another mug from Mrs. White.

As she put more filled mugs on the table, Mrs. White said, "Listen t'Ole Pete. A word to the wise is sufficient, so they say."

"Do they?" Neville gave her the smile that had melted much harder hearts.

Priscilla rose, drawing attention back to herself as Mrs. White abruptly simpered like a young miss. She had information to share with Neville from her conversation with the inn's landlady. "If you will excuse me, gentlemen, I think I shall retire."

The men came to their feet and bid her a good evening. Neville tapped the table to let her know he planned to remain a little longer. He must have seen or heard something he wished to investigate further. She had seen the excitement glowing in his eyes when he returned from the stable, and she was curious about what he had discovered.

As she walked to the front door so she could climb the stairs in the entry, she felt someone staring at her. She took the time she needed to open the door to sneak a glance back. One man, the young driver who had brought up the subject of Sir Thomas, watched her with an unsettled expression. He clearly was worried about what was happening in the fells. She suspected as well that he would be the target of Neville's questioning.

The stairs were as twisting as in a medieval tower, and more than one of the treads rocked beneath Priscilla's feet. She was relieved to reach the upper floor. The corridor's ceiling was low, and she realized the inn must be even more ancient than she had guessed. She could walk without bending, but Neville would have to duck his head. Their room was the second one on the right, the landlady had told her, and the door would be open.

The room's ceiling was sharply slanted. If Neville went to the single window, it would have to be on his hands and knees. One pane was coated with dusty spider webs that looked as old as the inn itself. However, the rope bed was freshly made, and a fire was lit on the hearth. It was, she decided, in no worse condition than Tarn's Edge, and it was far better than most of the roadside inns where they had stopped during their journey from Stonehall-on-Sea.

The door protested loudly when she closed it. She pulled the chair closer to the fire. As the minutes ticked by and Neville did not come upstairs, she pulled out the bag of knitting she had brought on the trip. She had recently rediscovered the craft. Neville had teased her about becoming interested in such housewifely tasks once she realized she was pregnant. She laughed with him, but, in truth, the click-click of the needles was soothing.

For more than an hour, Priscilla sat by the fireplace and worked on her knitting; then the door opened again with another squeak. Neville came in and closed the door behind him.

Walking toward her, he sat on one corner of the bed. His head brushed the low rafter. "Are you making something for our baby?"

"That would announce to the world that we are having a baby. No, I am making a shawl for Aunt Cordelia. A thank you gift for helping Daphne with the wedding plans."

"I am sorry to miss the first meeting between your aunt and Witherspoon's mother."

"I'm not!" Priscilla put her knitting on her lap. She was grateful to Aunt Cordelia for contacting Lady Witherspoon to work out the few undecided matters. "Though if Daphne and Burke are wise, they will remain silent."

He laughed. "Do you honestly believe they will be able to get a word in edgewise? Your aunt is determined to control every situation, and Lady Witherspoon is her match. If you recall, during our call in

London, the marchioness commanded most of the conversation."

"Enough about that. Tell me what you have discovered, and then I shall share what I have learned."

Priscilla listened, astonished, as Neville described the carriage in the stable. "Are you sure it is Lord Beamish's?"

"Who else has had a carriage abandoned here?"

"I don't know, but we cannot assume anything."

He shook his head with a grimace. "That is true, Pris. And to be honest, I would be glad to hear it belonged to some other lord in the south of England. Trying to get information on Miss Beamish takes away time from my real mission."

"Did you find out anything interesting from the men downstairs?"

"Interesting, yes. Helpful, no. Duncan was right about St. John being a favorite topic. They enjoy speculating about what St. John is doing behind his wall, but no one seems to know anything. What about Mrs. White? Did she tell you anything that will help?"

"She gave me the names of some men who have been to the new community." She pulled a slip of paper out of her knitting bag and handed it to him. "I wrote them down."

He scanned the list and smiled. "Excellent, Pris. I got only a single name from Jocko, and that man lives north of here."

"I asked Mrs. White for the names of men right here in the village."

"Smart of you, Pris. May I?"

She motioned for him to keep the page. "While you call on the men on that list, I shall visit some of the shops to see what else I can learn."

"An excellent plan." He pushed himself to his feet, hit his head on the ceiling, and cursed. "Why don't we get some sleep, Pris? I am chilled from the ride in the rain, and I would like to get warmed up."

"Another good idea." She set aside her knitting and stood on tiptoe as she locked her hands behind his nape.

He nuzzled her neck, sending waves of heated anticipation through her. "You are the antithesis of your aunt, you know."

"How so?"

"She can be a gabster. You, on the other hand . . ." His own fingers slid along her side to settle on the curve of her hip. "Say much with only a few words." Sweeping her up into his arms, he chuckled from deep in his throat. "I need to do this while I can. Soon you will be as big as those drays out there."

"You give me the kindest compliments."

He answered her with his lips on hers, and then there was no need for talking.

SOMETHING SQUAWKED. A short sound but enough to disrupt Priscilla's sleep. She opened her eyes and savored the warmth of Neville's shoulder under her cheek.

The noise came again.

Squeeeeak!

The door!

Priscilla sat up, but Neville had already sprung from the bed and toward the door. Before she could shout for him to be careful and to wait for her, he and the person who tried to sneak in had run out of the room. She groped for her dressing gown. By the time she had pulled it around her and buttoned it in place, the doorway was empty.

She started to call out Neville's name, then reconsidered. Caution was imperative.

But so was making sure Neville was not hurt by the intruder.

Where had they gone?

She knocked on other doors along the corridor. When she got no answer, she opened each one and looked inside. The faint light coming through the windows showed the rooms were empty.

She held her breath as she knocked on the final door. Again, she got no answer. Again, she opened the door.

The room was black. Either it had no window or the glass was covered.

"Is anyone here?" she whispered, then raising her voice, repeated the question.

A loud curse came from the hallway. She rushed out and saw a form silhouetted against a doorway that must lead to another stairwell. The form vanished.

She rushed forward and almost stumbled down the uneven steps. She slowed, making sure each step was solid beneath her foot before she took the next one. A door at the bottom led out into what looked like a stable yard because she saw horses milling about.

Two men were in the yard. Neville! She recognized his height.

Suddenly Neville tumbled off his feet, falling face first to the ground. Had he been shot?

Before she could run to him, her arm was grabbed. Something struck her head, and night rose up to consume her.

Chapter Six

NEVILLE WOKE WITH a headache bad enough for him to wonder if he had been too much in his cups. The last time his head had throbbed like this, he had spent the whole night at the card table and had given several bottles of cheap gin black eyes. It had been in the wake of getting the news that his good friend, Lazarus Flanders, had died without Neville knowing he was ill. He had no time to thank Lazarus for helping him turn his life around. He had waited a year before he called on Lazarus's widow to offer his condolences. He could not bear to see such grief in Pris's eyes.

Pris . . . his beloved Pris, who never made him feel worthless as many others in the *ton* had. Who had accepted him as he was. Who had helped him find his heart so he could give it to her.

No, he would not have drunk last night until he was floored. Then why did his head hurt so badly? He searched his memory and could not recall having more than a pint or two of ale at . . . The Rose and Thistle Inn!

Memory after memory burst out of his mind, each one bouncing off his tender skull.

Examining Beamish's carriage and learning from the stable lad the name of a man who had worked for St. John.

Pris obtaining even more names.

The plan to talk to the men in the morning.

Someone sneaking into their room in the middle of the night.

Giving chase after a man whose face he never saw.

An explosion of pain when he was struck from behind. All thought disappearing save for the fact that, in his enthusiasm to discover who had tried to sneak into their room, he had left Pris unprotected.

Pris?

Where was she?

Where was he?

As if he had spoken, he heard a female say, "Ah, you are awake at last. Welcome to Novum Arce."

"Where?" he tried to ask.

The woman must have understood because she repeated, "Novum Arce."

He forced his eyes open to see a face surrounded by a spun white halo. He could not make out any features because his eyes refused to focus. Flowing white robes fluttered when she moved. She seemed to be carrying something flat and thin.

Halo? White robes? And was that a harp she was carrying?

What was going on? What was Novum Arce?

"This cannot be heaven." He was able to get those few words out of his dry throat. He sounded like a croaking toad.

"Hardly." A hint of laughter filled the woman's voice.

"Why are you dressed like a wingless angel?"

He did not know if the woman was trying to avoid his question, but instead of answering, she ordered gently, "Tell me how you are feeling, Mr. Williams."

"Mister . . ." Neville halted himself before he could say something witless. For some reason, she believed his surname was Williams. He suspected the reason had to do with Pris. Who else would give him a fake name? And why had she lied?

Where was Pris?

He put the back of his hand to his forehead in an emoted pose worthy of the worst on Drury Lane and moaned. "Forgive me. What I meant to say is my head feels like the finish line at Newmarket track."

"What?"

"As if a dozen horses are trampling on it at top speed."

"Oh." She went to a small table near the foot of the bed and set down what he now could see was a tray with several dishes on it.

The very idea of eating made Neville nauseated. He ignored his roiling gut and tried to sit, but moving was not a good idea. He propped himself on his elbows and waited for the dizziness to subside. More than once, he considered collapsing into the pillows. He fought the temptation, and it took several minutes for the room to stop swirling around him.

The woman poured something into a cup and turned to bring it to him. He winced when she moved because she had blocked a bright flame in a low lamp. The light slashed at him, and he put his hand to his tender skull, groaning.

"It will be all right," the woman said.

He squinted, glad she now stood between him and the light. She was elderly, her face a pattern of ravines, but she stood as straight as an oak. Her gray hair was drawn back in a simple bun at her nape. A loose white tunic was caught at both shoulders by simple broaches, and a sash at her thick waist held the garment in place. Over one arm, she carried a light green cloak. When he managed to focus on her feet, he saw she wore sandals that laced across the top and up beneath her robe.

What was going on? Had he fallen asleep and woken in the midst of a costume ball?

"Drink," she ordered.

"What is it?"

"It will help with the headache."

Pain crashed through his head, and he grasped the metal cup with two hands. Anything to ease the agony. He downed the liquid in a single gulp. It sizzled on his tongue and scratched his dry throat. An acrid taste made him gag.

"I know," the old woman said. "It tastes awful."

Neville was about to reply the horrid flavor was not worth the help, but then the tight iron bands around his skull began to loosen. He had no idea what had been in the cup, but he would gladly drink more to banish his headache.

"Thank you," he whispered.

"Drink this." She held out a second cup, taking the empty one. "It will soothe your throat."

He did not hesitate as he drained the second cup. The liquid was sweet as if mixed with ripe strawberries. He wondered where she had found a summer fruit, but that was the least important of his questions.

"Who are you?" he asked.

"I am Tulita Easton, but you can call me Aunt Tetty. Everyone here does."

"Here?" He looked around the room. The cot where he had awoken looked like something the army would use. A wooden chest had been pushed against the wall beside the table where she had placed the tray. A backless bench held a bowl and ewer. The mirror over them was the only decoration on the wall that showed signs of dampness where plaster had fallen in chips to the worn wooden floor.

"Novum Arce." She gave him a small smile.

"That is what you said before, but it means nothing to me."

"I know."

He waited for her to go on, but she clamped her lips closed before she took the second cup and shuffled back to the tray. When she remained silent, he realized he would have to get a few answers on his own.

Swinging his legs over the side of the bed almost sent him crashing to the floor. He waited for the world to right itself again. With care, he stood and went toward the window. He felt like a drunken sailor on a high sea. Gripping the edge of the sill, he forced his quivering legs to steady beneath him. He had to be patient, something he did not do well, while the scene cleared in front of him.

And he did not believe his eyes.

Neville could not recall the last time words failed him, but every one fled his mind as he stared out at what appeared to be a perfectly recreated Roman village along the empire's northern border. Buildings were laid out in an exact grid, the streets as straight as the flight of an arrow. Many of the buildings were small, only a single story high. He saw a few larger buildings. Like the lesser ones, they had been constructed of stone and whitewashed. What looked like slate roofs topped each building. However, every window had glass, and the wooden doors were edged with iron hinges.

Men and women hurried past, intent on a task or errand. They wore the flowing clothes he had seen on ancient statues and cloaks in a variety of colors. The women's clothing resembled styles that had swept England twenty years ago, loose robes lashed under and between the breasts. The men's belted tunics hung over leggings and reached to the knee, but were not cut close to the skin like his knee breeches. Instead of boots, leather sandals rose to the ankle.

The wind struck his face, and he heard a sharp snap. Overhead fluttered flags emblazoned with an imperial eagle, the symbol of the Roman army that had last flown in England a millennium and a half before. He looked up at the fells rising in every direction around the settlement. On a high ridge where once Roman legionaries might have stood watch, men patrolled. He could not discern if they were dressed as these others were in the ancient costumes.

A shout came from his left, and he choked out a curse. Men in the white tunics of Roman legionaries practiced with shortened swords on the green between the stone buildings. Two men in the red of Roman centurions directed them.

Was he dreaming, or had the blow to his head undone his hold on sanity?

"It is real," Aunt Tetty said. "There was a fort here when the Romans ruled. Not so much a fort as a supply depot I have been told, though we are supposed to think only of the past glories recreated in Novum Arce."

"Novum Arce," he repeated.

"Yes. I am told the name is Latin for 'new castle.'" She laughed without amusement. "But Newcastle is a real city, isn't it?"

He nodded. "Newcastle upon Tyne. Ironic."

"What is ironic?"

"The ancient Roman wall built by Hadrian has one end east of Newcastle upon Tyne, and here is another town with the same name not far from the wall's west end in Bowness-on-Solway."

"You seem to know a lot about that old wall."

"Knowledge I never expected to have any use for." He watched a child run past, his sandals slapping the grass. "How long have you been here, Aunt Tetty?"

"It is *Aprilis*, isn't it? We use the Roman names whenever possible."

"Yes, it is April." He chuckled. "I mean, *Aprilis*."

"Then I have been here for quite a long time. *Biennium*."

Neville searched his mind for what he remembered of Latin and realized he could not recall much save a few phrases, but he guessed *biennium* meant two years. He had had no formal schooling in the dead language, for he had not had the luxury of a tutor or a classroom. Most of what he had learned back then was the language of the worst London streets. Later, though, he had studied Latin when he first played a part in Shakespeare's *Antony and Cleopatra*. Even though the play had been written in English, he had thought memorizing the speeches in the language of the characters would help him understand them better. He had discovered a fascination with languages, so he had learned more with Lazarus's help.

Usus est optimum magister. That was one phrase he remembered learning from Pris's late husband. *Experience makes the best teacher.*

He wondered what he was about to learn about a place called Novum Arce, but first he had to know where Pris was. "Was I brought here alone?"

"I don't know." She shrugged. "People come to Novum Arce all the time. It is not my task to keep track of them."

Hope skittered through Neville. Maybe the men who had tried to break into their room had not noticed Pris. She could be safe at the inn or on her way to Duncan to get help. Though she would be frantic about him, she and their baby would be safe.

"Is this the settlement established by Sir Thomas Hodge St. John?"

he asked, refocusing on the situation.

A smile teased Aunt Tetty's lips. "An odd question from a man who has no idea where he is. What else do you suspect, Mr. Williams?"

"Not much at this point, because I never guessed St. John's obsession in creating a utopia would lead him to choose ancient Rome as his model." He glanced again at the soldiers on patrol. The Prince Regent's instincts had been right. St. John had built an army.

The only questions remaining were: Why? And how long would it take Neville to sneak out past those soldiers to get the information to London?

"He has his reasons for the life he has established here," Aunt Tetty said, drawing his eyes back to her.

"And they are?"

"It would be better if you heard that from the Imperator's lips."

"He calls himself the Imperator, does he?" That, as much as what he had viewed, gave Neville a hint of what was taking place in this strange settlement. Imperator had been the title given to a Roman commander before it was taken by the imperial Caesars as part of their title. St. John had set himself up as the absolute ruler of Novum Arce for both civilian and military matters.

St. John had no military experience, and from what Neville had observed in London, the baronet disdained the company of military men. He had never imagined the reason St. John refused to speak to them was because he was jealous of their authority. And now the insane baronet was the leader of these crazy people who followed him.

Crazy people? He cut his eyes toward Aunt Tetty who was smoothing the blanket on the bed. Was she as insane as St. John? Maybe Neville should have thought twice before he drank the so-called medicines she offered. It was too late to worry about that now. Instead, he had to gather more information and then find a way out of . . . what had she called the place? Novum Arce?

"Yes, he is our Imperator, and he wants to meet you as soon as you have regained your senses." Aunt Tetty pointed to a pile of fabric at the foot of the cot. "I will leave you to clean up then I will escort you to the *principia*. It is the central building of Novum Arce." She walked out, closing the door without giving him a chance to respond.

Neville glanced from the towels to the men practicing with short Roman swords. Suddenly he felt totally disconnected from reality. This was a new world created out of St. John's irrational mind. Just as Jocko had said.

New world . . . a quote from *The Tempest*, his favorite Shakespearean play, whispered through his head:

"*O, wonder!*
How many goodly creatures are there here!
How beauteous mankind is! O brave new world,
That has such people in't!"

He hoped the residents of Novum Arce would prove to be goodly, but as he watched the soldiers training beyond his window, he knew he must be prepared if they were not.

Chapter Seven

THE *PRINCIPIA* WAS set at one end of an avenue broad enough to drive three closed carriages abreast. At the other end, barely visible through the rain falling from clouds clinging close to the fells, stood a smaller building that was a mirror image of the grand *principia* with its row of white columns and pediments decorated with bas-relief figures Neville assumed were Roman gods and goddesses. He wondered where St. John had found skilled sculptors. Maybe he had bought the figures from some archeological site and moved them to his new community.

Aunt Tetty did not speak as she led him to double doors that rose to over twenty feet. They were open, and she told him to go in and walk to the opposite end.

"You will have your questions answered there," she said.

"Isn't this a bit of an outrageous way to answer some very basic questions?"

A faint smile tugged at her lips, but she slipped past him and into the building.

Neville followed and found himself in a room as vast as the nave of a cathedral, but the ceiling was low and flat instead of arched. Like a cathedral, it had aisles on each side, set off by rows of columns. He recognized the simple lines and undecorated capitals as the Italianate Doric style favored by architects in the past century. However, no country house was crowded with people wearing Roman garb. His torn and dirty waistcoat and breeches and scuffed knee boots made him the odd man out, but he doubted he would find an odder group anywhere. The men stood on the left side of the room while women crowded together on the right.

A familiar face, though her golden hair was swept up in curls beneath a sheer veil, caught his eyes. Pris! His heart fell. He had been hopeful she had not been taken from The Rose and Thistle Inn, that she had given him the name Williams when talking to the landlady there. However, the curs who had attacked him must have brought her here, too.

More questions battered his mouth, but they must wait. For now, it took every ounce of restraint not to run to her and pull her into his arms.

From where he stood, she looked unharmed. He nodded his head toward the door, a signal he hoped she would understand. If possible, he would meet her outside the building after whatever was going to happen here was over. She gave him a smile, then looked away as if he were a stranger who had intrigued her for a moment. He followed her lead, continuing to scan the room from its ceiling painted with a primitive depiction of the sun and moon and stars to the mosaic tiles under his feet.

After everything else he had seen, it was no surprise to see a throne with an eagle banner hanging over it at the end of the long room. He almost would have been disappointed if there had been no sign of Imperial Rome. Beneath the banner was another flag with a bull in its center. It might be an emblem belonging to one of the legions that guarded the empire's borders. He wondered how accurate St. John had insisted his utopia be.

On the throne sat Sir Thomas Hodge St. John, dressed in the white toga of a Roman leader with a cloak of imperial purple draped around his shoulders. Would the man whose black hair was laced with silver recognize Neville, whom he had met on a couple of occasions? The last time, Neville had not spoken to him directly, so it was possible St. John would not remember him.

"A newcomer, Imperator," a voice intoned from behind the throne. Neville could not see who stood there, so the person might be behind the drapery.

St. John squinted at Neville and motioned him forward. "I am told your name is Williams."

"Yes, sir."

"Leonard Williams?"

He hoped this was not some test or trap. He shifted his eyes toward Pris. She gave the slightest nod, and he hurried to say, "Yes, sir."

"You look familiar, Williams."

He had to choose his lies with care. Anything he said could trigger a memory in the older man's head. "I once served as a footman and guest valet for gentlemen who came to Lord Stoningham's country seat near Newmarket to enjoy the races. Perhaps you saw me then."

"Possible, though I always have traveled with my own valet." Raising his voice, he spoke to the whole gathering. "But that is part of the old world. Now we have this new world. You will be part of that,

Williams, and you should be grateful such an honor has been granted to you."

"Yes, sir." He had no idea what else to say. If he spoke the wrong word, would these pseudo-Romans toss him to the lions for their enjoyment?

He realized St. John had not been waiting for an answer. St. John pushed himself to his feet and called out, "Here in Novum Arce, we have cut ourselves off from war, and we seek to live in peace. *In pace*. We have established a place to raise our children and their children and their children without interference from outsiders." His pale eyes focused on Neville again. "Pax Romana. Do you know what it is?"

"Would you explain, sir?" he asked because he needed to know how St. John defined the term that translated as "the peace of Rome." For a man who preached peace, St. John had plenty of men training to be soldiers.

Neville heard intakes of breaths behind him and then a sigh in unison. No doubt, St. John's followers had heard him prattle about his ideals for Novum Arce too many times before. He listened with half an ear as he scanned the great hall. A single door opened at the back, visible only because someone had pulled the draperies aside so the rain did not strike them. He did not need an escape route . . . yet. Everything he saw created more questions in his mind. He needed more answers before he left Novum Arce. But it was always best to be prepared, though he would never leave without Pris.

"Pax Romana was the greatest moment in Roman history," intoned St. John. "A time when the empire was united in peace. Imagine that, Williams! The whole of the known world under one government. Our beloved England, then known as Britannia, was part of the empire. That splendid time lasted, unfortunately, little more than two hundred years, but almost ten generations lived in peace and prosperity before the barbarians tore it apart. It was the most perfect time in the whole history of mankind."

Neville clasped his hands behind his back when St. John paused. He bit back facts that would contradict St. John's delusions. Pax Romana had not ended because of invaders but because of the ineptitude of its emperors who had quarreled among themselves, often using assassination as a tool to get rid of rivals. In the time when the Caesars had mollified their subjects with bread and circuses, Rome grew bloated and weak.

However, to say those words in Novum Arce would likely be considered the gravest heresy. In St. John's fantasy, which he was explaining in tiresome detail, Pax Romana had been destroyed by those who were jealous of what Rome had created. Until Neville was more certain of what St. John truly planned, it would be wise to play along as Pris was.

"The American leaders chose the words well for the preamble to their Constitution." He put his hand over his heart as if posing for a statue. "*We the People of the United States, in Order to form a more perfect Union, establish Justice, insure domestic Tranquility, provide for the common defense, promote the general Welfare, and secure the Blessings of Liberty to ourselves and our Posterity, do ordain and establish this Constitution for the United States of America.*' A fine goal." His gaze swept the room. "One that could describe us at Novum Arce."

Applause erupted as if St. John had spouted a cure for every disease known to man. Neville resisted rolling his eyes as Daphne did often. Silly St. John had made the settlement a success . . . at least thus far. Underestimating him and his followers could be foolish, and being a fool was one thing Neville Hathaway was determined never to be.

He suspected being one at Novum Arce was a quick way to find himself dead.

PRISCILLA LET THE other women walk ahead of her across the wet grass. Clouds still hung low over the fells, but the showers had stopped. She had no doubt they would start again soon. The women's light voices faded beneath the shouts from the training ground where the men were again practicing with swords and shields.

Her own heart sang. When she had seen Neville walk into the *principia*, she had to fight not to sob with happiness. She had feared he was dead, and asking questions about him had been risky.

She picked up an empty basket and settled it on her hip. She grabbed a length of cloth off one of the drying lines and draped it over the basket so it looked as if she carried a load of laundry. Pulling her stola over her head, she hoped nobody would take note of her. Already she had noticed how the many men in the compound ogled the women openly.

Another reason she was glad Neville was in Novum Arce.

Walking in the general direction of the laundry set near the stream flowing from beyond the walls, Priscilla looked for Neville. He had signaled that they should meet outside.

A motion caught her eye, and her heart leaped in a crazy dance. No, it was only one of the clerks who rushed around Novum Arce as if an angry bull gave chase. She kept strolling. It was hard to smile when someone greeted her, but she must pretend to have nothing more on her mind than getting the laundry done.

There! Was it . . . ? Yes!

Neville stood in the shadow cast by the back wall of the *principia*. Her feet begged her to run into his arms, but she kept her pace steady. She continued to check to make sure nobody was watching.

He pulled the basket from her hands and tossed it to the ground before he tugged her through the back door and into the deepest shadows near the banner draped behind the Imperator's throne. When his mouth claimed hers, she slipped into his arms. She had feared she would never feel his strong, firm body against her again.

His lips moved across her face, each kiss branding her with the heat of his eager passion. She murmured over and over that she loved him, knowing only now how deeply she had feared that she would never see him again. As tears ran down her face, he drew back to wipe them away as gently as if each one were a precious gem.

"I thought I had lost you," Neville said when her weeping slowed to unsteady hiccups. "Seeing you alive was the answer to a prayer my heart had been shouting from the moment I woke here."

She ran her fingers along his arm, loath to break the connection between them. "Should we look for some other place to talk?" She glanced along the length of the shadowed hall. The torches had been doused, and the light coming in from the door on the far wall did not reach across the floor.

"I have no idea where else we could go, and from here we have a good view if anyone comes in." He glanced at his dirty and torn clothes. "I stand out like a beggar at a ball."

"I can get you some other clothing."

"Resorting to thievery already? I can see your aunt is not wrong. I have been a very bad influence on you."

Surprised when a laugh tickled her throat, she said, "Yes, you have been a bad influence, but not in this case. Each of us in Novum Arce is assigned a workplace, and mine is in the laundry. I will get you clothes and clean yours as best I can."

"Good. I will need them when we leave."

She had much to tell him, but before she spoke of Novum Arce and the surprises she had discovered in the settlement, she had to ask, "How are you doing?"

"Better than I was a couple of hours ago." His fingers grazed the back of his skull, and he grimaced. "Whoever struck me did so with eager vengeance." His eyes narrowed. "What of you? How are you and . . . ?"

"We are fine. I was knocked out, too, but I have been awake since dawn." She glanced around then smiled. "As a woman, I did not warrant an audience with our leader."

"I should be honored?"

"I am not sure," she replied, "whether the whole of that welcome was for your benefit or the community's. No one speaks against Sir Thomas. In fact, they treat him as if he were Jupiter himself, but I could see those in the *principia* wished they were elsewhere while he rambled on and on about Pax Romana."

"Now he has a ready audience."

Priscilla looked down the length of the hall again to make certain no one else had entered. "Once I woke, I kept asking about you, but I remembered you said you had met St. John, so I chose a different name for you." She frowned. "He did not seem to recognize you."

"Lucky for both of us." He explained how excited St. John usually was when he was at the board of green cloth or by the final turn of the racetrack. "I think my image would have to have been on the cards he held for him to have noticed me." He brushed a vagrant strand of hair behind her ear, and she shivered. "I assume because you gave them a fake name for me, you have one for yourself."

"I am Mrs. Kenton."

"But that makes no sense if they think I am Mr. Williams."

She gave him a wry smile. "They don't realize we arrived together at The Rose and Thistle Inn, and the landlady must not play any part in their activities. I was not noticed until I was seen coming out of another room while I searched for you. When I discovered they thought we were two visitors who happened to be at the inn at the same time, I decided to let them continue with their delusion." Her expression became serious again. "They seem to be good at accepting delusions."

Neville considered her choice. It had been a good one. He intended to find out more about Novum Arce. If caught where he should not be, any punishment would be his alone. Not having to worry about Pris paying for his crimes would give him greater freedom to follow any clues he uncovered.

He reminded himself why they had come to Lakeland. "I saw soldiers in the village and up on the hills."

"I know. They want to make sure that no one gets a close look at this place, except for those of us who are stuck here."

"Is that the only reason St. John has built himself an army?"

She shrugged. "I don't know. I have been careful in what I have asked, because I didn't want to tip my hand. It is best that they think of me only as Mrs. Keaton who works in the laundry."

"Do you have a first name, Mrs. Kenton?" he asked, tensing when a shadow crossed the door at the other end of the hall. It vanished. The person must have walked past without stopping.

"Of course, I gave them a first name," Pris replied.

"What is it?"

Color flashed up her face. "Cordelia."

He shook his head in disgust. "Of all the names in the world—"

"It was the first one that came to me. I was thinking how glad I am the children are safe with Aunt Cordelia."

"Not all of them." He glanced down at her belly, which still was flat beneath her loose clothing. "Pris—"

"Stop," she whispered. "Watch what you say."

Neville berated himself. She was right to scold him. The throbbing in his skull was no excuse. He started to apologize but halted when someone entered the hall. Without a word, he took Pris's hand and drew her out of the *principia*. He frowned when he saw everyone along the walkway in front of them stop. Pris tensed beside him and he realized she thought they had been caught.

Or had she stiffened when she saw the fake Roman soldiers marching past in perfect unison, holding their shields and spears? Their short swords bounced with each step, and the feathers in their helmets danced in the breeze. Were those their only weapons, or did they have more modern ones stashed away, ready to be used upon St. John's command?

"Come on," Neville murmured, leading her away from the crowd cheering as the *faux* legionaries paraded in front of them.

Pris went with him without question, but he knew she had as many as he did.

As soon as they were concealed behind what appeared to be a well house, he said, "I see what is in front of my eyes, but I cannot believe it."

"It is exactly what Sir Thomas told you. He is trying to resurrect Roman Britain and the Pax Romana. I have tried to find out why he chose this particular time, but either the people don't know or they don't care because they feel safe here."

"In a madman's hallucination?"

"Despite Sir Thomas's state of mind, you can see that he has been working on the settlement for quite a while." She pointed along the straight street where the soldiers were now marching toward the small, columned building. "That is a temple to the cult of Mithras. It is on top of a cave because the worship must be below ground. The people believe the cave is the reason Novum Arce is here."

"Or they pretend to believe it."

"It does not matter. They are willing to play along with the fantasy that Mithras is the god of light and wisdom, and it was with his guidance that Sir Thomas came here to build his city. I have been told no women are allowed in the temple or the cave below it because it is the domain of warriors."

"We need to get the hell out of here. Tonight—"

"No, we cannot leave."

"Don't worry about the guards at the gate. We have slipped past others."

She shook her head. "We cannot leave because we have to figure out how she fits in here."

"She who?"

Pris pointed toward another group of villagers who stepped hastily aside as a tall brunette glided along the walkway, heading toward the temple. Thick bands of gold encircled her upper arms, and pearls were woven through her lush curls. More jewels glittered on her fingers. Her eyes were lined with kohl, making her look more like an ancient Egyptian than a Roman, and her lips were painted scarlet. The white gown accented her voluptuous curves, and her draped cloak, which was a vivid purple, offered a few glimpses of the pale skin of her shoulders and swanlike neck.

His eyes widened as he stared at the woman's long neck. "Is that who I think it is?"

She nodded. "Yes. That is the baron's daughter, though from what I have been told, she is calling herself Bellona now."

"The Roman goddess of war?"

"I am constantly amazed at the breadth of your knowledge."

"Knowing a little about a lot makes a man a good dinner companion, a vital skill among the *Beau Monde*." He looked past her. "I wonder why she chose that name."

"Though we are surrounded by people who are more than a bit insane, we are exactly where we should be. Not only can we learn about Sir Thomas's plans, but we can rescue Miss Beamish."

"Do you know if she is ready to leave or has any idea where her servants are?"

"I have not had a chance to talk to her. The other women who are assigned to the laundry are in awe of her and call her *magistra*. I think it is a term of respect."

Neville did not reply as he watched Beamish's daughter. He was not going to call her by the absurd name she had adopted. Had it been chance that they had been brought to the same place where she was? Or had something other than fortune played a hand in arranging for him and Pris to end up in Novum Arce?

If it were the latter, the person who had ordered their abduction must believe their lie that the only reason they had come north was to search for Miss Beamish. He had not guessed that the excuse would make them prisoners behind a great wall. Someone wanted to keep them from reporting to Beamish, but who? And why?

And did that person suspect the real reason they had come to Lakeland? If so, their situation could be even more perilous than he had guessed.

Chapter Eight

PRISCILLA PRESSED her hands to the small of her back then looked around. If Neville chanced to see her showing any hint of pain, he would insist they leave immediately. She had no doubts Neville could find a way to sneak them out of Novum Arce, but she did not feel right about leaving Lord Beamish's daughter behind. Reporting her location to her father could mean jeopardizing Neville's work because Lord Beamish would likely storm into the settlement before the government's forces could arrive. If Sir Thomas truly intended to use his army to attack England, any intrusion now could mean him taking his men and his plans underground where they could not be found until they were ready to start a war.

And what about Miss Beamish's servants? Where were they? If they were part of Sir Thomas's plans, that must be known, too, so Neville could report that to whoever sent him north.

She hung the heavy, sodden garment over the line strung between two cottages, then realized she would not have enough room for the rest of the laundry. With a groan, she began pulling the garments closer together. She heard threads snap and halted, knowing she must take each one off and readjust it. The very thought sent tears welling up in her eyes.

No! She would not be weak. Not when Neville had been sent to work in the fields, trying to turn the hard soil with primitive implements from almost two millennia ago. She had to complete her task if she wanted her midday meal, and she could not risk going without when her baby was growing within her. Besides, she must not stand out in any way. In the past week, the others seemed to have accepted her and Neville.

A twinge ached in her back, but she ignored it. If she could get a good night's sleep, she would do better. Several of the women with whom she shared a cramped cottage talked long into the night, not caring that others were trying to sleep. Another muttered in her sleep, and two or three were plagued by nightmares or sleepwalking.

Maybe that was why she did not notice the voice until it became sharp with impatience. "Cordelia, I am talking to you. Do you hear me? Cordelia!"

Belatedly, Priscilla recalled that everyone in Novum Arce, save Neville, believed her name was Cordelia Kenton. She folded the clammy garment over her arm and turned to see who had called to her.

Miss Beamish!

She chided herself. She must think of the woman as *Magistra* Bellona. A mistake in addressing the baron's daughter could lead to questions that would ruin any chance she and Neville had of getting to the truth.

She dipped in a curtsy. "Pardon me, *magistra*. My mind was soaring away on the spring breezes."

Bellona eyed her up and down. "Have we met?" Her voice did not match her loveliness. It was raspy and a bit too high pitched, an altogether unpleasant sound.

She decided to do the pretty for Bellona. "Everyone in Novum Arce knows *you*."

"No, I meant have we met before your arrival here?"

Priscilla had stiffened like a stone when she heard Sir Thomas ask Neville a similar question. Now she had to copy Neville's gentle puzzlement at what Cordelia Kenton would see as an extraordinary query. Pretending to consider what Bellona asked, she answered, "I was going to say no, but on second thought, it is possible. Did you ever call on Lady Whittingly in London?"

"Are you one of her relatives?" Bellona's nose wrinkled in distaste.

"No."

"A friend?"

"No." That much was the truth. Lady Whittingly had few friends because the bitter woman seldom spoke anything but insults.

"Then why would I see you at the lady's house?"

"I was her lady's maid."

"Lady's maid?" Bellona openly appraised Priscilla again then nodded. "That makes sense. You have an aura of gentility about you but obviously not the polish of the *ton*."

"True," she replied in the same respectful tone.

"Walk with me while we talk, Cordelia."

It was not a request, and Priscilla put the wet garment back in the basket. She motioned to one of the other laundresses. The woman frowned, but that expression quickly changed into a smile when she saw who stood by Priscilla. With a nod, she called that she would be glad to finish hanging the items.

The woman was wasting her time trying to gain Bellona's attention because the younger woman had already turned to walk away. Her assumption that her orders would be obeyed without question piqued Priscilla's curiosity. She had seen the young woman cause a stir wherever she went in the compound but had no idea why. Had Sir Thomas taken her under his wing? She recalled how Lord Beamish had said he spoiled Miss Beamish as a child. Such protection in Novum Arce would demand outward respect. Or was it simply the Beamish arrogance?

More questions Priscilla needed to find answers to, but she was not going to squander a moment of her chance to speak to Bellona. Hurrying to catch up with the younger woman, she waited for Bellona to say why she had sought out "Cordelia."

"How are you settling in?" Bellona asked.

"Quite well. Thank you."

"Some people are more trouble—have more trouble than others." She glanced at Priscilla, daring her to comment on a slip of the tongue.

Acting as if she had not heard, though it was important for Bellona to believe she was hanging on every word, she said, "What I have been doing here is not much different than what Lady Whittingly asked of me. And other people here have been kind to explain things I do not understand. Some houses I have been in were not as welcoming."

"*Some* houses? How many have you served in, Kenton?"

"Only two, but I do not wish to speak badly of either." She stared at the road, her eyes properly downcast. Most abigails spent their whole time in service at a single house. "And now here, of course."

That seemed to satisfy Bellona who must have believed her tale of being a lady's maid because she now addressed her as Kenton, as a lady spoke to an abigail.

"The fact you are fitting in here speaks well of your interest in Novum Arce."

"I had no idea such a place existed."

"Few do." Bellona smiled, but her eyes remained cool and evaluating. "You should count yourself lucky, Kenton."

"I do, *magistra*. I do." As they passed the *principia* and turned down the main avenue toward the temple, Priscilla said, "If I may ask a question . . ."

"Of course," she said as if granting a great kindness.

"Have you been here long? You seem at home in Novum Arce."

Bellona wore a benevolent smile. "In some ways, it feels as if I have been here my whole life. In others, it is like I arrived a short time ago." Her girlish giggle startled Priscilla, especially as it seemed sincere. "That sounds like a frivolous answer, but I am so happy here I have let the days slip by me uncounted."

"Did you know of Novum Arce before you came here?" Priscilla held her breath, knowing she was overstepping her role by asking a second question.

"I had heard rumors, of course, but I had no idea which ones were true and which were lies created by jealous outsiders."

"So you decided to come and see for yourself?"

"Not exactly." She paused as a very tall man wearing the armor of a legionary stepped out of one of the identical buildings along the avenue.

He was unlike most of the legionaries Priscilla had seen, who clearly had been recruited from farms among the fells and were still struggling to keep up with the demands of their training. He displayed well-contoured muscles that strained against his armor. His face was as perfectly sculpted as a Roman statue, and his black hair curled on his forehead. He was a man who would make a woman look twice and let her eyes linger the second time.

He rushed forward to take Bellona's proffered hand and press his lips to it. "*Carissime*," he breathed. He raised his head and stared at her as if she were the source of the very air he breathed.

"Livius." Her voice was low but sliced through the air like a riding crop. "I am speaking with Kenton."

"Forgive me. Forgive me for intruding." He dipped his head and took a step back.

Priscilla hid her astonishment. His accent sounded like Duncan's. She had not guessed anyone in Novum Arce had come from north of the Scottish border. That could add another dimension to the potential danger of St. John raising an army at Novum Arce. There were those north of the border who would gladly see England defeated. Such information would be of great interest to Neville. She sighed silently. Watching these two young people in love—or at least, Livius was in love with Lord Beamish's daughter—reminded her yet again how much she missed being with her husband.

"Of course, I forgive you, Livius." Bellona's voice drew Priscilla's attention back to the drama playing out in front of her. "You and I will talk later?"

"Aye. I will be counting every moment. I am eager to share something with you. Until we are alone . . ." He reached out, grasped her fingers, and squeezed them before hurrying away.

Bellona's smile was cool as she wiped her hand on her gown before looking at Priscilla. As if there had been no interruption, she said, "I traveled north to spend time with my late mother's family and get to know them better."

Priscilla recalled Lord Beamish saying his daughter had traveled from London to meet a suitor, so one of them had to be lying. She had no idea which. Or maybe she had not heard the real truth yet.

"Does your mother's family live here?"

"In Novum Arce?" Her eyes narrowed, and her voice became a sibilant hiss. "Why would you assume that?"

"I mean no offense. I only wanted to ask, *magistra*, if your mother's family lived in Lakeland."

"No. They live farther north." She looked in the direction Livius had walked. "North of the borders. Father was not happy with my plans." Bellona's mouth twisted. "He wants nothing to do with my mother's family."

Priscilla understood what Bellona was taking pains not to say. In the wake of the rebellion fomented by Charles Edward Stuart, the Young Pretender, almost seventy years before, few members of the *ton* would acknowledge having Scottish relatives in the Highlands. The battles culminating at Culloden had wreaked havoc on both England and Scotland, and the government's retribution had been both swift and brutal.

"That must be hard for you," Priscilla said when she realized she had to say something. "I am sorry."

"Father does not wish to speak of my mother's family." Bellona began walking again. With a terse laugh, she said, "His not wanting to talk of them made me, as a child, more determined to know the truth about my late mother's relatives."

Priscilla laughed with more ease. "I understand. I was much the same, and my . . ." She faked a sneeze to cover her pause. "Excuse me. I was about to say, my sister's children act like that as well."

"Children are curious. It is part of their nature."

She kept her shoulders from sagging with relief. A former lady's maid would not have children because any servant achieving that elevated post was expected to be at her mistress's beck and call at any time of the day or night. Combining those duties with marriage and a family was impossible.

"How did you come to Novum Arce, *magistra*, if I may ask?"

"Of course, you may ask. I was about to tell you." She gave Priscilla another gracious smile.

Priscilla was amazed at the volatile and rapid changes in the young woman's moods. That is, if they were true changes and not simply a way to control those around her. Instantly she scolded herself. She must not judge the daughter by the father. And, though Neville had his doubts, Priscilla was certain Lord Beamish's concern for his daughter was genuine.

As they strolled from sunlight to shadow beneath the recently planted trees lining the street, Bellona said, "There are two ways people come to Novum Arce. One is of their own volition. Most of those are local people who jumped at the chance for a new beginning."

"A new world."

"Exactly. The other way is by being chosen."

"Chosen?"

Bellona nodded, her smile becoming superior as she looked down her slender nose at the people they passed. "We are the ones selected because of our age, our beauty, and our intelligence. As I was." She laughed coolly. "And as you were, Kenton. You should feel honored."

Honored was not exactly the word she would have selected, but she was grateful she and Neville had ended up in the same place. From within the walls, Neville should be able to obtain the information he needed far more quickly. As well, they had found Lord Beamish's daughter. Reminding herself to play the part she had created, she asked, "I can see why you were chosen. But I am only a lady's maid traveling to a new employer."

"Being modest will get you nowhere in Novum Arce. You are not bad to look at for a woman of your age. How old are you? Thirty-two, thirty-three?"

Priscilla almost laughed. Bellona prided herself on her intelligence, but she had missed Priscilla's true age by almost five years. "The latter."

"So you are still fertile. That is a good reason to bring you here. It is ironic that the upper classes who can afford to raise children are less fecund than the lower ones."

Almost choking at Bellona's plainspoken discussion of something no lady should ever mention, Priscilla decided to move the conversation back to what she needed to know. "Who does the choosing?"

"There are agents who comb the countryside looking for possible candidates for our community. When they select a likely person, they make arrangements for that person to be brought here."

"Whether they wish it or not?"

Bellona's smile fled, but she quickly regained it. "Of course, if someone comes here and is unhappy, everyone makes sure they learn they can find their true joy here."

Did Bellona truly believe that drivel? Priscilla wished she could be blunt, but had to guard every word she spoke.

"Did your traveling companions come here with you?" Priscilla asked.

"Why do you ask about such a thing?"

"I cannot imagine a lady of your stature would travel alone, and I was curious to know what happens to those who are not chosen."

Bellona closed her eyes. "I don't know. Such questions should be posed to our Imperator. He is the one who makes the ultimate decision of who is welcome and who is not."

"Your family must be worried sick wondering where you are," she said, trying to decide if the young woman was being honest.

"I have thought of that." She stared past the wall to a freshet coursing down over the hillside in a slender waterfall. "Often."

"But you have not made any attempt to leave. Surely you want to return to the life you had."

"'Life I had?' I had no life, Kenton. My father refused to allow me to receive any callers until I met a man who cares enough about me to ignore my father's stupid rules. Of course, my father then disparaged the man to me and everyone else."

Priscilla wondered if she spoke of Clarence Sherman, the man whose very name was distasteful for Lord Beamish. Again, she chose her words carefully. "I am sorry to hear that. Yet there must be something that calls you home."

"If I wished to leave, where would I go?" She stretched out her arms. "Look around. Do you see any living things other than sheep?"

"There are people in the valley below."

"I am sure there are, but could I reach them before I was stopped? I saw one fool try to sneak away. He was trying to steal from the community." Her mouth twisted. "Don't ask me what happened to him. I don't want to think of it."

Priscilla bit her lip to keep from asking another question. Whoever had sent Neville here had been right to be worried. Despite its outwardly peaceful appearance and Sir Thomas's declarations of Pax Romana, there was a very definite dark side to the community.

"Let's talk about you." Bellona paused and faced her. "Are you happy in the laundry?"

"It is honest work."

"Bah, that is an answer you give to an employer. Surely you would prefer to work where you could use your skills."

Hoping the comment was not a test, Priscilla replied, "One always wishes to do the work one has been trained for."

"If you have served as a lady's maid, I am not sure what work you are suited for here other than the laundry. It is a shame there are no ladies besides myself here. The other women would have no idea what to do with a lady's maid." She laughed gaily as if she had made a hilarious jest.

Priscilla hoped her own laugh did not sound as fake as it felt.

"Do you have any other skills, Cordelia?"

"I am good at keeping accounts and records."

"Records? Why would you keep records for your lady's estate? Didn't she have an estate manager?"

Stupid! She could not forget Bellona was as familiar with the ways of the *ton* as she was.

Making sure her obsequious smile did not waver, she hurried to say, "Forgive me. I did not make myself clear. I handled the accounting of my lady's personal funds along with assisting the vicar with his." At least that was the truth. She had always overseen the household and the church accounts while married to Lazarus. "It pleased my lady that I was involved in helping with the parish."

"Yes, doing your Christian duty would reflect well upon her." She pursed her lips. "That is a side of Lady Whittingly I have not seen before."

Priscilla remained silent. She needed to let Bellona make her own assumptions. Saying anything might lead to her lie unraveling completely.

The younger woman began walking, cutting across an area between the low buildings. Beneath their sandals, the grass was just beginning to grow. Priscilla was not sure where they were bound until she saw a tall, thin woman sitting on a stone bench. She was embroidering a piece of white cloth with an intricate design.

"Ah, Parker, I had hoped we would encounter you," Bellona said as if the meeting were a chance one.

The brunette wore a gown and stola of lesser quality than Bellona's. When she rose and dipped in a curtsy, her gaze slid toward Priscilla before her eyes focused on Bellona. That, as much as anything else, told Priscilla that the thin woman Bellona had called Parker was a servant.

"Do you need something, *Magistra* Bellona?" The young woman's voice was a stark contrast to Bellona's strident tones. It was lyrical and lilting like notes rising from a violin played by a master.

"I want you to meet Kenton. You have much in common. Kenton has experience as a lady's maid. I will leave you to your conversation of matters that you are familiar with." Her tone suggested anything of interest to two ladies' maids was nothing she wanted to hear.

Parker curtsied again as Bellona walked away. Priscilla hurried to copy her, wishing she had picked a different profession for Cordelia Kenton. How could she have guessed a real lady's maid would be among the residents?

But at least one of Bellona's servants was alive. Maybe she knew where the others were.

"My full name is Roxanne Parker," the abigail said.

"I am Cordelia Kenton." The lie tasted bitter on her lips, but she could not trust anyone in Novum Arce except Neville.

"You came here not too long ago with Mr. Williams, didn't you?"

"So I have been told, though I must own, I have no memory of my arrival. I do recall seeing Mr. Williams at a wayside inn where I stayed before I came here."

Roxanne smiled shyly. "Mr. Williams is a very handsome man. He could not take his eyes off you when he came into the *principia*."

"He probably remembers me from our evening meal that night."

"If you are interested in him, you should make that clear before some other woman turns her eyes on him." She ran her fingers over the low nap on her stola. "The Imperator has urged us to find mates among the residents of Novum Arce. He prefers we are married and happy."

Priscilla remembered Neville's half-teasing words about Sir Thomas building a utopia and filling it with children. He had not been wrong.

"You came here with *Magistra* Bellona?" she asked, steering the conversation back to where she needed it to go.

"Yes."

"Alone? The two of you traveled so far by yourselves?"

Roxanne shook her head, and bright tears filled her blue eyes. "Of course not. She is the daughter of a baron."

Priscilla faked surprise. "A baron's daughter? That explains her mien."

"Yes, she is a polished lady. That is why she was accompanied by her companion, Miss Redding, as well as one of Lord Beamish's footmen, a tiger, and the coachman."

"Lord Beamish?"

Roxanne flushed. "Oh, I should not have said that."

"But if she is Lord Beamish's daughter and you are his servant, then you are the ones reported missing. Do you know where the others are?"

"No, I have not seen any of them since our last night at the inn."

"Inn?"

"The Rose and Thistle Inn. Do you know it?"

"Yes. Like you, we were staying there."

"We?"

Priscilla flinched. Forcing a strained smile, she said, "You know already. Mr. Williams was there, too."

"Oh, I thought you might have been traveling with someone else. Someone who might be looking for you." She sighed. "Were you?"

She shook her head. "I don't know about Mr. Williams, but I was on my way to a new position. The lady who hired me must be thinking I changed my mind."

"Would she send someone to be certain?"

"I doubt it."

Roxanne sighed again. "Forgive me, Cordelia. I hope each time someone new comes . . ." She glanced around nervously. "I should not be speaking of this. I should be grateful I can continue to serve my miss, even here. Have you been given your assignment yet?"

"I am working in the laundry."

"That is ridiculous!" Roxanne frowned. "You are a lady's maid. You should not be consigned to cleaning soldiers' sweaty clothing."

"The *magistra* said there was nobody here other than herself who would know how to make use of a trained abigail."

With a saucy grin, Roxanne said, "My miss sees the situation from a lady's point of view. You and I know part of an abigail's job is training her employer."

"True." Priscilla chuckled.

"There are several highly placed ladies in Novum Arce. I am sure one of them would be delighted to have an experienced lady's maid." A devilish smile banished the stress from her face. "In fact, they have been jealous of my miss for having me. I will make a few discreet inquiries, and you will be done with your job at the laundry in no time."

"Thank you. But am I allowed to change assignments?"

"Maybe. Maybe not, but don't worry. A pretty woman like you is certain to attract the eye of one of the commanders of the legion. That will free you from the laundry." Roxanne's face was taut. "I know how that sounds, Cordelia, but it is the way of life here. I count my blessings every night Miss Beamish—I mean, *Magistra* Bellona insisted I continue as her abigail."

"But aren't you worried about the others who traveled with you?" Priscilla hated pushing Roxanne toward what she knew was a tender subject. But she needed all possible information.

"Terribly." Tears pooled in her eyes. "Especially my betrothed. His name is Asher. Asher Snow. He is a footman at Lord Beamish's estate, and he came north with us." The tears tumbled down her cheeks. "I don't know if he is dead or alive."

"Someone here must know."

"I am sure someone does, but nobody will answer my questions. It is as if he and the others have vanished. At first, I thought my miss was dead, too, but then a week or more after I woke up here, I saw her, and I was relieved to discover she was alive. But I haven't seen Asher or the others."

"Have you asked *Magistra* Bellona if she could find out what happened to them?"

"Yes, but I hesitate to press because Miss Redding has been her companion since the *magistra* left the classroom. Before that, Miss Redding taught her deportment. My miss has to be heartsick with worry for Miss Redding. When we first saw each other here, she embraced me as if I were her sister, and I have served her for only a few years."

"Has *Magistra* Bellona said anything about what she believes might have happened to the others?"

"She refuses to talk of them. I can understand, for it must be as painful for her as it is for me to think of them. Yet I cannot stop wondering where Asher is. I don't know if I will ever see him again." Her voice broke into sobs.

Priscilla put her arm around the abigail's quaking shoulders. "Roxanne, don't forget one fact. To anyone living beyond Novum Arce, it will seem as if we have disappeared without a trace, too. But we are alive."

"True." She dashed away her tears. "I wish I could be sure Asher is safe. The others, too."

"I know." She did not add that she suspected being within the walls of Novum Arce was no guarantee of safety.

Chapter Nine

A WEEK LATER, NO closer to solving the puzzle of where Bellona's missing servants were, Priscilla was grateful to learn that Roxanne had arranged for her to work as a lady's maid for the commandant's wife. The woman, who called herself Domitilla in honor of a mother of two Roman emperors, wanted Priscilla to help her dress and do her hair in the morning and again in the evening before her husband came home. Otherwise, she preferred Priscilla make herself scarce because having to deal with an abigail was a constant reminder to her of how much Domitilla did not know about managing servants.

Domitilla was kind to her. Whenever Priscilla suggested new hair arrangements that suited the Roman style, Domitilla was thrilled. Not just because the styles suited her better than the mess she had made of her own hair, but because she could brag about how her abigail had designed it especially for her. She gave Priscilla a new gown and stola so Priscilla could get rid of the stained one she had worn at the laundry.

But Priscilla was never comfortable when Domitilla's husband, who called himself Trajanus, was in the grand house which was only slightly smaller than the grand villa Sir Thomas had built for himself. He had been court-martialed from the king's army for killing a man with his bare fists. The thought brought chills to Priscilla because she could not help thinking of Bellona's warning about what had happened to the man who tried to flee from Novum Arce with stolen items. Had the commandant been the one to order his beating or had he done the deed himself?

Her hope that he might have meetings with his men at the house came to naught. She had no chance to eavesdrop on their plans. Her attempts to learn something from Domitilla were just as doomed to failure because the commandant's wife had no interest in what the troops were doing.

Yet, not having to wait on Domitilla day and night gave Priscilla a chance to explore Novum Arce. She was impressed with the simple architecture that looked classical but had been designed for the cold and damp weather in Lakeland. She had no idea if the Romans had glass in their windows or enough fire pits to keep the buildings warm.

She began to understand why some of the nearby people had come to Novum Arce with their children, their sheep, and their skills. The living conditions were better behind the walls than in a small cottage on the fells. In exchange for comfortable surroundings and good meals, they were willing to accept Sir Thomas's absurd dream of rebuilding Britannia.

But she had had no time with Neville. She had not spoken to him since she became Domitilla's personal maid. She had no excuse to go to the fields being plowed and sown. Her hope that she could steal a moment with him at the evening meal had been dashed because the fieldworkers were fed before everyone else so they could go to sleep early and rise before dawn the next morning. Even in Sir Thomas's utopia, a hierarchy was already settling into place.

She wanted to tell him what Roxanne had related about the missing servants. If they were alive, they must be imprisoned somewhere. Otherwise, they would have returned to Lord Beamish's estate and let him know what had happened to them and to his daughter.

Where were they? Were they being held in Novum Arce or somewhere else? Had Sir Thomas built a prison to hold those who he did not want in his community? Why would Sir Thomas want to banish servants who could work hard within the walls? The male servants could have been added to the army which spent almost every waking hour of each day training.

She was missing something important. And she was missing Neville more. Talking over information with him always helped her clarify her thoughts, but more than that, she ached to have his arms around her.

As she sat by the well in the courtyard in the commandant's house, she ran the toe of her sandal along the intricate mosaics. They made a picture of a horse leaping over a shrub. She had no idea if the pattern was Roman or from Sir Thomas's imagination.

She needed to take the facts she had and try to arrange them to see the full picture. The problem was she had too few facts. Maybe Neville had discovered something that, put together with what she had learned, would help them see the truth.

"Cordelia!" came her mistress's voice. "I need my best comb. Do you know where it is?"

Pushing aside her thoughts, Priscilla went to do Domitilla's bidding. Tonight the commandant's wife was joining her husband at a gathering at Sir Thomas's house. Priscilla intended to put the hours when they would be occupied to good use.

The answers were there. She simply needed to discover what they were.

"YOU LOOK QUITE pleased with yourself."

Neville looked up to see Pris walking through the shadows. As he had hoped she would. He had been on his way from supper with his fellow fieldworkers when he saw the commandant and his wife leave their grand villa. Letting the other men go ahead of him, he had waited to see if Pris would slip out of the house. From afar, he had taken note of how she had been exploring the compound while he was stuck in the fields, clearing rocks and sowing the seeds he had been given.

He motioned for her to follow him past the *principia*. Taking her hand, he savored the warmth of her slender fingers curling around his. The ache of missing her that had plagued him, keeping him from sleeping when his body was desperate for rest, grew stronger. But he was aware of how many eyes could be on them. In Novum Arce, one was always watched, whether by guards or other residents. Sir Thomas's utopia was built on distrust and the ambition to gain power within its walls.

Pris said nothing as he paused by a big building beyond the *principia*. Not a light shone through the narrow windows. He opened the door, drew her through, and shut it behind them. He considered dropping the bar into place, but that would be a sure sign someone was inside. Better to remain alert.

"This way," he murmured, tugging her hand.

"Should we be in here?" Her voice was a balm for his soul, and he realized how much he had missed its sweet warmth.

"No one is using it." He led her through an open courtyard and opened a door on the far corner. "It looks like St. John is hoping to lure another mungo here."

"Mungo?"

He laughed. "I never am sure which parts of London street cant you know and which you don't. A mungo is an important person."

"But who is he asking here?"

"I have no idea if he has someone in mind or if it is a rumor."

"Most likely a rumor. I cannot imagine Sir Thomas sharing the power he has given himself with anyone else. Or Bellona stepping aside as the highest ranked woman in Novum Arce."

"If we were dealing with sane people . . ." He did not bother finishing.

She took his hand. "Come with me. I know a better place for us to talk."

Neville hesitated, not wanting to waste a moment they could have together, then nodded. Some of the soldiers used empty house for trysts with women who hoped to enhance their status by marrying well. Though he doubted making a match with one of the incompetent soldiers would do anyone much good. He had watched the practices for the past week, and the only thing that had improved was their boasting and swaggering. Even so, while Pris was with him, he did not want to stumble over a soldier and his ladylove.

Maybe the threat to the Crown was only an illusion, like everything else about Novum Arce. What he had seen pointed to having nothing to worry about, yet his gut still warned that there was a threat here. All he needed to do was pinpoint it. Maybe Pris had seen something that would help.

On the other hand, he really did not want to talk about his mission while he was with her. He would prefer to bring her into his arms and delight in the feel of her lips against his.

"All right," he said. "Lead the way."

The moon was rising over the fells when they emerged from the great house. He made sure the door was closed then took Pris's hand again, wishing he would not have to let go of her once more. A motion high on the fells caught his eye, and he froze.

"What is it?" Pris asked.

"I saw someone. Up there."

She peered through the dark, lit only by the moonlight. "I don't see anyone."

He looked again. "Nor do I. Now."

"Sir Thomas has patrols along the fells. Maybe you saw one of them."

"Impossible. The guards are up there only during daylight. Once it grows dark, they return to Novum Arce."

"That makes no sense."

"What here does? From what I have been told, one of the fools lost his way and fell, breaking a leg and an arm. Since then, the patrols go out only when the sun can light the way." He squinted at where he had seen movement. "Maybe it was a trick of the light."

"Maybe. Maybe not."

Her confidence in him urged him to draw her close and hold her while the rest of the world disappeared.

Disappeared.

Blast St. John and his inept army who could not even manage to patrol their own hills!

He quelled his vexation as Pris guided him around the back of the commandant's house. She went, without slowing, to a small outbuilding and opened the door. Leaving his side only to collect a dark lantern from another building, she motioned for him to go inside.

He took the lantern from her, so he could see the interior. It might have been intended to be a stillroom, a wine cellar, or a private laundry, but it was empty save for a few puddles on in the stone floor close to the two windows.

Closing the door, Priscilla said, "You watch the window past my shoulder, and I will do the same with the one beyond you. That way, we can make sure nobody chances by."

"An excellent idea." He wished his mind could work as quickly as hers, but it was mired in exhaustion. "How are you being treated in the commandant's house?"

"Quite well. Both of *us*," she said, touching her stomach so he could not fail to understand she spoke of their child, "are happy with the circumstances, and Domitilla is so proud to have an abigail that she never chides me, even if I drop something."

"And her husband?"

"I rarely see him. The few times I have, he acts as if I am not there." She told him how disappointed she was that she hadn't had the chance to listen to the soldiers making their plans.

"That would have been almost too easy." He lowered her stola off her hair and ran his fingers through her soft tresses. "I am relieved your work is less strenuous than at the laundry."

"As am I." She took his hand and sandwiched it between hers. "How are *you* doing? The work you have been given is strenuous."

"True, but the team I am on finished our section earlier than anyone else today. Our reward was a chance to visit the baths behind the temple."

"That is why you don't smell as pungent as other workers I have passed."

He laughed. "I will take that as a compliment. While I was there this evening, I kept thinking what a good idea it would be to have a real Roman bath built at Tarn's Edge."

"Just one? For men? Do you intend to build another for the women?"

He waved a hand to dismiss her questions. "One would be sufficient. Just think. The two of us in a heated pool and . . ."

"Enough!" She wrapped her arms around herself. "Enough! It is bad enough that we have to sneak about to talk. I don't want to think of how long it has been since you last kissed me."

"One week, two days, five hours, and two minutes."

"Really?"

He chuckled. "Possibly. I don't know it to the exact second. I know it feels like it has been an eternity."

"You can be annoying when you are trying to be nice. Did you know that?"

"You may have mentioned it once or twice."

With a laugh, she slapped his arm. He winced at the ache that coursed through him. Every muscle protested the backbreaking work he had been doing. An hour in the baths trying to loosen them had helped but not enough.

Tears filled Pris's eyes as she said, "I am sorry."

"No need for you to apologize, Cordel—by all that's blue, I find it impossible to call you that."

"Call me Kenton. An abigail is addressed by her last name, and it may be easier for you. I have been waiting to tell you what Bellona and Roxanne Parker told me."

"Who is Roxanne Parker?"

"Bellona's abigail."

Ah, now that was interesting. He had not realized any of the servants from Beamish's household had joined Miss Beamish at Novum Arce. He listened while Pris outlined what Beamish's daughter had told her about how people arrived at the settlement. Not that he was surprised, for the explanation fit their experiences, but for Miss Beamish to speak of it so openly was unexpected. He stood straighter when he heard what the abigail had shared with Pris.

"It is, indeed, troubling to hear," he said when she finished, "that Miss Parker has no idea of the fate of the other servants."

"I suspect they are—or at least have been—here."

"But nobody's seen them."

"Roxanne has not seen them. That does not mean they are not here. She did not see Bellona for a week after they arrived."

"True." He considered the import of her words. If the other servants were alive, they were being kept from returning to Beamish's estate. Assuming they were still alive. Pris seemed certain, but she was not as familiar with the blackness of men's hearts as he had become through hard lessons.

Madmen became dangerous when their addled plans were thwarted. Though St. John did not have a villainous reputation, how would he react if someone challenged him? Even if his army was incompetent, people could be hurt or killed in a melee.

"One other problem," she said with a sigh. "Bellona has no interest in returning home. She is out from under her father's thumb and is enjoying an elevated status here while not having to comply with his unreasonable expectations."

"Her father is unreasonable?" He gave her a wry smile. "It *would* be simpler if our fair Roman princess was eager to leave."

She whirled to look out the window behind her. "Did you hear that?"

He strained his ears for the sound she had heard. There it was! A faint scratching as if something were in the walls. That was impossible, because the building had been constructed from stones pulled from the fells.

Ignoring his aches and bruises, Neville dashed to the window. He looked both ways and saw nobody. "Wait here!" He threw open the door and went out.

A group of four or five people was walking along the street leading from the commandant's house toward the center of Novum Arce. In the other direction, two guards stood at the gate. If there was anyone closer, he could not pick them out of the shadows.

Turning, he went back inside. He shook his head. "Someone may have been spying on us, but I could not see anyone nearby."

"We said nothing other than the fact that we know Miss Beamish's real identity." She wrapped her arms around herself. "We need to find a place where we can speak without being overheard."

"That will not be easy for me. We are watched constantly in the fields."

"I can find excuses to walk through Novum Arce. I have been watching everyone . . . to see if I can discern the truth you are looking for."

"Be careful. You are watched closely, too."

She nodded grimly. "If I am questioned, I can pretend I am on an errand for Domitilla and went to the wrong place by mistake."

"I don't like you wandering about alone. I have heard the comments the men make about any woman they see out walking."

"I know the risks. Roxanne has warned me how women are expected to marry."

He turned toward the door, fighting back a grimace at the return of the ache through his muscles. "Let's go."

"Where?"

"Out of Novum Arce. Now. I will not have you leered at and pawed like some doxy."

"It is too dangerous."

"Too dangerous for you to stay, I agree."

"No, I mean it is too dangerous for us to try to sneak away."

He listened, appalled, as she repeated Bellona's tale of the man who had tried to leave the settlement.

"And," she continued as he cursed colorfully, "we cannot go until we discover the truth. You promised to find it out, and I will not let you break your promise."

He drew her into his arms and captured her mouth. Her need for him branded his lips, stealing his breath and setting his heart pounding at a fierce tempo. Her pliant curves caressed him as she melted against him. Whispering her name, he relished the shiver that swept along her skin.

He tipped her face back so he could gaze into her loving eyes. "All right, but if one of these over-zealous pseudo-legionaries comes too close—"

"I will let you know."

"You better." He pressed his mouth to hers, not wanting to think how long it might be before he had a chance to kiss her again.

Chapter Ten

THE NEXT TIME Neville had a chance to see Pris was only two days later at a command performance that required the attendance of everyone, save the gate guards, in the great hall of the *principia*. Neville would have liked to find an excuse to avoid attending because it would have been the perfect time, when everyone was occupied, to sneak into portions of the compound that were off-limits to a mere laborer. However, the other fieldworkers had insisted he go with them while they enjoyed the Imperator's wine and not thinking about the toil awaiting them at sunrise tomorrow.

He wondered how they could forget it, even with a few jugs of wine. At least his muscles no longer cramped so badly he could barely move in the morning. He occasionally woke at night when he shifted and a muscle complained. He reminded himself that Wellington's soldiers worked as hard every day toting gear and marching across the heated plains of Spain to fight Napoleon's troops again. His admiration for them increased threefold. At day's end, he collapsed on his cot and wished Pris was beside him to kiss away his pain. He wanted more than a few stolen kisses. She was his wife, and she was risking her life trying to find the information he had vowed to uncover while he was stuck digging up worms and grubs.

The first thing that struck him when he entered the *principia* was the deafening noise. Everyone seemed to be shouting. The cacophony pressed painfully on his ears.

"Mr. Williams!"

He heard the voice only because Pris's reached into his heart as well as his ears. He looked along the hall and saw Aunt Tetty waving. He was about to wave back and look for Pris when he realized she and a woman he did not know were sharing a low couch with the old woman.

"Be right there," he yelled back. With a wink at the other field hands, he told them to save him a spot. "Near the biggest wine jug."

That brought a round of laughs as they hurried to claim good seats near the walls where they could listen without being observed emptying several jugs of the Imperator's good wine.

Striding to where Pris sat, he wove past other lounging sofas where groups of women and men were talking. Their voices faded and their noses wrinkled in distaste as he moved past them. He heard an intentionally loud insult behind him, but ignored it. He found it more difficult to elude the fingers of women who were interested in him sharing their couch. Some of the women looked to be well born, but they acted like harlots on London's lowest streets.

How much coercion was St. John putting on his subjects to marry and reproduce? Such an edict was guaranteed to cause trouble. It already had. One of the fieldworkers had come to work that morning with two black eyes and a broken nose. Though he claimed the injuries had been caused by his clumsiness, the truth was that he had flirted with a woman already claimed by a stronger man.

Neville smiled when he reached where Pris sat. When she gave him a playful grin, he knew she had seen his efforts to disentangle himself from the bolder women.

"Will you join us, Mr. Williams?" Aunt Tetty asked over the din.

"Thank you, but I should sit with my comrades from the fields instead of among these fine people."

"Nonsense," the old woman said. "Everyone is equal in Novum Arce, so you are welcome to stay with us."

"Do stay," added the dark-haired woman he had not met. "Like you, we are servants."

Pris's smile broadened. "You do not know Roxanne Parker, do you? Roxanne serves as the *magistra's* abigail. Roxanne, this is Leonard Williams."

"Mr. Williams, it is a pleasure to meet a friend of Cordelia's."

He had to hold back a laugh at the idea he and Cordelia might ever describe themselves as friends then realized she was talking about Pris. How he wished Pris had chosen a different name!

The three women shifted, and he found himself sitting between Pris and Aunt Tetty who kept them laughing with her tales of medicines she had tried—very unsuccessfully—to distill.

He frowned when he heard a muffled sound in the distance. What might have been a sharp retort had its edges sanded off, so he could not tell what it was. It repeated a couple of more times. Even so, he could not identify it when his ears were battered by the tumult in the *principia*, though he guessed someone was shooting on the fells. He wondered what prey could be found on the barren hills. He hoped it was not human.

Suddenly Roxanne tugged on Aunt Tetty's arm. With a lame excuse about finding a clean goblet for her wine, the brunette drew the older woman away.

"So," he said with a leering grin, "we are alone at last. What would you like to do about that?"

Priscilla smiled at Neville, wishing she could throw her arms around him. She was grateful for Roxanne's attempts at matchmaking, but must be careful not to show a preference for Neville's company when she had seen men brawling over a woman.

"How is the planting going, Mr. Williams?" she asked.

He leaned an arm along the curved back, and she could not help but notice how bronzed he had become. The last time she had spoken with him, the light had been dim. Now she admired how muscles rippled along his arms.

"It is going apace. Or so I am told. And you, Kenton? Is everything all right for you?"

"I would say we are doing fine right now."

"That is good to hear." He glanced around the space. "Are you enjoying yourself?"

She laughed and lowered her voice. "I keep seeing resemblances to a large assembly at Almack's."

"How so?"

"The hierarchy is well-established, and certain people speak only to other certain people. A few guests have arrived already into their cups, and nobody seems interested in dancing when they can gossip."

Neville grinned. "Trust you to see such similarities. We could go out and kick up our heels in a dance to entertain the *hoi polloi.*"

"*Hoi polloi* is Greek. Not Latin."

"But, as I recall, the Romans revered the Greeks and borrowed liberally from their culture. We could swirl about in a waltz and shock everyone."

"The waltz is not unacceptable any longer. I have heard it is danced at Almack's now."

"Why not do so at our Roman version of Almack's?"

With a laugh, she shook her head. "I should have guessed you would take my comments to *reductio ad ridiculum.*" She tilted her chin and regarded him like an impatient tutor. "That, my dear sir, *is* Latin. It means—"

"Take an argument to its most absurd conclusions. I am not completely unlettered." He leaned closer to her and whispered, "I trust you are feeling well enough to shake a toe in a waltz."

"Stop worrying. As I told you, I am—*we* are fine, save I have had no luck in my search."

"Nor have I, but . . ." His voice trailed away.

"But what?"

Neville did not reply as his gaze swept the room.

"What are you looking for?" she asked.

"Any clue to the real reason for this feast tonight."

"Roxanne told me today is the day the Romans celebrated *Vinalia Urbana*, a festival to celebrate the gods' influence on wine."

"That explains the abundance of wine being poured, but what is the real reason for recreating a festival that has been forgotten for the past millennium?"

"I think we are about to find out."

He stood as the curtain behind the throne fluttered, showing people were moving on its other side. "I need to join the other fieldworkers."

Priscilla wanted to argue and ask him if they could meet after dark, but he was right. She watched as he wove a path toward the main door. He crossed to the other side and was welcomed heartily by the other sowers. As he sat, the blare of a horn resonated through the *principia*.

With as much pomp as if the whole royal family had entered the hall, Sir Thomas and a small group appeared from behind the curtain. Bellona stood on his right as he took his throne. She put her hand on the top, making it obvious she was accepted within the inner circle. None of the others stepped as close to Sir Thomas as she did. Instead, they arranged themselves in a half circle behind her. If Sir Thomas was their emperor, then Bellona was declaring herself his closest advisor.

Heads bent toward each other throughout the hall, and a whispered buzz filled the space. Sir Thomas did not act as if he heard, but Bellona's shoulders straightened and her chin lifted in a satisfied pose.

Priscilla groaned. Lord Beamish's daughter had no reason to leave Novum Arce. Why should she when she was the highest ranking lady in the settlement? That honor was never offered by the *ton* to a baron's daughter.

Across the hall, Neville was scowling, and she guessed he had come to the same conclusion. There had to be something Bellona wanted that would lure her away from Novum Arce. But what?

Her mind went round and round as she tried to figure out ways to persuade Bellona to return home. She had already spoken of how her family must miss her, and Bellona had talked about how dangerous it was to try to slip away. But if they were able to promise Bellona a safe passage out of Novum Arce . . . would she go? Certainly, the troops training here were incapable of putting up much of a fight.

She shuddered as she recalled Bellona's words about the thief who tried to flee from Novum Arce. Someone had been able to capture him and drag him back behind the wall. Maybe the legionaries were not as incompetent as they appeared.

Sir Thomas stood to speak, and the *principia* became as silent as a tomb. Even the clink of wine glasses halted.

Priscilla tried to listen but Sir Thomas was not an inspired speaker. His droning voice seldom rose or fell. The only exception was when he mentioned Pax Romana. Real enthusiasm filled his words then.

She struggled to stay awake. To fall asleep in the middle of Sir Thomas's speech would draw attention to herself. She blinked and blinked, but each time it was more difficult to reopen her eyes. She remembered how much sleep she had required when she was pregnant with her other children.

Cheers met a pause in Sir Thomas's speech. From the other side of the room, Neville's eyes caught hers. She could not read his thoughts, but the tension in his shoulders told her that, though he was applauding like everyone else around them, he had taken note of something unsettling. Something more than the misplaced fervor ringing through the room.

During the cheers, Roxanne slid back onto the low couch. She clasped her hands in her lap, her knuckles white. While the others watched Sir Thomas as he continued in the same monotone, Roxanne's gaze was focused on Bellona. Priscilla could tell the abigail was as worried about the change in Lord Beamish's daughter's status as she was.

But instead of speaking of her disquiet after Sir Thomas left to fervid applause, Roxanne asked, "What do you think of Mr. Williams? He seems quite taken with you."

"He was kind to talk to me after you and Aunt Tetty left abruptly," Priscilla replied, though she would rather have asked if the abigail had known Bellona would appear at Sir Thomas's side.

"We left because we felt he wanted to talk with you alone."

"He did."

"Did he ask you to walk with him in the moonlight tonight?"

"What?" she choked out, hoping Roxanne was not suddenly able to discern her heart's cravings. "Why would you say that?"

"Because he looked at you as if you were a treasure he had been searching for his whole life. You don't have to remain an abigail forever. You can marry."

Pris smiled. "You are a romantic, Roxanne."

"I know." Her smile wavered. "If I cannot be happy with the man who holds my heart, I would like to see someone else happy."

"Have hope that you will be reunited."

"I try. I know, if he could, Asher would have come by now."

"But if he does not know where you are—"

"He knows. He was with me when one of the men who confronted us at the inn mentioned Novum Arce and Sir Thomas by mistake. Even though they wore masks to conceal their faces, I could tell the other men were furious with him. If Asher could get here, he would straightaway." She brushed away tears.

Priscilla embraced her friend and considered this new information. To what lengths would Sir Thomas go to keep his community secret and secure?

"CORDELIA?"

Priscilla turned carefully from where she was placing Domitilla's extra stolas in a cupboard. She did not want to bump the small statues of household *lares* in their wall niche. She had been told the woman with a flute was the guardian-goddess of the household while the male holding a spear was a *lar militaris*, who watched over the commandant on the field of battle. There had been a similar female in the quarters shared by the women who worked in the laundry, and she had been told no true Roman household would be without one or two of the statues.

"Is it time for the midday meal?" Priscilla asked. Domitilla had decided earlier in the week the servants should dine at the same time. Priscilla was not sure what led Domitilla to such a decision. She had not given any reason, and no one had asked.

It was becoming simpler every day to respond to her aunt's name. She smiled at the young girl behind her. Juno worked in the kitchens. In a normal house, she would have been called a scullery maid because her duties focused on cleaning the pots and taking out the scraps.

Juno giggled, looking younger than her thirteen years. "It is for you, Cordelia."

"For me? What do you mean?"

"Come with me." She grabbed Priscilla's hand and almost ran toward the back entrance to the house. Flinging open the door, she crowed, "See what I mean?"

Neville stood there, holding a small reed basket. He tilted it toward her. "A friend of yours suggested you might like to be properly courted, so with her help, I prepared a grand nuncheon for us."

"And you thought I would like to be courted by going on a picnic?" She shook her head. "That is not very Roman."

"Then we shall call it an *al fresco* meal. Maybe not Latin, but close because it is Italian." He held out his hand.

She heard muffled giggles as she put her hand on Neville's. Juno must have been joined by the other kitchen maid who worked in the stillroom.

"Your audience approves," she whispered as he drew her closer.

"Not mine, yours. They recognize a rare presence upon the stage before you utter your first line."

She laughed with him, happy they could tease each other again. Walking away from the commandant's house, she was surprised when he led her past the barracks. She steeled herself, waiting for the rude calls that were shouted whenever a woman walked past. There was only silence, and she realized the legionaries were gathered on the training field for yet another seemingly pointless session of practice. They never improved, which made no sense. Even clumsy oafs should get better after all those hours of training.

"Where are we going?" she asked as they climbed toward the uppermost wall. "Not up on the fells, I assume."

He lifted a single brow. "It would be lovely to have you there alone, but as we would never be allowed through the gate, I thought we might dine close to the stream where it first enters the wall."

"To check the upper watergate?"

"Perhaps you did not notice, but that spot presents an excellent view of the gate and its guards."

Priscilla smiled. "The very thing I wanted to see while I was enjoying whatever you have in your basket. It smells luscious."

"A few sandwiches, a bit of meat pie, and a dried fruit tart." His grin would have better suited her son on his naughtiest day as he added, "And a slab of our great leader's finest cheese."

"How . . . ?" She shook her head. "No, don't tell me. That way I can plead innocence of the crime."

It did not take long to walk to the spot Neville had chosen. A newly planted tree offered sparse shade on the soft, new grass as they spread out the cape he had brought.

While they sat together, enjoying the food and the cold water from the stream, Priscilla could pretend they were out of Novum Arce. She had to tell him what she had learned from Roxanne, but that could wait a little longer. She was content to be with him, his arm brushing her back as he leaned his hand on the ground behind her. They did not have to talk. Being together was enough.

Neville reached into the nearly empty basket and offered her another sandwich.

She shook her head. "I am stuffed."

"Maybe *you* are, but what about . . . ?" He glanced at her abdomen.

"Right now, I am the only one who gets a vote on how much to eat." She laughed. "For now. In a few months, if this is like before, I shall be eating everything in sight. So you should eat now because you may not get much later."

He took a big bite of the sandwich. After chewing and swallowing, he grinned. "Thanks for the warning." He shaded his eyes as he watched the activity at the gate. "They have two men posted at all times, but they seem more interested in their conversations than guard duty."

"Why not? Nobody is trying to batter down the walls. Those within the walls are unlikely to try to slip out if the risk of leaving is great. They are there more for show than protection."

"After the shabby skills I have seen them use in training that probably is for the best. They are as likely to stab each other as an intruder." He chuckled.

"What do you have planned?"

"Nothing specific." He plucked a piece of grass and stared at it. "But I have been wondering what Duncan is up to."

"He surely has begun to search for us once we did not return as planned."

"As long as he does not trigger the same trap we did."

"Don't tell him I said this, but Bellona mentioned that Sir Thomas's agents look for young, handsome, and intelligent people. He is only two out of the three."

Neville sat forward and spun the piece of grass. "He considers himself a youthful, dashing blade still."

"That is neither here nor there. We need to figure out a way to contact Duncan. With his help, we may still be able to succeed in escaping so you can make your report."

He tossed the piece of grass aside and wiped his hands. "Contacting him is not necessary."

"What did the two of you concoct before we left Tarn's Edge?" She asked herself why she had not considered before that Neville and Duncan would have some scheme.

"He said if we were not back in a fortnight, he would call out the militia. By my count, he should be gathering his troops about now."

"Troops? What troops?"

"Duncan knows many of the same people I do."

"People who will do anything if you cross their palms with a few coins?"

"Such folks are good to know when one is in a jumble."

"Which we are."

He smiled. "In fact, I first met Duncan when he was in a pickle of his own with the sort of person you would never receive. There was the issue of several hundred pounds unaccounted for, and the gamester thought he could get it from Duncan."

"Did Duncan owe the debt?"

Neville shook his head. "No, though he was well-known at the time as a man who often punished his pockets with losses. That fact did not deter the cheat who wanted Duncan's deep pockets to cover *his* losses."

"And how were you involved?"

"Let's just say I convinced the swindler to look elsewhere for money. That gained me Duncan's eternal gratitude and, more important, his friendship. During the ensuing years, before you came back into my life—"

"As I recall, *you* came back into mine. Disguised as a masked swordsman and frightening my household half to death."

He tapped her nose. "But I did not fool you for a second, did I?"

"Not that I will admit to." She leaned her head on his shoulder, watching the two men at the gate as he did.

"As I was saying, Duncan often helped me when unpleasant matters had to be handled with finesse." He suddenly scowled.

"What is it?" she asked.

"I need to speak with Prinny again about what he promised he would offer Duncan in thanks for getting him out of the mess that earned me my title. I will do so once we leave here with the information I need. Beamish can come and get his daughter."

"But what about her servants?"

"We cannot be certain they are even here."

"They are. Or at least they were." Priscilla's contentment vanished like a soap bubble popping. She faced Neville as she told him what Roxanne had said during the wine festival. He listened without any questions, but a storm erupted in his eyes.

"They could not let the servants leave, though they did not plan to bring them to Novum Arce," he said, his gaze turned inward as his fingers closed into a fist. "That suggests a more evil side to this settlement than I had guessed. There are many things that we are not seeing, things that they are concealing."

"The very things that created the request for you to come here."

He nodded. "I agree, but where to look?"

"Wherever it is, we must be more careful than ever. I wonder what they will do to prevent outsiders from learning the truth about this place."

"Sir Thomas speaks of peace, but the ones who do his dirty work may not agree. Up until now, I had assumed the servants were hiding somewhere, unwilling to return to Beamish without his daughter. Now I am not sure they are alive."

She put her hand over the fist on his lap. "We have to believe they are."

Neville did not answer, and she realized he was staring at the training field.

"What is it?" she asked as she had before.

"Don't they look more skilled than usual today?"

She watched the men swing their small swords and block their opponent's blows with shields. "It would seem they are improving."

"So quickly? Yesterday, they were stumbling over their own feet, more of a threat to their allies than any enemy. Look how fluid their motions are today."

Priscilla appraised the men, and she saw what Neville had noticed. When the men lined up to practice throwing their spears, most hit the targets instead of landing short. The ones practicing with the swords were not wielding them wildly, but with purpose. A third group was doing laps around the field faster than usual. At the most distant side of the field, two more groups of men, obviously the less proficient ones, were struggling through the exercises the others did with ease.

Five groups? She had never counted that many on the training field at the same time.

"Aren't there too many legionaries on the field?" she asked.

He counted then nodded. "I would say a good score extra."

"It would seem that Sir Thomas has conscripted some worthy soldiers we may not have seen before."

"Apparently we need to look more deeply into Novum Arce." He bit off a curse.

"What is it?"

"More soldiers mean more stomachs to fill, and that requires more food." He put his hand to his back and groaned. "And that means more fields to plow and sow."

"Maybe some of the least skilled legionaries could be put to work in the fields."

"If all the incompetent ones were reassigned, the rest of us could sit back and watch *them* work." He stood and held his hand out to her. "On that note, I need to return to work. The other men have been covering for me."

She came to her feet. Gripping his arm, she said, "You are not going to get into trouble, are you? I loved spending this time with you, but it is not worth it if you are punished."

"If I slacked off for any other reason, I would be chastised in ways I will not repeat for your tender ears. But with our great leader's decree that there needs to be more marriages and more babies by this time next year, the field boss is willing to allow one or two of us a short absence to court a potential wife."

"I am glad you think of me as a potential wife."

He laughed and pulled her to him. "I am more than willing to court you from the beginning again." He caressed her lips with his own before releasing her and picking up the empty basket. "Whenever I can, I will be calling, Mrs. Kenton."

"I look forward to it, Mr. Williams." She brushed his hair back from his forehead.

He caught her by the wrist before pressing his mouth to her palm, setting her skin ablaze. His gaze was as heated as he looked up at her, holding her with his eyes. Her knees weakened like softened butter, and her breath grew uneven.

She had no idea how they were going to get the answers Neville needed. She was unsure if they would ever be able to persuade Bellona to leave. She could not guess if they would even find the missing servants. But she knew one thing for sure: She could not wait until she and Neville escaped Novum Arce, and she could be his wife in truth once more.

Chapter Eleven

DOMITILLA WANTED some fabric for a gown, so she sent Priscilla to the storerooms on the lower side of the settlement near where the stream exited from Novum Arce. It was the excuse Priscilla needed to see if she could discern any sign of the missing servants.

Her hopes of looking around were dashed when the quartermaster, who was in charge of supplies for both the military and civilians, kept his hawklike eyes on her the whole time she walked from his office to the storeroom where the fabric was kept. He did not follow her, but stood in front of his office, his arms folded over his full belly, so he could make sure she went to the proper building.

When Priscilla entered it, she gasped. The storeroom was about the size of the commandant's house, and every inch of it was packed with crates. Had Sir Thomas spent his whole fortune on cloth and thread and buttons and broaches and sandals and the other items stacked in neat rows? Then she saw the guns lying in open boxes along the left hand wall. She started counting the boxes and gave up when she reached thirty.

Here was the proof Neville had sought. The thought sent a shudder deep into her soul. Only now did she realize how much she had hoped that the person who had sent him north had been misled by rumors. These weapons were as real as the new soldiers who were so highly skilled.

There were four other storage buildings. How many weapons were cached in them? Were they planning for a siege or an attack?

She gathered up the fabric Domitilla wanted and hurried out. She needed to talk to Neville as soon as possible.

Thanking the quartermaster who grunted an answer, Priscilla hurried up the hill toward the commandant's house. She grew calmer as she realized what was in the buildings could not be a secret from everyone in Novum Arce. Otherwise, the quartermaster would not have allowed her to go inside. Her heart thudded harder again when she thought about how it did not matter what anyone *within* the walls knew. Nobody could escape to reveal the truth to the rest of the world. She had to talk to Neville.

Which field was he working in today? She would scour each one until she found him. He had to know what she had seen.

Priscilla reached the commandant's house just as someone stepped out of the main door, the one only highly ranked guests were allowed to use. She stopped, surprised.

Bellona!

Since their one conversation, Bellona had cut Priscilla direct on the few occasions their paths crossed. What would Bellona do when they stood face-to-face? Priscilla held her breath, anticipating a tempest.

Instead, Bellona gave her a wide smile that suggested they were bosom-bows. "Ah, Kenton! Exactly the person I had hoped to speak with."

"I am honored, *domina mea*." She had heard others address Bellona so. If she remembered her Latin correctly, it meant *my lady*. "What may I do for you?"

"Do for me? Aren't you the most generous soul?" She laughed but it sounded feigned. "I must admit to being intrigued. I never have met a lady's maid who also handled ledgers. An odd combination of skills, I must say."

"It was my lady's wish I learn both."

"And a good abigail always complies. Right?"

Priscilla did not lower her eyes, because that might suggest she had been lying. "Most certainly, *domina mea*. It was my pleasure to allow her the opportunity to avoid the task she found bothersome."

"You are an excellent abigail, Kenton. Domitilla has been singing your praises, and she does not give praise lightly. She says she has no idea how she would get along without you. I thought you should know that."

"Thank you, *domina mea*."

Bellona leaned her cheek against one finger and regarded Priscilla as if she were an unsolved puzzle. "As I said, I am intrigued that you have experience in handling ledgers."

"I am no expert as an estate manager or a solicitor must be."

Bellona frowned, and Priscilla realized she was not expected to speak unless asked a direct question. Their first friendly conversation had been, Priscilla suspected, simply for Bellona to learn more about the newcomer and ascertain if Priscilla was a threat to her vaulted place in the settlement's hierarchy.

"We need an *actuarius*," Bellona said, her smile returning. "A clerk to handle the accounts of Novum Arce. It seems to me that you are better suited for the task than anyone else here."

What did it matter how Priscilla replied? Surely she and Neville would be planning their escape from Novum Arce as soon as she showed him the cases of weapons. Bellona would become suspicious if she turned down the offer. She forced a smile and dipped in a curtsy. "It would be an honor to serve."

"Of course it is, so see you do not bungle the duties of the position. Neither Sir Thomas nor I would be pleased." Bellona walked away.

Staring after her, Priscilla swallowed her gasp of shock. Bellona spoke of herself and Sir Thomas as equals. She was unsure what the change might portend for Novum Arce, but for the first time, she was glad she had seen those guns. She was ready to leave the community.

Now.

PRISCILLA HAD expected she would oversee the ledgers in addition to serving as Domitilla's lady's maid, but the day after Bellona tapped her for the position of *actuarius*, Roxanne and another young woman came to the commandant's house and removed Priscilla and her few possessions. Only then did Priscilla understand the true reason behind Bellona's generous offer. By giving Priscilla another job, Bellona was denying Domitilla the chance to have an abigail. Now the commandant's wife could not challenge Bellona's status as Novum Arce's premier lady. Domitilla could rage at the unfairness—and she did by throwing things across the bedroom and yelling at the servants who could not hide from her fury—but Priscilla left the commandant's house as ordered.

She was delighted to discover she had a tiny room of her own at the back of the small building where she would work. There was enough space for her cot, a chest for her extra clothing, and a washstand. The chamber had been freshly whitewashed, and best of all she did not have to share with other servants. She began to imagine ways for Neville to sneak in at night and out in the morning, so they could be together. It would be a challenge because the building was set at the crossroads of two of the busiest streets in the compound.

After two days, Priscilla discovered her work was difficult, but not onerous. No one had kept records since the settlement was first established over two years ago. She was tempted to remind Sir Thomas that the Romans were renowned for their record keeping, but she had no idea how he would react if someone openly challenged the illusion he had built.

She liked her office. It had large windows on either side so the softening spring breezes could slip through on sunny afternoons. On stormy days, she closed the window shutters and left the door ajar. A small porch kept the rain outside, and she could enjoy fresh air.

By the time she had worked there for almost a week, only clerks bringing her stacks of papers and receipts to sort out and put in the ledgers interrupted her. The rest of the day she was on her own. It was the perfect arrangement because when she could no longer fight the smothering fatigue that came over her without warning, she could slip into her room for a quick nap. By leaving the door to her private quarters half-open, she was able to be at the table by the time the heavy-footed clerks came inside. It helped that the clerk who came most often always whistled while he walked.

The only problem was that she had no chance to talk to Neville. She found excuses to walk in the direction of the field being seeded each day, but she had no chance other than to wave a greeting to him. Any conversation she tried to have with him was interrupted by other men or a request for her to return to her office to deal with some matter.

She did not even dare to try to convey the message through some sort of code. Someone else might be able to figure out whatever simple cipher she devised, or it might be so complicated that even Neville could not read it. She stewed in her frustration as she waited for the chance to tell him what she had seen.

Roxanne stopped by each day so they could go to the evening meal together. It was the safest way to avoid the amorous advances of the lonely soldiers who wanted to settle down with a wife and bring Novum Arce its next generation. Priscilla had received more marriage proposals than she could count. On more than one occasion, she politely told one man no, only to be asked by the man standing next to him.

It was probably the most bizarre aspect of Novum Arce, but she endured the offers of marriage and helped Roxanne deflect the ones presented to her. For the abigail, it was more complicated because Bellona was insisting Roxanne marry right away as an example for the other unwed women, while Bellona herself showed no signs of selecting a husband. Each time Priscilla saw Bellona, she was with a different man. In London, she would have been called a coquette or worse, but Priscilla could not help wondering if the intoxicating freedom from Lord Beamish's domineering ways was what led her astray. No one dared to speak poorly of her in Novum Arce for Sir Thomas had made her elevated position official by having her stand right next to him whenever he made a proclamation.

Now that she had gotten the upper hand on Domitilla, Bellona acted as if Priscilla did not exist. Left to her own devices, Priscilla worked alone every day, copying information into the ledgers. That was why the sound of her office door opening and the heavy thump of a legionary's sandals on the stone floor startled her. She did not look up as she continued adding the long columns of numbers. There were several more pages of reports to put into the ledger that day, and she had no time to try to persuade another man she did not want to marry him.

"*Ave, domina mea! Quid agis?*"

Her mind began to translate the greeting and the question of what she was doing, and then the voice penetrated her concentration. Her head jerked up to see Neville's eyes twinkling at her.

"Nev—!" She clamped her lips closed. Or she tried to, because her jaw had dropped the moment she realized his dark brown eyes were shadowed by the brim of the Roman legionary's helmet. "If someone were to see you—"

His laugh halted her. "Don't you understand? These uniforms with their bright and shining armor are meant to be seen. Let the enemies of the empire quail at the very sight of Rome's might."

"I didn't mean that. I meant—"

"Don't worry. For some reason that escapes me, I have been promoted from field hand to the newest member of the Novum Arce century." He grinned. "Even though we don't have enough men to rightly be deemed a century, that is what our two officers call us."

Priscilla knew a century was a force of eighty Roman soldiers because she had argued about it with her governess while in the schoolroom. Her governess had insisted that a century should be one hundred men until Priscilla had shown her a diagram in a book. After that, her governess had declared that teaching a young woman history was a waste of time. Priscilla's father, Lord Emberson, had listened then hired a male tutor to continue his daughter's education. Aunt Cordelia had been appalled and let everyone in the family know it.

Aunt Cordelia! If she discovered Priscilla and Neville were missing, she would be frightened. Had Duncan let her know, or was he making an attempt, as Neville believed, to find them before sharing the dreadful news with Aunt Cordelia and the children? Priscilla wanted to hurry to her children, drawing them into her arms and hugging them as she had when they were small.

Standing from behind the table covered with books and papers, she smiled again when Neville turned around, giving her a view of every side of his uniform. As before, he wore a long tunic over leggings that ended at his knees. His sandals beneath were decorated with brass that caught the light coming through the windows.

She had to admit that the uniform with its breastplate and bronze helmet fit him well. It emphasized the breadth of his shoulders and the lean length of his body. But Neville as an infantry soldier! It was ludicrous because he was more suited to the task he had been given: to be a spy, skulking about and collecting information.

"Well, what do you think?" he asked.

"I have seen you wear sillier things."

He pressed his hand over his breastplate and struck a mournful pose. "To quote the great bard: '*Now my charms are all o'erthrown . . .*'" His brows lowered in a more genuine expression. "Odd, how many quotes from *The Tempest* are playing through my mind of late."

"That play was set in a fantasy world, and we are living in one. Isn't it in *The Tempest* that someone says: '*We are such stuff as dreams are made on*'?"

"Prospero says that." He grinned. "I am impressed with your knowledge of Shakespeare."

"A classical education comes in handy at times." She closed the door. Glancing out both windows, she asked, "You have no idea why you were tapped to join the army?"

"I have my suspicions." He leaned back on the table, the bronze pieces on his uniform clattering against the wood.

"Which are?"

"I see Bellona's fingers in this, just as in your promotion from the laundry to being a lady's maid and now clerk. After she watched us working in the field yesterday, she went straight to the man overseeing us then stormed away wearing a very determined expression."

"You didn't tell me she came to where you were working. Do you know why?"

He touched her cheek with his fingertips, a motion so gentle and loving she longed to throw her arms around him and beg him to take her away from this insanity.

"No. I was not sure if her appearance augured good things or bad," he murmured, running a single finger lazily along her jaw and up behind her ear, leaving a path of heated tingles in its wake. "Worrying needlessly is not good for you now."

"I have told you that I am fine. *We* are fine, but we shall not be if I have to worry that you are being less than honest with me."

One side of his mouth tilted in a grin. "If you had guessed Bellona planned to worsen my lot, do you think you could have hidden your thoughts?"

"Probably not." She eyed him up and down again, enjoying the view. "So you are now a soldier. I never thought I would see the day."

"I look rather dashing, don't I?" He struck another pose, this one with his helmet set in the crook of his arm.

"You look like you will soon have pigeons on your head." She smiled when he laughed, but she became serious again. "Have you been able to garner any hint of what the army is being trained to do?"

"Not yet. I have been issued this uniform and armor by the quarter-master, but nothing else. I have no idea when I will receive weapons to train with."

She slanted closer to him and lowered her voice to a wisp of a whisper. "Did you see what was in the storeroom along with the clothing?"

"The tools?"

"No. Guns."

His face grew taut, and he shook his head. "I didn't see any guns. Are you sure what was written on the crate was what was within it?"

"I saw an open crate, and it was filled with guns. I saw them more than a week ago, and I have been trying to let you know."

"Talking to you alone has been a challenge."

"I know. I saw the one open crate and thirty more identical ones by the wall to the left of the door."

"That area was empty today."

She sank to sit at the table. "Someone must have moved them."

Squatting next to her, he took her hands. "And they could be any-where within Novum Arce or beyond it."

"Why would anyone bring them here and then take them away again?"

He stood. "Another mystery for us to solve. But it would seem that I was not sent here in error."

"I am hoping that if we can get one answer, the others will follow."

His broad hand cupped her face tenderly, then he lifted his helmet to set it on his head. "I hope your optimism turns out to be justified. Soon."

"Very soon," she said to his back as he walked out of her office.

Chapter Twelve

IT TOOK LESS TIME than Priscilla had guessed to check the buildings in Novum Arce to discover if the guns were stashed within the walls. Returning to the storerooms on the pretense of needing ink, she saw Neville was correct. The crates were gone. A walk past the armory where the century's practice weapons were stored revealed only those flimsy swords and spears. She found excuses in her post as the keeper of the account books to visit every other public building, but to no avail. Two public places she could not go—the legionaries' barracks and the Temple of Mithras—Neville had already checked.

She had no luck with the private homes of the married soldiers and laborers. Accepting an invitation from one of the women she had met at a gathering at the *principia*, she enjoyed the best cup of tea she had tasted since leaving Tarn's Edge as well as a comfortable coze. But there were no signs of the weapons inside the small, three-roomed houses.

That left one public place where she had not checked. The granary storage beyond the barracks. From what she had seen in the information she was compiling in the ledgers, only one was in use. The other two would be filled with the harvest. Until then, the buildings would be the perfect place to hide something. She should have considered that from the beginning.

Going there by herself would be foolish when the soldiers were desperate to advance themselves by following Sir Thomas's orders to marry. She had heard that whispers of proposals had become more forceful. She must not take any chances, so she waited until late afternoon when she saw the legionaries going toward the Mithraic temple for whatever service was being held

When she was let into Bellona's house by a servant, she asked to speak with Roxanne. She was told in a clipped voice to wait in the center courtyard and not to touch anything by the man who was as arrogant as Lord Beamish. He flexed his arm muscles as if in warning. She almost laughed in his face but restrained herself.

Priscilla forgot about him as she entered the courtyard. It was grander and larger than the commandant's and set in a quiet corner of the community. Beneath her sandals, the black floors were smooth. Were they marble?

The mosaics around a fountain were fashioned into an exquisite design of mermaids. Each mermaid's face was unique, and their tails glittered with metallic tiles. Looking into the fountain, Priscilla saw fish. Real ones and tile ones. All were bright colors of yellow, gold, and red. A single white fish scattered the others before it.

She resisted the temptation to sit on the side of the fountain and dip her fingers in the water after the servant at the door had told her *twice* not to touch anything. Instead, she kept a cautious eye on the promenades around the courtyard. Encountering Bellona might be uncomfortable because despite the young woman's obvious annoyance at her father for putting a limit on her callers, she might not appreciate her abigail receiving visitors in the late afternoon.

When she saw Roxanne coming toward her, Priscilla waited until the slender brunette caught sight of her and rushed across the courtyard.

"What are you doing here?" Roxanne asked.

"I wanted to ask you a favor."

"Ask and I will be glad to help you if I can."

A man, not the one who had let her in, moved along the columned aisle to the right, glancing at them and then away as he increased his pace until he was lost to the shadows again. Priscilla had no idea Bellona had so many male servants. It should have been no surprise because she had surrounded herself with men in public.

"Let's go for a walk," Priscilla said, motioning with her head toward the door leading to the street.

"All right." Roxanne dimpled. "I need some fresh air anyhow."

Priscilla linked arms with the abigail who regarded her with astonishment at the motion until Priscilla whispered she did not want their words to be overheard.

"And it would be a brave man to approach us both and propose marriage."

Roxanne's laugh was such an unusual sound that it startled Priscilla. She wondered what the abigail had been like before being brought to Novum Arce. Living in the Beamish household could not have been easy, even though she had fallen in love and made plans for a future with Asher Snow.

In the same low voice, Priscilla asked, "Will you come somewhere with me?"

"I am already."

"Not here. Somewhere else?"

"Where?"

"I have been exploring Novum Arce, and there are some areas where it is unwise to go alone."

Roxanne halted and faced her. "What are you up to?"

"Trying to escape boredom." It was the first excuse she could devise that did not sound completely ridiculous. "I spend so much time inside with the accounts, and I have found that taking a different walk each day eases my ennui."

"I understand." She looked back at Bellona's house. "I know how it can be to spend too much time indoors."

"I thought you might, which is why I asked you to come with me." She smiled, but every falsehood she told tasted more bitter on her lips. As much as she wanted to trust her friend, if Roxanne let a single word slip in Bellona's hearing, the young woman could refuse to allow Priscilla to see Roxanne again.

"I am glad. Where do you want to go?"

"Out by the barracks."

Roxanne's face lost all color. "That is no place for a woman by herself."

"That is why I came to ask you to go with me."

"Do you think two women will be safer than one? Maybe on the street like this, but strolling past the barracks is sure to be seen as proof we are looking for a man's company."

Priscilla sighed deeply. "You are right. It is a foolish idea, but the only one I had."

Before she could add more, Roxanne's name was shouted by a woman standing near Bellona's house. The woman waved anxiously, making it clear that she wanted the abigail to return immediately.

"I have to go." Roxanne waved back to the woman who went into the house. To Priscilla, she added, "But before I go, promise me that you won't go near the barracks alone."

"I promise." She sighed again. "I was curious what was out that way."

"If you really want to go there, ask Aunt Tetty to join you."

"Why?"

"None of the soldiers will bother you if she is with you. Half of the men are scared of her because they believe she is a witch. The other half treat her like a beloved grandmother."

"That is a good suggestion. I will ask her."

"I hope you enjoy your walk." Tears abruptly rushed into Roxanne's eyes. "I know how precious time is and how foolish it is when one discovers how easily it can be wasted. Make sure you don't waste yours."

For a second, Priscilla considered telling Roxanne that she had a legitimate reason for taking a walk that afternoon. She could not speak of the guns because even a hint of the truth could endanger the abigail.

"Thank you," she said sincerely. "That is excellent advice."

Roxanne put out her arm to block Priscilla's way. "Before you go, let me give you a warning."

"About what?"

"I have heard Mr. Williams has been reassigned."

Priscilla nodded. "From fieldwork to serving with the century."

"That is the first time I have heard of such a change."

"What about me? I went from the laundry to being an abigail to working on the community's accounts so fast I barely had time to get used to one place before I was sent to another."

Roxanne's cheeks became pale. "You know why that happened. The *magistra* made those arrangements."

"Mr. Williams believes *Magistra* Bellona may have arranged his transfer as well."

The abigail's face grew more wan. "I assumed as much, but hoped it was because of some extraordinary act of his own."

"Not according to him."

"Oh, my! It must be what I thought."

"What is that?" Priscilla asked, though she guessed Roxanne's suspicions matched her own.

"Listen to me." She grasped Priscilla's shoulders and stared at her with an intent expression. "You must listen to me."

"I am."

"I have seen you and Mr. Williams together on several occasions, but I hope you have developed no feelings for him."

"Why?"

"If *Magistra* Bellona has him in her sights, he will be hers."

"But what if Mr. Williams and I are courting?"

Roxanne made an unladylike snort. "Do you think that will matter? The *magistra* does not care, for she wants what she wants."

"The man—"

"Has no choice if he does not wish for his woman to be consigned to the worst jobs. Trust me, Cordelia. I have seen it happen at least twice already."

An icy frisson slithered down Priscilla's spine. "I will warn Mr. Williams to be careful."

"Didn't you hear me? It is not only Mr. Williams who needs to be cautious. You have to as well. If she thinks you are trying to keep her from getting what—or whom—she wants, she can be a dangerous enemy."

"I will keep that in mind." She did not need the warning because she already had witnessed Bellona bullying Domitilla.

"One more thing." Roxanne's voice dropped so low Priscilla could hardly hear. "Warn Mr. Williams as I am warning you not to make a complaint to anyone of higher rank. They would be required to take it to Sir Thomas, and the Imperator will not halt the *magistra* from doing whatever she wishes."

"Why?" The question popped out before Priscilla could halt it.

"I don't know." The abigail stepped away and turned to look at Bellona's vast house. "I honestly don't know."

Many other questions filled Priscilla's head, but she had no chance to ask them as Roxanne hurried away. The abigail might not know what the connection was between Sir Thomas and Bellona, but she must have some ideas. Somehow, Priscilla had to convince her to share them. Maybe one of them would lead to the truth.

It was a short walk to Aunt Tetty's house next to the temple of Mithras. Men were going in and out of the temple, but they avoided Aunt Tetty's home by a wide margin. That confirmed what Roxanne had told her.

Aunt Tetty sat out in front. Scents, both pleasing and not, came through the open door behind her. She held a cast iron pot on her lap and was stirring a thick paste the deep green color of grass. Pausing, she motioned for Priscilla to take the chair beside her.

"Come and sit, Cordelia. It is about time the two of us had a real talk instead of one disrupted by speeches and hullabaloo."

"I would like that." She sat on the simple wooden chair. "What are you making?"

"It is spring, and in the spring, measles spread fast. This soothes the eyes so the spots don't take away one's sight. It is a simple medicine I learned from a wise old woman who had learned it from her granny." She gave the bowl one more stir and set it on the porch. "But you did not come here to talk of my medicines. Do you have questions about Novum Arce?"

Priscilla heard the affection in Aunt Tetty's voice as she spoke the community's name. Though she was curious how and where Aunt Tetty's and Sir Thomas's lives intersected, she said, "I need your assistance, Aunt Tetty."

"With what?"

Priscilla gave her an abridged explanation, leaving out anything about the guns. She let the old woman think that as part of her duties, Priscilla needed to check on the granary buildings.

"But I cannot go out there alone, or so Roxanne has told me."

"She was right to warn you."

"She suggested that I ask you to accompany me."

"What about that handsome man I have seen you with? Mr. Williams?"

"He is training with the other legionaries."

"It was," Aunt Tetty said with a nod, "a wise decision to give him a job better suited to his skills. One look at the man, and you can see he was born to be in charge." She pushed herself to her feet. "I will go with you. I need to deliver some skin softener to Domitilla, so I can combine the trips."

"If you tell me where the skin softener is, I will get it," Priscilla said as she stood, too.

After Priscilla collected a small jar of the lotion like the ones she had seen on the commandant's wife's dressing table, she handed Aunt Tetty a cane that had been beside a chair. The old woman took it gratefully and then slipped her arm through Priscilla's as they walked along the street.

She noticed how the other residents avoided Aunt Tetty. A few made an ancient sign against the evil eye when they thought nobody was looking. Priscilla frowned at them, and they scurried away.

"Pay them no mind," Aunt Tetty said. "Old superstitions are deeply ingrained in Lakeland." Without a pause, she asked, "You do know that not all dangers are unseen, don't you?"

"Why would you say that?" she asked, startled by the old woman's confident tone.

Aunt Tetty gave her a warm smile. "Because, Cordelia, you strike me as a woman who knows her own mind. Be careful what you want to do is the right thing. A misstep now could be disastrous."

"Is that a warning?" she asked, shocked by the old woman's words.

"If it need be, it is."

Chapter Thirteen

NEVILLE WHISTLED a tuneless melody as he rubbed the bronze on his shield with vinegar and salt, with a bit of flour added to the mix. It removed the patina that turned the bronze to a dull green.

He looked across the empty room where rows of beds would soon be filled. The men played cards and dice so late into the night that it was no wonder they were ineffectual on the training field. They had gone to the temple for some sort of celebration to their war-mongering god, and Neville had begged off, pretending he was being punished by their commanders. Jack, the red-haired man whose cot was next to Neville's, had invited him along, telling him, partly in jest, there would be no intelligent conversation unless "Leonard" was there.

Jack had helped Neville get to know the others in the barracks. Though he had refused to take a Roman name as many of the others had, he was trying hard to learn a soldier's skills. He never spoke of his last name, saying only he had been called by it too many years. Neville guessed he had been a servant. Curious as to why he had come to Novum Arce willingly, Neville appreciated that Jack did not want to talk of the past because Neville did not want to be quizzed about his own. They had become friends, training together and talking while the others wagered. Unlike the others, Jack kept his word and never bragged.

Tonight, Neville had told Jack to go ahead without him. That made Neville the butt of good-natured jokes about sneaking off to spend time with Cordelia Kenton.

If only it were true . . .

A soul-deep sigh erupted out of him. It was time for him and Pris to cut their losses and admit defeat. Even if the crates she had seen were filled with guns, they had vanished. Once he and Pris left, they could contact Beamish and let him know where to go to collect his wayward daughter. Trying to convince Miss Beamish to go home could put Pris and their child in jeopardy if the young woman realized she had been lied to from the beginning. He had seen enough of Miss Beamish to know she was as hungry for power as her father. If he hadn't been as eager as

Pris to discover what had happened to the guns as well as Beamish's missing servants, he would have insisted they depart Novum Arce days ago.

A soft sound brushed his ears. He put down the shield he had been polishing. Yes, he heard voices. Light ones, not the bass bellows of his fellow legionaries. He smiled ironically. Neville Hathaway, a Roman soldier. When he told Duncan about what he had been doing while in Novum Arce, his friend was going to succumb to paroxysms of laughter.

His smile vanished as he stood and went to the window to peer into the deepening twilight. Two people were walking close to the barracks.

Two women!

Had they lost their minds?

". . . and I have not walked in this direction before today," said a lyrical voice that tantalized him.

Pris!

For a moment, he let his eyes feast on her golden hair and gentle curves. His fingers itched to slip along both as he brought her mouth to his, melding them in the crucible of their passion. Then fury sped through him with the power of both lightning and thunder.

Neville stormed out the closest door and onto a path that intersected the women's. His steps faltered when he saw the woman with Pris was Aunt Tetty. He had thought the old woman had more sense than this. On the other hand, Pris could charm a thief into giving her his stolen loot as well as a confession.

He could not keep his anger and fear for her out of his voice, "What are you doing out *here*? I thought both of you knew better than to tempt those lecherous fools."

"I need to finish an inventory before supper." Pris glanced at the older woman. "Aunt Tetty agreed to come with me." She grinned. "Besides, when we passed the *principia*, your comrades-in-arms were listening to Sir Thomas inspire them with an enthralling speech."

"Enthralling is not the word I would use," Aunt Tetty said with a smile. "Our Imperator seems to have fallen in love with the sound of his voice." She looked from Pris to him. "The evening is growing cool on my old bones. If I leave Cordelia in your protection, Mr. Williams, I trust you will see her safely home."

"You may trust me, Aunt Tetty," he said with a bow worthy of courtier.

"But can Cordelia trust you?"

"As much as any woman can trust a man who finds her lovely and wishes to win her affection."

With a throaty chuckle, Aunt Tetty patted his arm. She turned back toward the center of the settlement.

"Go with Aunt Tetty," Neville ordered, though he did not want Pris to leave again soon.

"But I need to check the grain storage buildings." She explained her theory.

It was a good one, he had to admit. Even so, he said, "Not until after dark. The soldiers will wonder why I am not at the *principia*. If I don't show up, they will start asking questions." He put his hands on her shoulders, letting his fingers edge down her arms in a slow caress. "I will come to get you as soon as night falls."

She nodded as she put her hands over his. "All right. There should be no moonlight tonight because the clouds are thickening on the highest fells. We will be obscured by the shadows and rain."

"I am glad you are rational." He drew one of his hands out from under hers and ran his fingers along her face, wishing he could touch her more sensuously. But he knew someone else could walk by at any moment.

"One of us must be." She chuckled and patted his cheek as she turned to leave.

His hand clamped her fingers to his face before he could halt himself. As she gazed up at him, he breathed her name and tipped her mouth beneath his. The kiss had to be swift, and it left him with a raw longing that no quick brush of her lips could satisfy.

As he raised his head, he said, "I will be there as soon as possible, and we will go and check the granaries."

"And after . . . ?"

"I am sure I can think of an excuse not to sleep in the barracks tonight."

"Good." She stood on tiptoe and kissed him again before she whirled to catch up with Aunt Tetty.

He watched her and wondered how long it would be until they could spend more than a few moments together again. His promise to the Prince Regent had cost them too much time apart already.

NEVILLE WAS surprised how easy it was to take a dark lantern and slip out of the barracks a few hours later. Some of the men were asleep while others wagered and finished off the bottles of wine served with their evening meal. He had gained their respect because his skills with a blade and a sword, though he had not used them in years, were superior to theirs. He wondered why the more talented legionaries did not help them. The men had looked at him in confusion when he asked that. It was as if the idea had never entered their heads. They asked him to teach them, but he found excuses not to or acted as if teaching was something beneath him. As long as they were not battle-ready, they could not attack others. For a moment, he considered teaching them some defensive moves, but surrender was all they needed to be prepared to do.

"Off to do some courting?" asked Jack from where he lay on his cot, his hands clasped under his head.

"Is there anything better to do on a pleasant evening?" Neville asked as he flung his dark cloak around his shoulders before making sure his knife was in his belt. He did not intend to chance another man trying to contest him for Pris's affections.

"I would not know." He sighed.

Neville felt sorry for Jack, who was interested in a lass who had worked with Pris in the laundry. Unfortunately she had her eye on someone else and did not return his friend's attentions. Maybe Pris would know someone to match up with Jack.

He almost laughed aloud. This was not London where matchmaking was a favorite sport among the *ton*.

As he walked to the door, other men fired knowing grins at him. He gave them a wink and went out to the sound of their laughter.

A gust of wind swirled along the street, sending dust into small cyclones. He glanced in both directions. As always, guards stood by the gate, visible only as shadows in the pair of lanterns they had set on either side of gate leading into Novum Arce. He was surprised they used the lights, which would be a beacon across the empty fells, pinpointing the settlement through the thickening mist. Did they use them every night, or only on ones when the clouds lowered to conceal the higher reaches?

Making sure the door on his lantern was closed, he pulled his cloak over his head. He noticed how the ornaments on his ankle-high sandals caught the lights coming from the commandant's house as well as the barracks. He bent, gathered up some dirt, and scoured the brass until its sheen was gone. On the morrow, he would be yelled at because he had let his sandals fall into such a state, but better a dressing-down than having the small bits of brass betray him.

He walked away from the barracks, not bothering to conceal himself now. After dark, there was little activity in the community.

Neville realized his mistake when he heard someone say, "You are Leonard Williams, aren't you?"

He silenced the curses searing his tongue as he stared at Beamish's truant daughter. The light from a nearby window burnished her hair beneath her dark stola that was wrapped to accent her full breasts. Jewels glittered at her long neck and along her arms and hands. She could have been the perfect sculpture save for her calculating gaze that slid over him from head to toe and back.

"Yes, I am Leonard Williams." He waited to discover why she had spoken to him when she never had before.

"I am *Magistra* Bellona. Perhaps you have seen me about the settlement." She gave him what she must believe was a come hither smile. It might have appeared more genuine if she had been able to hide the way she gauged his reaction to each word she spoke.

"Everyone in Novum Arce knows who you are."

She preened, patting her intricately styled hair. "How kind of you, Mr. Williams."

"Not kindness. The truth."

"Yet it is kind of you to make a lady feel special, Mr. Williams." She fluttered her heavily kohled eyelashes at him. "May I call you Leonard?"

"Of course. The name is yours to use as you wish." *Just as I have.* He did not let his amusement show on his face.

"Thank you." She moved closer and gazed up at him with an obvious invitation for him to take her into his arms. She plucked the lantern from his fingers and set it down beside the walkway. "Being granted the privilege of using first names can be so . . . so intimate."

He wondered where Beamish's daughter had learned to be this brazen and how many times she had practiced with other men. Had Beamish been betwattled by his daughter, or had he worked very hard to keep her reputation intact despite her hoydenish ways? A man who could keep ministers in his pocket surely could cover up his daughter's improprieties.

How much did Miss Beamish know about what was really going on in Novum Arce? Playing along with her crude seduction might get him some answers. He had seldom bested Pris in any game of wits, but he doubted Beamish's daughter was Pris's match, so . . .

He returned her flirtatious smile. "And talking on the public street is so . . . so not intimate."

She laughed. "You are a lady-killer, Leonard, aren't you?"

"The name has been associated with me before." He caught her hand. Pressing it to his bare arm, he bent toward her. "But that could be changed by the right woman."

"And what type of woman is that?"

He opened his mouth to reply, but she put her three longest fingers against his lips.

"No," she whispered, "this is not the place for such a conversation." She slid her fingers slowly down over his bottom lip. "Don't you think it would go better with wine? It is not common knowledge where the Imperator stores his best, but I happen to know. A bottle of an excellent vintage would make our conversation more convivial . . . and intimate."

"Thank you, *domina mea*, but—"

"You can call me 'Bellona.' That would please me." She leaned forward to brush her breasts against his chest. "It would please greatly. And I enjoy showing my gratitude to those who please me."

He stepped back, trying not to show his disgust. She acted like the most slovenly whore in London. "I must complete an errand for the commandant."

"*He* can wait." She seized his hand. "I cannot."

Neville drew his hand away before she could press it to her breast. Hoping his regret sounded sincere, he said, "On this matter, he made it clear he cannot wait, *domina mea*."

"Bellona!"

"He cannot wait, Bellona," he repeated obediently, then dropped his voice to a murmur. "I will be with you as soon as I can. An hour, no more. Imagine the delicious anticipation we can savor." He lifted her hand to his lips and heard her quick intake of breath. He lowered it, unkissed, as he whispered in her ear. "Delicious anticipation."

She moaned and smiled. "I was certain there was something about you that I liked, Leonard. Now I know. You remind me of me."

He could not imagine a worse insult.

"You are," she continued when he did not speak, "not afraid of going after what you want. I admire that in a man." She looped her arm around his in a quick motion he had not expected. "But one glass of wine will not keep you from your task for the commandant . . . or the one you will be performing for me afterwards."

Every instinct told him to rip his arm away from her, but he said, "One glass and one glass only now." He picked up the lantern with what he hoped looked like a careless motion. "We will finish the bottle . . . afterwards."

"I like how you think, *my* dear Leonard." Her slight emphasis should have been a warning to any man who might believe he could have the upper hand in any *affaire* with Bellona.

He sent a silent apology to Pris, because he was certain Bellona would drag out that glass of wine for as long as she could in an effort to seduce him into forgetting his duties. That would be her goal. His would be to flirt and to escape as quickly as possible.

PRISCILLA HEARD the faint tap on the window. Finally! Pausing to peek into the darkness, she hoped the motion beyond the glass signaled Neville had arrived at last. He should have been there almost an hour ago. She had wavered between annoyance and worry something was amiss.

Irritation kept her from giving into her body's demand for sleep. The waves of exhaustion she had experienced during the wine festival had returned, and every movement felt as if she carried ten pounds of iron on her shoulders. She had considered maybe it was for the best that Neville had been delayed and that she should blow out the lamp and get in bed to sleep her fill.

But now he must be here!

She wrapped her stola around her hair and over her shoulders. She left a drooping section in the front so she could pull it across her face if she needed to mask her identity. When she opened the door and stepped into the night, scattered raindrops pelted her face fiercely, driven by the wind that sent the clouds scudding across the night sky.

Where was Neville?

A motion to her left! She heard the flapping of a cloak being pushed aside and caught a quick glimpse of light reflecting off a white uniform.

"Here," came a low whisper in Neville's beloved voice. "Beneath the window."

She rushed to his side. "I started to think you were not coming."

"I was delayed by Beamish's daughter. It seems she has taken a personal interest in me."

"A very personal one; Roxanne warned me."

"Warned you?"

She slipped her arm through his and leaned into him, taking care not to kick over the lantern by his feet. "Roxanne wanted to be certain I had not grown attached to Mr. Williams, because her lady disliked competition."

"You could have warned *me*."

Her laugh was filled with relief. "I have not had a chance, and, to own the truth, I assumed a Roman legionary could hold his own against one lusty wench."

"I was not so sure of that when she clamped her talons on me." He chuckled. "Beamish has got a surprise coming when she gets home."

Priscilla waved aside his questions as she came to her feet. "We cannot delay any longer."

He pulled his cloak back up over his head even though the spitting rain had halted. He put his arm around her shoulders and drew her close so to anyone glancing in their direction, they might pass as a single soldier on his way back to the barracks. Overhead, the moon played peek-a-boo with the clouds, illuminating the ground before slipping away again. They tried to avoid the pools of light and had to come to a stop more than once to wait for the light to fade again. She held her breath the whole time they passed by the windows where the legionaries' voices reached into the night.

Once they were past, she released it and drew in another filled with the scents that were uniquely Neville's. She had not guessed how she would miss such minor aspects of him when they were kept apart, day after day, week after week.

"Any word from Duncan?" she asked.

"No, but I am not worried. I know that he is looking for us, and he is like a foxhound when he gets the scent."

"And he will have to discover a way to get a message to us inside the walls."

He chuckled. "Duncan has done more than that in more harrowing circumstances."

"I would ask, but I suspect I do not want to know."

"Probably not." He lifted his arm from around her shoulders and pointed to the right. "There are the granaries. How many are there?"

"According to the records I have been copying into the ledgers, there are three." She saw they were set at the three points of a large triangle, an odd configuration, but then again, what was not odd in Novum Arce?

"Let's hope one of these three is the charm then."

Priscilla shared his hope as she climbed up two steps to the door on the first granary. It opened, and she stepped aside to let Neville shine the light from his lantern inside the building. Quickly, they realized it was completely empty. The second one was as well. *All we need is one*, she reminded herself as she had too often in the past few days.

She walked up the two steps to the door on the third stone building that, like the other two, had no windows. She put her hand on the latch and murmured a quick prayer before she raised it.

Wheat spilled out onto her toes, and she hastily shut the door. Or tried to. The grain beyond it prevented her from closing it completely. When Neville told her to step aside, she obeyed and took the lantern. He pressed his shoulder against the door and shoved it shut. She sighed when she heard the latch click into place.

"If the guns are in there," Neville said as he jumped down from the top step, "we will never find them. I can check back here regularly, but if I had to wager a guess, I would say nobody would be foolish enough to store them beneath piles of grain that could collapse on one at any time."

"Then where are they? I have checked every public building in Novum Arce and most of the private ones." She came down to stand beside him. "Maybe I was wrong, and the guns were never there. So much of this place is make-believe. Maybe they were, too."

He shook his head. "I don't believe that."

"How can you be sure?"

"Because the guns would not have been moved after you chanced to see them." He gave her a wry grin. "After all, why would someone play a trick on someone they barely know?"

"For the fun of watching us scurry around the compound, trying to look into every building?"

"I don't believe that," he said again. "We will figure it out."

Priscilla gave him a tight smile. She appreciated him trying to keep up her spirits, but her heart was heavy with the prospect of returning to her lonely room and playing a role she had come to hate. She wanted to see her children and the silly puppy Isaac had brought home. For the first time, she even looked forward to Daphne's daily drama about the upcoming wedding.

The idea of admitting defeat was not as horrible as she had imagined before. Whoever had sent Neville out to spy on Sir Thomas would have to be satisfied with what information they had. They could inform Lord Beamish where his wayward daughter was, and then he could do his fatherly duty and collect her himself. Only the thought of never learning what had happened to the other Beamish servants kept her from urging Neville to find a way to sneak out of Novum Arce right now. How could she go back to her family and leave Roxanne never knowing what had happened to the man she loved?

Sudden tears appeared in the corners of her eyes. She pressed her face to Neville's chest, gripping the front of his tunic and wanting never to let go.

"Pris," he said against her hair, "you have told me many times to have faith. Now it is my turn to say the same to you."

"I am tired." Her voice was uneven with the emotion she could no longer contain. "Every day, it feels as if I am trudging through mud. I want to go home and put my feet up and take a nap until I am not tired any longer."

"Oh, sweetheart, it is time to put an end to this charade."

"I know, but we need to . . ."

Priscilla stared toward a passage between the two granaries.

"What is that?" she asked.

As if on cue, the clouds drifted from the face of the moon to send a shaft of light to earth in front of them. She drew in a sharp breath when she saw what looked like another granary storage building hidden within the triangle created by the others.

"It is a fourth building!" She stepped away from him. "But there are only three in the ledgers. Maybe they don't intend to use that building for grain."

"Or maybe they use it when they want to hide something in plain sight."

She agreed. There was no reason to have a fourth building that did not appear in the ledgers unless it was for times when the Imperator did not want anything about it in the community's records. Would they find the missing guns behind its door? Or would it be something else altogether? Or nothing?

No, she refused to give into pessimism again. Taking Neville's hand, she led the way, slipping between two granaries as the moonlight vanished again. He wove his fingers between hers and squeezed gently. Warmth spread from his skin to hers, and her exhaustion fell aside as if it had never existed.

"Try the door," he whispered.

She stepped up and reached to raise the latch. It would not move.

"It is locked," she and Neville said at the same time.

She turned to face him, and he motioned her aside. Only then, as the light from the lantern struck the door, did she notice a heavy metal lock hanging from a hasp about a foot above the latch.

Neville handed her the lantern and drew his knife. She watched as he put the tip in the lock where a key should go. He shifted it with care and patience. It took several minutes, but then a click as loud as a shout echoed through the space between the granaries.

"I had forgotten you know how to pick locks," she said, shaking her head. "You always amaze me."

"It is a skill that often comes in handy, whether I need to get out of a Cornish cell or into a Lakeland granary." He lifted the lock off and threw the hasp aside before he opened the door.

She slid back the front of the dark lantern enough to allow a finger of light to splash out then followed him through the doorway.

Four pairs of wide eyes caught the light and stared back at them. An old woman crouched on the floor behind three men. No, two men and a gangly youth. The men and the boy wore ragged clothing that might once have been dark blue livery. The woman's simple dress was as ripped and filthy, but the fabric was appropriate for an upper servant.

"Is one of you Asher Snow?" Priscilla asked.

The younger of the two men stepped forward. "You know my name. Will you tell us yours?"

She pressed her hands over her mouth to silence her cry of joy. They had found Lord Beamish's missing servants.

Chapter Fourteen

WHEN PRISCILLA stepped past the door, she quickly introduced herself and Neville by the names they had taken in Novum Arce. She glanced around. Except for the door, which Neville had closed behind them so no light would betray them, there was no break in the stone walls. Some hessian jute had been tossed on the stone floor in two corners for makeshift, very uncomfortable bedding. A bucket by the door held water and another at the back of the space reeked. A single trencher held a small amount of food that smelled almost as bad.

Asher Snow was as tall as Neville and looked to be in his early thirties. His black hair was unkempt, but he kept his shoulders back in the pose every good footman learned. He gestured to the old woman. "Allow me to introduce Miss Redding, who has, until recently, served as companion to Miss Beamish."

Miss Redding tried to struggle to her feet, but when she began coughing hard, Priscilla hurried to her and urged her to remain where she was. In the lantern's light, the old woman's lined face was the gray of death. She hoped Miss Redding was in better condition than she appeared. Pulling off her stola, Priscilla draped it over the shivering woman.

"Thank you, madam," Miss Redding said in an obviously educated voice.

Asher pointed to the man on his left and said, "This is Harrison, Lord Beamish's coachee."

"Madam, sir." The coachman bowed his head to her and Neville. His thinning hair was steel gray. He must have been of much wider girth before the servants were taken from The Rose and Thistle because his clothing hung on him as if draped from a single peg.

"Davis is our tiger," Asher continued.

The lad, who could be no more than sixteen or seventeen years old, dipped his head as the coachman had. He was good-looking with shoulders too broad for his form, the very type of youth who could handle the luggage in the boot and would make a fine figure riding on the back of the carriage.

"You don't have anything to eat, do you?" he asked.

"I am sorry—"

Priscilla was interrupted by Neville setting the lantern down and pulling a pouch from beneath his cloak. "It is not much, but I took it during an encounter I had earlier this evening." He arched a brow toward her, and she realized he had taken it while trying to elude Bellona's seduction. "Like I said, it is not much, but . . ." He held out the pouch, and the boy seized it, almost tearing it open.

As the lad pulled out a slice of bread and some cheese, Asher said in a slightly embarrassed voice, "Sometimes a day or two goes by without any food being delivered to us."

"Who brings it?"

"We never see a face because the deliveries are at night, and the person wears a cloak." He exchanged a weary look with the coachee. "We learned trying to rush him was useless because the person never comes alone. The others are armed."

"With swords?"

"No, with pocket pistols." His mouth twisted. "That is why we did not rush forward when you unlocked the door. We figured it was being opened to deliver us food." Glancing at Davis who was examining the other food in the pouch, he sighed. "It's been almost four days since the last visit."

"Have you been imprisoned since you were snatched from the inn?" Neville asked.

"Yes, but not always here."

Priscilla glanced at the men then continued draping her stola over the older woman's shoulders. Letting Neville handle the questions now would give her a chance to comfort Miss Redding. She watched Davis, the tiger, pull a few slices of fruit from Neville's pouch. A growing boy needed more than the scanty meals served to the prisoners.

She fought her outrage that these people had been starved while there was plenty of food for the residents of Novum Arce. Lord Beamish would be furious because he would see their mistreatment as a slap to *his* face. What mattered now was getting these people healthy enough so they could escape when she and Neville found a way to slip them past the guards at the gate.

Davis stood and came over to the old woman. He held out a thick piece of bread and some cheese. "Here, Miss Redding. You need to eat."

Tears welled up in Priscilla's eyes. The boy was hungry himself, but thought first of Miss Redding.

"You eat it, boy," she said, wheezing on each word.

He pretended to tear the bread in half before offering her the same piece again. "Why don't we share?"

"Snow and Harrison—"

"There is enough for all of us, so eat up."

Miss Redding rolled her eyes. "Such language!" Despite that, she took the bread and took a ladylike bite. She began coughing again.

Priscilla rose and got a ladle of the brackish water from the pail by the door. She sniffed the water, hoping it was safe to drink. Priscilla held out the ladle, and Davis took it and offered the old woman a sip.

"I will take care of her," the lad said.

"Thank you." Priscilla went to where Neville was talking with Asher and Harrison. Hope mixed with fatigue on Lord Beamish's men's faces.

"We have not always been together," Asher was saying as she joined the group. "For the first fortnight, we were separated. We all arrived here about a month ago, by my calculations. But I have not always been able to see the sun rise and set. I have no idea why we were moved here. It was night when we were each brought here, and we were blindfolded. Nobody will tell us anything but we must wait while the Imperator decides our fate. He is the one in charge here, right?"

"So we are told," Neville replied as his gaze caught Priscilla's.

She nodded. Like her, he had seen the power shift that was taking place.

"You don't know what is beyond the door?" asked Priscilla.

The coachee said, "We have not seen anything or anyone but the ones who bring us food and now you. You are wearing strange clothing."

As Neville explained about Novum Arce, the men stared at him as if he had taken leave of his senses. Priscilla did not blame them for finding it impossible to believe. In spite of her time in the community, she still was astonished every morning to wake and discover it was not a nightmare.

"What about Miss Beamish and Roxanne Parker?" Asher asked with such intensity Priscilla realized that he had wanted to ask this question first. "Roxanne Parker is her—"

"Abigail," she said gently. "We know."

"You have seen her? Is she all right?"

She gave him a smile. "Yes, save for being worried about you. She and Miss Beamish are here."

"They are not imprisoned." Neville's voice was flat, hiding his emotion.

"Thank God for Miss Beamish," called Miss Redding from where she was eating the bread, and, much to Davis's obvious relief, was no longer coughing. "She must be the one who has kept us alive."

Asher's mouth worked, but he said nothing. Priscilla guessed the footman did not share Miss Redding's opinion. If Bellona had wanted her servants released, they would have been. She must have some reason to order them kept in the granary building, but why would she allow them to starve?

She put her hand on Neville's arm and gently squeezed. When he glanced at her, she shook her head. Reluctance tightened his face, but then he nodded. It would do no good to upset them further. Now was not the time for recriminations or demanding retribution. It was the time for devising a way to keep these four people alive long enough to get them away from Novum Arce.

"You two should have something to eat as well," she urged.

"Davis was correct. There is enough for all of you." Neville motioned to the lad who came over and held out the pouch to the footman and coachee.

The two men gratefully pulled bread out of the pouch and sat to eat it.

Priscilla leaned toward Neville. "Why did you have that food in your pouch?" she asked.

"When I saw the banquet the *magistra* had waiting, I thought some of my fellow legionaries might be willing to gamble for it." He grinned. "I could use a better pair of sandals."

"I might be able to arrange that. I know someone who keeps track of the inventory of such things." She stroked his arm.

"Good! But I have to say I am glad I helped myself while she poured the wine."

"Wine with the *magistra*?" she asked arching her brows as he did often. Like him, she did not speak Bellona's name.

"Is that jealousy I hear?"

"You would like that, wouldn't you?"

He slipped his arm around her waist. "Though you have no reason to worry, it pleases me that you might be a bit jealous."

She would have loved to remain listening to his silly banter, but she could not forget the four people watching them closely. She saw distrust on their faces. They had been treated appallingly by their captors.

As if she had spoken aloud, the footman stood. "How does Roxanne fare?"

Priscilla was glad to be able to speak the truth for once. "As well as can be expected. She is still serving as Miss Beamish's abigail, so she is exempt from the manual labor others are required to do. She is, however, very anxious to know that you are unharmed."

A storm of emotions crossed the footman's face. "My poor Roxanne. She does not know if we are dead or alive."

"She told us what happened at the inn when one of your captors mentioned the name of this place and the others seemed to panic," Neville said.

"I know she will want to come—" Priscilla began to say.

"No!" Asher lowered his voice as his fellow prisoners' heads swiveled toward him. "Don't bring her here. She cannot conceal her feelings, and Miss Beamish would learn quickly she had found us." He swallowed and looked at the floor. "I should not have suggested Miss Beamish would not help us."

"Your assumption may be quite accurate, Snow," Neville said as quietly.

Asher's head popped up. Sparks of frustrated anger burned in his eyes. "She knows we are here and being barely fed?"

"We cannot be certain," Priscilla said. "She seems to be in a position of some authority, but there may be secrets the Imperator is keeping from her."

"Who is this Imperator?"

"Have you heard of Sir Thomas Hodge St. John?"

His mouth grew round. "Not only heard of him, but I have encountered the man on multiple occasions."

"At Beamish's house?"

"Yes. Up until about a year and a half ago, he was a frequent visitor there. I was often stationed at the door when he arrived to spend a fortnight or two with Lord Beamish."

"Now that is very interesting. I had thought they had a falling out years ago." Neville tapped his chin. "And Miss Beamish was there during the baronet's calls?"

"Miss Beamish has acted as her father's hostess for several years now."

Priscilla could almost hear Neville's thoughts because they must be the same as her own. If Bellona was well-acquainted with Sir Thomas, not only as a child but as an adult, convincing him to let her work with him on his dream would not be difficult. Once he had welcomed her assistance, she could use the connection to start amassing authority within the compound.

"We should leave before we are missed." Neville held out the dark lantern to Asher, but the footman shook his head.

"If it is seen here," Asher said, "there will be questions as to how it got here. We have become accustomed to the darkness."

From the corner, Miss Redding said with a bit more vigor in her voice, "You have been kind to us."

Neville nodded. "We will do what we can to bring you food and other supplies you can keep hidden. For now, we need to go." He reached for the door.

Priscilla put her hand on Asher's arm. "Roxanne has never lost faith that the two of you will be reunited. I will let her know that you are alive, but warn her to take care not to reveal anything."

"Thank you," the footman said.

She turned to the other three servants. "Be patient. We will get you out of here."

"When?" asked Davis.

"As soon as we can," Neville said, "without endangering your lives or anyone else's. I promise." He glanced at Priscilla with an expression that told her they could not linger any longer.

As he closed the dark lantern and opened the door so she could step out of the granary, she heard Miss Redding cough and one of the men trying to soothe her. They did not have much time to fulfill *that* promise.

NEVILLE MADE sure his cloak concealed Pris's white gown before they emerged from between the two granaries. He kept his steps short so she could match them. No one must guess that two of them were within his cape.

"Promise me that you will not go back there by yourself," he said quietly when they had passed the barracks where the games of chance continued.

"I must bring them food and supplies."

He stopped and tilted her chin with his thumb. "Pris, it is too risky for you."

"Is it any less risky for you?"

"I don't know, but it will be easy for me to slip food out of the soldiers' mess. I see plenty others doing that. Whether they are stealing it for themselves or to trade with others, nobody would notice me doing the same."

"Good and I will get some blankets for them, so they don't have to sleep on hard hessian jute." Priscilla smiled. "It feels good to be able to do something to help."

"I know, but let me bring the supplies along with the food." He gave her a quick smile. "And, unless you have developed an ability to pick locks, you will not be able to get in on your own."

"You could teach me."

"Not quickly enough." He became grave again. "Let me handle this by myself."

"If you need my help . . ."

"I will." He looked at the community that was slumbering in the night. "Keeping them fed is the least of our worries. We need to find a way to help them escape. Getting the three men away would be tricky, but could be done if the conditions were right. Lazy guards on duty on a moonless night would be best."

"You might as well wish for a giant eagle to fly in and carry them off."

"A good idea, Pris, but do you have any idea where we can get our hands on a giant eagle?"

She chuckled. "I will keep my eyes open in case someone has one they want to get rid of. But you said the three men. What about Miss Redding?"

Neville began walking again. "She is frail. I doubt she could step out of the granary on her own at this point. She would not survive traveling through the fells on foot."

"She should not be in the cold, damp granary. It will make her cough worse."

"It should not be too hard to slip her out of the granary if there was a place where we could hide her."

"My room behind my office."

"That is too dangerous."

She shook her head. "I usually keep the door to my room closed, so nobody would notice anything different. She can use my bed, and I—"

"I can probably borrow a cot from the barracks. There are plenty of empty ones."

"Good. If you cannot, I will simply take more blankets from the storerooms. The quartermaster does not keep track of those. I know, because he could not give me an accurate accounting when I asked him for one. When can you bring her?"

"I will try tomorrow at the same time I take them more food."

He could tell she was smiling even though he was unable to see her face. "Good. One step forward. Now the next . . ."

"Which is?"

"Telling Roxanne what we found."

He said, only half-joking, "If you are talking about us going to Miss Beamish's house tonight, I am not as brave a man as you think I am. *She* is waiting for *her* dear Leonard to return. I know you are not a jealous woman, but don't consign your husband to that viper's den."

She laughed. "Don't worry. As far as Bellona knows, I am a former lady's maid, and I am unworthy of her notice should I come to her house on an errand. However, if you want to flee, I will enter the den alone."

"No, I will gird my loins and go with you."

"Your loins, eh? You might want to consider other ways to protect them than girding." She chuckled again.

Neville squeezed her closer. How did she know his every mood before he did? She had seen through his jests to know he was concerned about the choices he would have to make to protect Pris and the others. That she trusted him to make the right decision was a gift he had despaired of ever receiving until she offered him her heart.

When Pris led him around to the back of Miss Beamish's large house, she opened a door to a storage room. It was filled with crates that must hold enough food for the century for weeks. He was curious why it was stored there, but Pris motioned for him to follow her into the kitchen.

A banked fire on the hearth gave off enough light for him to see the large wooden table in the middle of the stone floor and a stack of pots next to the fireplace.

"Wait here," Pris whispered, pointing to the shadows in the corner. "I will bring her here."

When she left the kitchen, he edged into the shadows. And it was just in time because a man strode into the kitchen as if the house were his. The arrogant set of his shoulders identified him as one of the skilled warriors who trained separately from the rest of the century. Neville thought his name was Livius.

The man walked out the door Pris had used, not looking once in Neville's direction. Knowing he should stay where he was, Neville tiptoed after him. The warrior seemed to know his way through the warren of rooms that opened onto the central courtyard. Neville hung back as the man entered it. He watched, not surprised, when Miss Beamish met Livius near the fountain. She gave him a fierce kiss.

Neville stifled a laugh. Apparently, Leonard Williams had missed his opportunity with her.

Livius drew back. "We must talk, Bellona," he growled, his Scottish burr strong with his intensity. "The men grow restless."

"The time is soon. It is your duty to remind them." She was annoyed he had interrupted their kiss with talking. "For now . . ." She reached for him again.

"They want to practice with the other weapons."

She put her hands on her hips and scowled. "It takes time to arrange that. Swords and spears don't make any noise that will call attention to you. The other weapons do."

"They want to know if the old man—"

"Tell them not to worry. He will heed me, but others may not."

He laughed. "Those fools who call themselves legionaries are no threat."

"I am not speaking of them." She seized his arm. "I don't wish to talk of these things where we can be overheard."

"Don't you control your own servants?"

"Most of them, and the others will learn the cost of disloyalty," she said before tugging Livius across the courtyard.

Neville pushed away from the wall and retraced his steps to the kitchen. Noisy weapons? Bellona and her lover had been talking about guns. The same ones Pris had seen? If so, he wondered how much time he had to get that news to London. He could slip away tonight, but he could not leave the others here. He knew without even asking that Pris would not abandon Beamish's servants to their fate in Novum Arce. His plan for escape must include all of them.

He reached the kitchen a few seconds before Pris arrived with Roxanne. When Pris started to speak, he motioned her to silence.

"Outside," he whispered.

Pris frowned at him. "Why—?"

"Outside." He put his finger to his lips. "Not another word."

She did not argue as they slipped out of the kitchen with Roxanne between them. When he led the way to where a bench was set beneath some saplings, both women followed. Roxanne sat and rubbed sleep from her eyes as she looked at both of them.

"Cordelia," she asked, "why are we out here at this hour?"

Pris sat beside her. Dropping her voice to a whisper, she said, "We found them."

"Them?" She paused. "Oh, my! You found *them*! How—I mean . . .?"

"They are alive."

"Alive? Thank God. How is—?"

"No names," Neville said sharply but quietly. He could not be sure that there was not someone listening. The night could have dozens of ears trained on their conversation. "But *he* is fine."

Roxanne pressed her hands to her face and began to weep.

Putting her arm around the abigail, Pris murmured to her. Neville could not pick out a single word, and he doubted Roxanne could. It did not matter because there were no words that could convey both the woman's relief and joy.

Roxanne raised her head. "When can I see him?"

"We cannot say yet," Neville replied.

"What do you mean?" she asked, turning to him. "If you know where he is, why can't I see him?"

"Because we must continue to act as if we have no idea where they are. Until we have a way to get them out of Novum Arce, all we can do is make sure they have food and whatever else they need."

"I want to help—"

Pris smiled. "I know you do, but the best thing you can do right now is pretend nothing has changed. Mr. Williams will take them food."

Roxanne nodded. "All right, but isn't there something I can do?"

"Nothing but be patient." Priscilla gave her a sad smile and put a comforting hand on her arm. "I know that is the hardest task."

Neville wondered how many times he had witnessed her offering someone solace. He had lost count, but every single person had been comforted by her genuine kindness.

"She might be able to help you with the oldest one," he said, taking care to follow his own advice and not mention any of the servants by name.

"Oldest? Woman or man?" the abigail asked as she looked from him to Pris.

"Woman," Pris answered. "She is sick, and we are bringing her to my room to recover. I will need help making sure nobody discovers she is there." She looked at the house. "Nobody."

"I will find time to sit with her." Roxanne held out her hands and took one of Pris's and one of his. "Thank you so much. I barely dared to believe they were alive after all this time."

"Don't thank us yet," he said drearily. "Until we can make a plan to get them out of Novum Arce, they are prisoners." He cursed under his breath before adding, "Just like the rest of us."

Chapter Fifteen

SHORTLY AFTER breakfast two days later, Jack stamped into the barracks and threw his equipment on the bed. Swearing, he turned to ram his fist into the stone wall.

Neville grabbed his arm. "Whoa there, mate! You will break your knuckles, and how will that help you win your lady's heart?"

"It is not about her!" Jack jerked his arm, and Neville released it. "We will never be anything but a joke."

"We?"

"The soldiers in this end of the barracks." His fingers curled into fists again, but he opened them when Neville frowned at him.

"What has gotten you at daggers drawn?"

He hooked a thumb toward the side of the building where the skilled soldiers slept. "Them. They have been whispering about a meeting at the baths for those who have been welcomed to the Temple of Mithras, a group to which every soldier should belong. It is a good time because the baths are seldom used in the morning. But when I asked them about it, they told me only *real* warriors were invited. They laughed in my face and told me to keep my mouth shut and go back to trying not to kill myself with my own weapon."

"They were trying to rile you."

"They succeeded." He sat heavily on his cot and shoved his armor onto the floor. "Because they are right. Some of the men here can barely control their swords or spears. Our so-called officers are worthless, more concerned about the amount of wine in their goblets than helping us learn to defend Novum Arce."

"Let me see what I can find out," Neville said. He stuck his dagger in his belt and reached for his helmet.

Jack snorted. "Good luck with your doomed quest."

"Thanks." He clapped his friend on the shoulder. "Wait here, and don't try to ram your hand through the wall . . . at least until I get back."

He gave him a reluctant smile. "I can promise that much."

Neville hurried out of the barracks and toward the center of the compound as he considered ideas and tossed them aside. He had to have what would appear to be a legitimate excuse to enter the baths when the elite soldiers were holding a meeting. If he did not, they would guess Jack had told him, and then they might punish Jack for talking about what they wanted to keep a secret.

He paused as he passed Pris's office. He should not involve her, but the two of them going to the baths on the pretense of being together in one of the rooms was the only idea he had. It would not be dangerous. People came and went at the baths throughout the day, which made the soldiers' plans to congregate there surprising.

Walking into Pris's office, he saw her writing in one of the great books open on her table. She looked up and smiled. Warmth flooded him. Each of her smiles was a precious gift that reached right into his heart and banished his usual cynicism for a few heartbeats.

"This is a wonderful surprise," she said, coming to her feet and around the table. She kissed his cheek in a greeting appropriate for very good friends, but the longing for more glowed in her eyes like twin versions of the evening star.

As he did each time he saw her, he checked to make sure there were no visible signs of her pregnancy. They needed to be away from Novum Arce before that happened. Her form still was trim and showed no signs of the changes going on inside her.

"I need your assistance." Neville lowered his voice. "At the baths."

She looked over her shoulder toward her bedroom door. "I should not leave my guest alone."

Getting Miss Redding to Pris's room after dark last night had been more complicated than they imagined. Neville had recruited some of the other soldiers to help him carry weapons to the training field. When he had asked his fellow legionaries to wrap the swords first in blankets to protect them from the dew on the ground, they had been hesitant until he promised them some excellent bottles of wine if they followed what he let them assume was the commandant's order. Miss Parker had told them where those bottles were stored, a fact she learned when Miss Beamish had sent her to get one or two to share with a favorite lover. Pris had retrieved a dozen while pretending to do an inventory.

When Neville went to get Miss Redding, she did not want to abandon the others and had to be convinced it was part of a scheme to free them. He wrapped her in a blanket to match those used to transport the weapons and carried her to Pris's office with no undue notice. There, Pris and Miss Parker helped the old woman into bed while he had carried the wine, carefully wrapped in the blanket, to the barracks before rejoining the other soldiers on the training ground.

Complicated, yes, but it had worked without anyone else being the wiser.

"How does your guest fare?" he asked.

"She is asleep, thanks to one of Aunt Tetty's powders."

"I will need your help for a few minutes." He outlined his nebulous plan. "Once we are seen going into the baths, you can sneak back here before your guest awakens."

He took her hand, thrilling in the feel of her soft fingers against his work-hardened skin. He did not release it as they walked toward the baths. When they passed the entrance to the Temple of Mithras and began down the hill toward the baths beside the stream, he glanced at the temple with its simple columns. He had gone inside when he and Pris had been searching for the elusive crates of weapons. Seeing no doors in there, save for the one that opened into the cave below, he had left. Now he wondered if he should have explored farther. He would do so as soon as he had a chance.

They passed more than a score of people between Pris's office and the main door to the baths. Neville made sure he greeted each of them, so they would remember seeing him and Pris.

Inside, they walked through the apodyterium, the area where anyone could leave their clothing while they enjoyed the baths. Individual cubicles were available, so items did not get mixed up or lost. Nobody guarded the space. Whether it was because there were no thieves in Novum Arce or no one could be spared for the task, he had no idea.

He held his finger to his lips and listened for voices. He heard them, faint and distant. No words, only voices rising and falling.

"Where are they?" Pris whispered.

"In the caldarium, I would wager." He took her hand and walked through the door into what should have been the hottest room in the baths, the place to sweat and wash. It was cool. The hypocaust fires which heated the space beneath the stone floor must have gone out overnight.

The room was empty. Where were the soldiers?

"Listen," Pris murmured. "I can still hear them." She knelt. "Down here."

Under the floor? Neville lifted a stone and looked down into the area where fires were lit to keep the caldarium hot. All he saw were ashes.

Leaning down, he held his breath. The voices were definitely louder beneath the floor.

He stood. "All right, Pris. This is as far as you go. I will let you know what I find."

"You cannot be thinking of crawling under the floor. There could be hot embers."

"I need to find out what is going on."

"Then I am going with you."

"No!"

She stared at him in disbelief at the tone he had never used with her before. Curving his hands around her shoulders, he bent until his eyes were even with hers.

"Don't argue with me on this," he said, brushing a loose strand of her hair from her face. "I have to go, but you must stay here where you are safe."

She sighed and closed her eyes, complying with his request. When she put her hand on his arm, her fingers trembled. He set his hand over hers and gave it a gentle squeeze. He hoped the motion would say what words could not.

"Wait for me with something cold to drink." He tried to give her a jaunty smile, but it was impossible when her expression was bleak.

"I will," she whispered. "Be careful, Neville."

"I always am."

Her golden brows rose. "Really? Since when?" She pressed her lips to his and ran out of the caldarium.

Neville stared after her, knowing she felt she had failed him because she could not be at his side.

He rubbed his hands together then knelt by the stone he had shifted to one side. The space was narrow, but he should be able to fit through it if he held his breath.

Dropping into the space that was no more than three feet high, he grimaced as he pulled the stone over him, leaving a small gap so he might escape back into the caldarium. He could not go out the way the boys did after clearing the ashes without being seen.

Light trickled between the stones, and he saw where ashes had been brushed aside to his right. His eyes widened. There should not be an opening in that direction. He was near the front of the baths, and he should be looking at a stone foundation like the ones on the other three sides.

He listened and was not surprised to learn that the rumble of voices was coming from the tunnel. It was magnifying the sound enough so it could be heard in the baths. He could not pick out individual voices.

As he crawled on his belly toward the tunnel, he realized the embers had been kicked aside by someone else who had also come in this direction. That person might be ahead of him. He peered down its length and saw faint light. Nobody else was in the tunnel unless there were branches or niches off it. But he could not discern that from where he was.

Neville inched into the tunnel. The scrape of embers threatened to betray him, but he left them behind after he was a few feet into the cramped space. There was enough room to raise his head to gauge how close he was to the end as he clawed his way through, gripping the edges of bricks to propel himself forward. If he had to beat a hasty retreat, he would be in deep trouble.

Making sure there were no vagrant embers or other debris in front of him, he eased as close as he dared to the end of the tunnel and looked out. A string of curses rattled through his head as he stared at what he had not expected to see.

It was a large, earthen-sided chamber. A cave. The tunnel must be near the roof. Smoke came from a trio of braziers set equidistant along the long room. He saw a pair of identical statues on the floor near the bottom of stairs leading up from the cave. The two figures wore legionaries' cloaks, helmets, and weapons. Each had a drawn sword pointed at the other stone warrior.

At the other end of the room, three square columns were set beneath a mural of a man slicing the throat of a bull. That was the altar of Mithras. The three columns were about three feet tall. Though close to the same size, each one was topped with a different sort of pediment. The one in the middle held a carved figure, and the two flanking it were covered with crudely carved writing. He guessed the words were in Latin, but he could not read them from across the cave. He could see the figure on the middle one. It was a torso of a man dressed in armor. From the left side of his helmet, three indentations were shaped like chubby feathers. They were not feathers, but light flowing off the god.

He was looking at the secret cave beneath the Temple of Mithras, the one sacred to the warrior god's followers. As he watched, a half a dozen men wandered into his view. They came toward him, but did not look up to where he hid.

More men followed, and he picked out faces he recognized, though some of the men remained in shadow. The ones he could identify were from among the elite warriors in the century. St. John walked among them as if he were a soldier, too. Everyone but the Imperator stopped by one of the statues. St. John continued to the altar and bowed before turning to face the others.

"We are well-assembled here this morn." St. John raised his arms, and Neville saw he held some sort of staff in his right hand. "Our way will be blessed."

A man Neville recognized as one of the leaders of the skilled legionaries stepped forward and took the staff. Holding it aloft, he said, "It is time to stop talking and set forth with what we plan to do."

"Not yet." St. John took the pole back, and Neville wondered if they believed the one who possessed it had the right to speak. "For over two years, we have lived in peace here in Novum Arce. It can remain that way."

"Thomas, will you stop mewling like an old woman?" asked a voice from the shadows. A female voice!

Neville frowned. He had not expected to hear a woman speaking in Mithras's cave. Who was it?

A tall, voluptuous woman emerged from the shadows. Lord Beamish's daughter! What was *she* doing in the temple of Mithras where only men were allowed?

She walked up to St. John and plucked the staff from his fingers. He sank to sit on a bench beside the three short columns, looking suddenly less like a great leader and more like a beaten dog.

As the other man had, Miss Beamish held the staff over her head. "Heed me well! The time is coming, but it is not yet."

Grumbles trickled through the cavern.

Miss Beamish cut the complaints off with a single command. "Heed me well!" she repeated. "Our time is coming, and I can promise you the rewards at the end will be worth the wait. Who is with me?"

The cave echoed with excited shouts. Again, Neville looked at St. John. The man had his face hidden in his hands. His shoulders shook as if he were laughing or weeping. Neville guessed it was the latter. As he watched the soldiers cheering and moving to surround Miss Beamish, he bit back a curse.

Everything that the Prince Regent had feared might be happening at Novum Arce was unfolding in front of his eyes. He had to find a way to alert the government. But how could he without endangering Pris and Lord Beamish's servants more?

PRISCILLA BLEW out the lamp in her bedchamber and tiptoed to the door. Miss Redding was asleep, her cough eased by a powder Aunt Tetty had sent with Roxanne. Priscilla kept hot water available on the hearth so it would be ready if Miss Redding needed another dose.

Now Roxanne was back at the *magistra's* house. Neville had sent a message he would share what he had found at the baths as soon as he could, but the century was undergoing long hours of training and no one was excused. After the evening meal, Priscilla had carried an armful of blankets that would become her bed into her office. She could have slept on the floor beside her bed, but she did not want to chance someone happening to see Miss Redding when Priscilla came out to start her day.

Closing the bedroom door, she shivered. One of the windows had been left open, and the chilly night air flooded her office. She dropped the blankets on the floor then went to close the window. A furtive motion caught her eyes. Someone was crossing the century's training field. Who was out there at such a late hour?

For a moment, she dared to hope Neville had slipped out of the barracks. She wanted to learn if he had found anything significant at the baths or if it had been a dead end. She hoped he could remain at her office tonight. Not that they would have any privacy with Miss Redding in Priscilla's bed, but they could have some time together in the darkness while the older woman snored through the night.

A flutter of a long skirt shattered that hope. The person skulking across the training ground was a woman. Dousing the dim lamp on her table, Priscilla drew the shutters back so she had a good view of the street and the open area beyond it. The moonlight sparked off the woman's jewelry, and she gasped. Only one person in Novum Arce wore that much silver, gold, and gems.

Bellona!

Was she on her way to a tryst? But why would *she* be sneaking across the compound instead of having her paramour come to her luxurious home?

An anger she did not recognize twisted through her middle as she wondered if Bellona was on her way to coerce Neville into becoming her lover. Imagining tearing out the young woman's hair was not a proper thought for the former wife of a vicar, but she did not try to curb it. Neville was her husband, and she was not going to share him with another woman.

She trusted Neville, but she also trusted that Bellona would not care about anything and anyone as long as she got what she wanted. If

Bellona threatened Priscilla, Neville would capitulate in order to protect
her. She hoped he realized surrendering one's will to Bellona could mean
never escaping the webs she spun. Oh, how she wished she had told
Lord Beamish that he needed to get someone else to find his missing
daughter!

Grabbing her dark cloak, Priscilla tied it around her neck. She drew
the hood over her head and pulled it across her gown so no hint of her
light hair or her white gown would catch the faint moonlight and pinpoint her location. As she reached for the door, she paused, wondering
if it was safe to leave Miss Redding. Still, an earlier dose of the powder
had left the old woman sleeping for almost ten hours. She would be back
long before the woman awoke.

The streets were silent. Priscilla kept to the shadows as she hurried
to catch up with Bellona without letting the baron's daughter know she
was being tailed. Her eyes widened when she realized Bellona was on a
direct course to the gate. Bellona came to a sudden stop. Priscilla jumped
into the deeper shadows and pressed against the cold stone wall of a
building. Why was the *magistra* looking up at the fells?

A light flashed once, twice, then a third time from high on the hill.
Someone was up there, but who? The patrols were recalled into Novum
Arce once the sun went down.

From the corner of her eye, she saw another flare. It was coming
from where she had seen Bellona only moments ago, and it blinked
twice more, as had the light on the fell. She must be signaling to someone.

Then Bellona was moving again. This time, directly toward the gate.

How was she going to slip past the wall? She recalled what Bellona
had told her about the man who tried to flee the community. But was
any of that true, or had Bellona made up the tale to frighten others into
staying within the settlement?

Priscilla started to push away from the building to follow then
gasped when she saw a person hurrying toward her. She waited until the
woman came closer before she called in a stage whisper, "Roxanne?"

The abigail halted and looked wildly in every direction.

Priscilla stepped out of the shadows. "Here."

"Cordelia," she gasped in a strangled whisper. "You scared a year
off my life."

"What are you doing out here at this hour?"

"I could ask you the same." When Priscilla did not answer, the
abigail hurried on, "*Magistra* Bellona left to call on the Imperator without

her warmest stola. I thought I would bring it to her."

"Will you help me with something first?"

"Certainly. I can deliver the stola to her later. Her visits to the Imperator can last half the night."

Priscilla's curiosity was piqued again because Bellona was not heading toward the Imperator's house. "Before you agree, it could be dangerous. Do you want to know what I am up to?"

"Don't tell me." She glanced toward where Bellona was walking toward the gate. "I don't want to know. All that matters is that you are keeping Asher and the rest alive. Mr. Williams has agreed to let me go with him tomorrow when he visits them. He said I was such a good collaborator in moving Miss Redding that he believes I can see Asher and still hide my joy. To repay that kindness, I will do whatever I can to help you."

"I am glad you are going to see your beloved tomorrow." Priscilla gave her friend a big hug, then whispered, "Now I need to slip past the guards at the gate."

Again, Roxanne looked toward where the *magistra* was disappearing into the shadows. "And then back in later?"

"Yes." She frowned. "How did you know I was not going to keep going once I was past the wall?"

"Because Mr. Williams is here, and I have seen how you look at him. You would not leave him to the *magistra*."

Priscilla chuckled. "You are astute, Roxanne Parker." She motioned for Roxanne to come with her toward the gate. She needed to keep Bellona in sight. Though it appeared as if the gate were the *magistra's* destination, Priscilla did not trust her not to go somewhere else entirely.

They used the buildings to hide them as long as they could, and Priscilla was grateful the commandant's house had few windows on the side overlooking the training field. When they reached the end of the large house, she motioned for a pause. She scanned the open area. As she had expected, Bellona was at the gate and appeared to be in deep conversation with the guards.

Roxanne put a hand on Priscilla's shoulder. "I should not speak of this, but I want to warn you before you are hurt."

"In what way?"

"If you are following the *magistra* to make sure she is not meeting Mr. Williams, you should know she has probably forgotten him by now. There are others willing to do what she wants in exchange for what she offers. She learned her skills well before our arrival at Novum Arce."

Priscilla did not try to hide her shock. "She was with as many . . . ?" Choosing other words because even if Lord Beamish's daughter's reputation was sullied, speaking of it bluntly was abhorrent, she said, "She was as inconstant in her affections before she came to Novum Arce?"

"Yes."

"I thought she was to be married to Mr. Sherman. That is what my former lady mentioned," she added hastily, again uncomfortable she could not be completely honest with the abigail who was risking so much to help her.

"I learned the truth one day when Mr. Sherman called. I should not have been listening to their conversation; yet when she sent Miss Redding away, I wanted to make sure she had a proper chaperone. What I heard shocked me. She struck a bargain that allowed her to use him as an excuse to see other callers when her father was busy elsewhere." She shuddered. "He did not mind sharing her with others, and it allowed him his own pursuits as well. If we had not been brought here, I suspect they would have married and kept the same arrangement."

"I am sorry."

"Don't be. When Asher asked me to marry him, I was able to say yes without a pinch of guilt. We intended, after escorting her to visit her family, to take our leave of that horrible household and make a life for ourselves elsewhere." Her eyes widened so much Priscilla could see them in the faint light. "Oh, my! She has gone past the guards."

Knowing there was no time to waste, Priscilla said, "I must see where she goes. I need you to distract the guards so I can sneak past them."

"I will." She threw the stola over her head and shoulders, then kissed Priscilla's cheek. "Good luck, my friend."

"Good luck to both of us."

Roxanne nodded and walked as boldly as Bellona had toward the gate. Priscilla followed more clandestinely by hurrying to a section of the wall about ten yards from the guards and letting the shadows cover her once more. She held her breath as Roxanne paused by the guards.

"Good evening," the abigail said, putting her hand on her hip in a motion she copied from Bellona.

"What are you doing here?" demanded the taller of the two men who was silhouetted by the lanterns set by the gate.

"I could not sleep, so I decided to take a walk."

"Walk somewhere else."

"Don't be hasty," the other man said. "Don't you recognize her? That is the *magistra's* maid. You don't want the *magistra* angry with us, do you? We will be back on the training field with those incompetents in no time."

Roxanne leaned toward them, but kept her voice loud enough to reach Priscilla. "You, sir, are a very smart man." She walked her fingers up his chest. "My lady likes smart men."

"Does she now?" The man preened like a rooster in a yard of hens.

The tall man pushed forward. "You can tell your lady that I am smart, too."

"I will have to remember to mention that to her."

"Are you chasing after a cat, too?" the taller man asked.

"A cat?" Roxanne's voice faltered for a moment, then she laughed. "Why don't we leave that to the *magistra*?" She crooked a finger at the men. "Unless you want me to say, 'Here, kitty, kitty.'"

"You were not supposed to speak of that," the shorter man said, punching the other man in the upper arm.

"To anyone who doesn't know. This is the *magistra's* maid. She knows what her lady is doing." He glanced toward Roxanne. "You do, don't you?"

"What kind of abigail would I be if I didn't?" Her voice was so convincing Priscilla almost believed her. The young woman could have a career on the stage. The two men continued to argue with each other and flirt with Roxanne. Priscilla edged along the wall. When Roxanne put an arm around the shoulders of both guards and turned them away from where Priscilla lurked, she rushed through the gate. She crouched close to the ground, letting the shadows beyond the lanterns conceal her. She held her breath, waiting for shouts or a spear being driven into her back, but the conversation by the wall continued uninterrupted with Roxanne telling the men it would take her no more than a half hour to return with enough wine for them to enjoy the night together.

Half an hour. That was all the time Priscilla had to chase after Bellona, discover why she had left the compound, and return. She hoped it would be enough. But it would have to be. Because there was no way she was leaving her friend to the lascivious guards.

Chapter Sixteen

IT HAD TO BE Bellona. No one else would be abroad on the hill when the narrow curve of the crescent moon offered little light. Priscilla had lost sight of her several minutes ago. Aware of every second ticking away, she knew she had only about twelve minutes before she had to be back inside Novum Arce.

Hoping she was right and what she thought was Bellona was not a sheep, Priscilla followed the moving form up the steep fell. She placed her feet with care, not wanting to disturb the loose stones strewn across the hillside. Ahead of her, Bellona was not being cautious, and pebbles tumbled down the hill to pelt Priscilla.

One hit her hard on the bridge of her nose. She blinked back tears as she bit her lip to keep from crying out. She flattened herself against the ground when Bellona looked behind her before continuing the climb.

Priscilla inched close enough so she could hear Bellona's straining breaths. A rest would be good, but that would eat away precious seconds.

The new grass bursting from the tangle of last year's mat threatened to trip her on every step. Each time Bellona halted, Priscilla froze close to the ground or behind a boulder. The few trees on the hillside were too scattered to shield her.

But Bellona did not seem worried about being followed. Why should she? The guards at the gate served her well by keeping anyone from giving chase.

Staying low and keeping her stola tight over her shoulders, Priscilla used every trick Neville had taught her about trailing someone. She moved when Bellona did and stayed still whenever the young woman slowed or stopped, so no errant sound or movement could betray her.

Then Bellona disappeared again, her silhouette no longer visible against the clouds rolling down toward the fells. Priscilla pushed forward, hoping Bellona would think any rustles in the grass came from the sheep grazing on the hillside.

The crown of the hill was flat, which was why Bellona had seemed to vanish. In its center was a stone circle. Almost a dozen stones stood upright with several more lying on their sides, poking up through the grass. The area was preternaturally flat, and Priscilla guessed ancient Britons had prepared the space before dragging the stones up the steep fell. To them, it had been a sacred place, a place to come and celebrate their gods, but, for Priscilla, the great stones provided a place to hide.

She squatted, clinging to the shadows before she scanned the hillside. Letting someone else sneak up on her would be foolish. She wished for eyes in the back of her head or Isaac's excitable pup Beowulf who would bark if anyone approached.

Satisfied nobody else was climbing behind her, she peered around the rock. Bellona stood in the middle of the circle, by a stone that was smaller than the others. It only reached as high as her waist. The young woman flicked her fingers, and water spewed from the top. She bent and opened a dark lantern enough to illuminate the grass around her feet.

And then she waited.

Priscilla fought her frustration as time slid past. Bellona had not come up here simply to be alone, so she must be meeting someone.

As she counted down the time before she had to leave, a man stepped out of the shadows. Priscilla had to force her gasp down her throat. She had not sensed he was waiting beyond the light of Bellona's lantern. He walked confidently toward Bellona who waited as if she were a queen and he, the least of her subjects.

The man bowed his head. "Gracious lady, we are well met on this night."

Priscilla pressed her hand over her mouth before another gasp could escape. The man's accent was French. Why was a Frenchman sneaking around the countryside? England was at war with Napoleon's French Empire. He must be a spy, but why was he meeting Bellona on the fell?

"Do you have news for me, M. LeChat?" Bellona asked.

M. LeChat? Was that a real name? *Chat* was French for cat. The guards at the gate had asked Roxanne about a cat. Was this why?

"Nothing yet, gracious lady."

"My allies grow impatient," she replied in the petulant voice she used whenever she did not get her way immediately.

"It cannot be helped, gracious lady. To move too soon would be a mistake. Everything must be in place if we are to succeed. Other attempts have failed because people did not wait until the conditions were right."

She folded her arms over her chest and tapped her toe against the ground. "M. LeChat, you might believe you have nine lives to wait on what is to come, but the rest of us don't."

"Ah, gracious lady, why is a young and beautiful woman like yourself listening to the counsel of those who wish only to win glory for themselves? They don't know, as we do, that battle should only be engaged when the odds are in our favor. The time is coming, gracious lady, when England will accept her rightful ruler."

"Soon?" Her voice became silky and seductive.

"Very soon. Now have we not talked about that long enough?"

Priscilla ducked behind the stone as the man pulled Bellona to him, kissing her hard. Hoping they were too focused on each other to notice anything else, she slipped away.

All the way down the fell toward Novum Arce, she replayed their words in her mind. First, she had to get Roxanne away from the guards; then she had to talk to Neville. More was going on in Novum Arce than either of them could have guessed.

TAKING A DEEP breath and continuing to walk through the thick grass, Priscilla chided herself. She should have insisted Livius, the legionary with the Scottish accent, come with her to the dairy instead of leaving her at the crossroads by the *principia*. His directions were convoluted and had taken her on a roundabout route. And she had not yet found the dairy.

What had he said? *You will find it just the other side of the storerooms. It has red brick walls. You cannot miss it.*

But she had. Somehow she must have walked right past it. She went to where the stream exited under the wall and began to follow the bank upstream toward the Temple of Mithras and the baths beyond it.

Why had Neville sent Livius with a message to meet him at the dairy? She had asked Neville, in the short note she had sent the first thing this morning, to come to her office. They could talk there without being overheard. Nobody else must learn what she had seen and heard last night. Had she failed to stress the importance of coming as soon as possible? No, she had written she needed to see him right away. He must think the dairy was a more secure place to talk without the jeopardy of being overheard, but he could have come to her office and told her himself instead of sending that leering legionary.

She smiled when she saw a wooden door built into a short red brick tunnel beneath the bank. At last!

Unsure if the door was secured, she put her hand on the latch. It lifted easily. She opened the door, startled by the sudden rush of cold. Stepping inside on black and white tiles, she saw an inner door. She could hear rapidly running water beyond it.

That made sense. Some of the water rushing down from the fells had been diverted beneath the hill. Fresh milk could be placed in containers and set in the icy water to keep it from spoiling. She wondered why this building had not appeared on any of the ledger entries she had made. Maybe it was because the community had no cows. There was not enough grazing for them on the barren fells. Erecting a dairy was another of Sir Thomas's addled ideas.

Priscilla pulled her stola closer. She shivered. She wished Neville would arrive to explain why he had asked to meet her in such a chilly place.

Wrapping her arms around herself, she concentrated on not shivering with the cold. The big quivers stopped, but not a faint one beneath her heart. She gasped and put her hand over her abdomen. Had it been . . . ? She held her breath, willing the small flutter to come again.

There!

A tiny motion like an awakening butterfly deep within her.

The baby!

It had grown large enough so she could feel it move. She wanted to sing with joy and gratitude at the miracle that was as precious now as it was the first time she had felt Daphne quicken within her.

Where was Neville? Now she had wondrous tidings to share along with the disturbing events she had witnessed last night.

Priscilla heard a soft sound past the inner door. Had he been waiting inside all along? What a laugh they were going to have once their teeth stopped chattering!

"Mr. Williams?" she called as she rushed into the other room, unable to bear waiting a moment longer to tell him about their baby's movement.

Hands grabbed her and flung her away from the door. With a scream, she teetered on the edge of a great well that went deep into the earth. She leaned away, praying those hands would not push her again, this time into the chasm.

Somehow, she threw herself back and landed on her bottom in a cold puddle. The concussion of hitting the stone floor raced up her spine, and she cried out in pain. She dug her fingers into the cracks between the stones, determined not to rock forward into the pit.

Once she was secure on the floor, she looked around and saw no one. Whoever had seized her had fled before determining if she lived or had fallen to her death. Using her feet to push herself back, she counted herself lucky. If the person had stayed, he might have finished what he began.

She pressed her spine against the wall and forced herself to her feet. She did not move for several minutes, fearful she would miscalculate and tumble into the great well. Taking deep breaths, she waited, watching her breath form clouds in front of her face until her heartbeat began to slow and her knees were steady.

It took almost more courage than she possessed to inch to the edge. In the light of a lantern set on the floor across the opening, she could see stairs winding down. A faint glimmer at the bottom was not a stream as she had expected, but blocks of ice covered with straw.

This was not a dairy. It was an icehouse.

She had made a terrible mistake. Neville was probably waiting for her at the dairy now.

Turning, she reached to push the door open. It had slammed shut, catching one corner of her stola. She had to get out of the cold before the shivers shook her bones apart. The latch lifted, but the door refused to open. She pushed with her shoulder. The door would not budge. Raising her fist, she banged on it and shouted for help.

She got no answer, though she screamed until her voice was gone. Her wet clothes clung to her, dank and stiffening while they froze to her. She leaned against the door because she did not dare to take her stola off and leave her arms bare.

The lantern sputtered and went out.

She was afraid to move in any direction, lost in the stygian darkness and unsure where the pit was. She did not know when she slid to her knees and then to the floor. By then, every breath was a separate torture as the frosty air urged her to close her eyes and stop fighting its promise of warmth if she would surrender to it. She placed her hands over the spot where her baby now was still.

"Forgive me," she whispered in the moments before the cold wrapped her completely in its unforgiving embrace.

NEVILLE CHECKED over his shoulder, but nobody was paying attention to him or the basket he carried. He guessed it was because Roxanne Parker walked by his side, her fingers lightly trembling on his arm. Anyone looking in their direction would believe they were courting.

The abigail had not said a word since he met her not far from the barracks. Her face was rigid. Telling her to relax would be useless when she was eager to see her betrothed.

He took a roundabout route before they slipped between the outer granaries from the rear, so the buildings blocked them from view.

"Say nothing," he whispered, though she had been silent, "until we are in the granary and have closed the door behind us. We cannot afford to alert a chance passerby there is another building in the middle of the others. Someone might be curious what is in it."

"I know."

He gave her a bolstering smile. "I know you do, but I always feel better saying that aloud."

Miss Parker's lips quivered when she tried to smile back. Her tension stiffened every step. He understood too well. When he awoke in Novum Arce, he had been frantic with worry for Pris. He did not want to imagine how the abigail had felt, day after day, week after week, month after month when she had no idea if her betrothed was alive or not.

He heard her draw a quick breath when they reached the center building. Handing her the basket, he unlocked the door. If she was shocked at how he used his dagger instead of a key, she wisely said nothing.

"Miss Parker, after you, if you please . . ." He bowed and motioned toward the door.

With a half-sob, she gave him back the basket and rushed past him. "Asher!" she sobbed as she threw herself into the footman's arms.

The footman looked over her head with a steely glare. "I thought I told you not to bring her here," he growled as soon as Neville had shut the door. "You have put her in danger."

"No," said Miss Parker. "Mr. Williams did not put me in danger. We have been in danger from the moment we agreed to come north with the *magistra*—I mean, Miss Beamish."

"I know what she calls herself here." The footman's voice was still taut.

The abigail smiled as the coachee and young Davis stepped forward to greet her. "Thank heavens you are alive."

Neville handed the full basket to Davis who unpacked the food onto an extra blanket. The tiger picked up some strips of bacon and offered them to the other men before taking a bite out of the one he held. He grinned at the salty, greasy flavor Neville had enjoyed a few hours ago.

"We are alive," Harrison said, "because of Mr. Williams and Mrs. Kenton." The coachman raised the rasher of bacon in a salute to Neville. "I don't know how much longer we could have gone before we starved to death."

Miss Parker's eyes widened as she looked from her betrothed and his comrades to Neville. "How can that be?"

"They had become a liability," Neville said quietly.

"How?"

"Do you remember telling Cordelia," asked Neville, taking care not to trip over the name, "that when you and Bellona were taken from The Rose and Thistle Inn, one of your kidnappers mistakenly mentioned where you were being taken?"

"Yes."

Neville smiled coldly as Snow put his arm around Miss Parker's shoulders. "Because of that slip of the tongue, the men who had been sent to get you and Miss Beamish had no choice but to bring everyone else, too. However, that did not mean your kidnappers were going to give your companions *carte blanche* to wander freely in Novum Arce." He locked eyes with Snow. "You might be able to identify them to the constable or justice of the peace, though they wore kerchiefs over their faces."

"But I was not imprisoned." Roxanne blinked back tears.

"If I were a wagering man, which I am, I would put a small fortune on the fact that was because Miss Beamish wanted you to continue as her abigail."

"But that would mean . . ." Miss Parker's face became as gray as a misty morn.

"Miss Beamish was privy to what happened before it did," Snow finished. "It would explain why she was willing to spend the night at a simple inn when she insisted on the best every other night of our journey."

Everyone began speaking at once, louder and louder.

Neville silenced them with a sharp whistle. As the four servants turned to him, he said, "Nothing has been proved one way or the other about her complicity. To own the truth, what Miss Beamish did before you came here no longer matters. We have to flee and make sure we find the person at The Rose and Thistle Inn who betrayed us, so nobody else is brought here against his will."

The male servants shared a glance before the coachman asked, "Don't you know who their agent is at the inn?"

"It is not Mrs. White, the landlady. That much I know." *Otherwise*, he added-to himself, *they would know Pris and I are man and wife.*

Snow grimaced. "'Tis no one inside the inn. 'Tis the one who can best keep a close eye on who stays there and alerts his despicable allies."

"The stableboy," Neville said, barely able to believe the words as he spoke them.

"Aye," said Davis, his face twisting in a scowl. "If I had any suspicions that little weasel was involved, I would have anointed him with both fists in his lying mouth."

Neville sighed. "I would not have given him even a farthing for his time."

His tone was so droll the four servants burst into laughter.

"Williams, before you leave . . ." Snow held out his hand. "The key."

"We don't have one." He drew his dagger. "Other than this."

"You have been picking the lock each time you come here?" The footman stared at him in astonishment.

"Our only choice. We have no idea where the key is."

"I may," Roxanne said slowly. "The *magistra* has a box where she keeps her best jewelry. I saw several keys in there when I went to get a necklace for her a few nights ago." A cool smile eased across her lips. "I can borrow them one at a time to discover which one works on the lock here."

"Then you could bring us food," Davis piped up, the young man's voice cracking on the few words.

In quick order, Neville arranged with Roxanne for her to let him know when she had one of the keys. If they found the key for the lock, they would have it at ready for when they all could escape Novum Arce.

"But we will need to know when it is you unlocking the door instead of our jailers," Snow said. "Some sort of signal before you open the door, so we know we don't have to pretend to be debilitated as we were before you began bringing us food."

It made good sense, but something about the idea made Neville uneasy. He reminded himself nothing would change. Only he, Pris, and Miss Parker would have the signal. Still, he hesitated.

"If we have no choice but to flee," Harrison said, "we can be prepared to do that, too. We don't know what plans they have for us."

Neville nodded. He could not argue with that logic, especially when he would have asked for the same if their situations had been reversed. "The signal will be two quick knocks, a pause, two more quick knocks, a pause, and then a single knock. Simple, but unique enough so you will know it is one of us."

The servants repeated back the code. He could not miss the expectancy in their eyes, something he had not seen before. They would need every ounce of that hope when the time came to attempt an escape. Their greatest trial might yet still be in front of them.

"THANK YOU, Mr. Williams," Miss Parker said once he had locked the door behind them. "I don't think I truly believed they were alive until I could see and touch Asher. If I can get one of the keys out of the *magistra's* jewelry box, may I return with you again tomorrow?"

"I cannot promise." Neville took her arm to steer her through the narrow opening between the other buildings. "We must take care that nobody sees a pattern in when we come here, or they may try to investigate what we are doing."

As they stepped away from the granaries, Miss Parker chuckled. "No wonder you and Cordelia get along well. You both are willing to risk everything for what you believe in. She must be the bravest person I know to do what she did last night."

"And what was that?" he asked, though his stomach knotted.

The abigail stopped and faced him. "Didn't she tell you?"

"I have not seen her today. What did she do?"

It took every bit of Neville's self-control to keep his frustration contained as Miss Parker gave him a quick account of what she and Pris had been up to while he slept, oblivious, in the barracks. She finished with, "I am sure Cordelia told me that she planned to send you a note this morning to come to her office as soon as you could."

He frowned. "I never received any note."

"Well, no matter. Now you know she wants to talk to you."

Shoving the basket into her hands, he said, "And I want to talk to her. Good day, Miss Parker."

Neville crossed the compound in angry strides. What had Pris been thinking to go after Miss Beamish? Even if she was willing to chance her own life, what about their unborn child's? If she had been seen, it could have been tragic.

Then he reminded himself that Pris was not interested in being a hero. She would have weighed the risks last night as she had each time she made such a hazardous decision. But the idea of losing her and their child was a piercing pain so strong he almost looked down to see if someone had driven a knife into his chest.

Greetings were called as he passed other residents. He ignored them, not caring if they considered him rude. Stepping into Pris's office, he saw no one.

Where was she?

He heard sounds coming from the back room where she slept. He tore open the door.

Miss Redding sat propped against pillows on the bed, holding a cup of what smelled like freshly brewed tea.

"Where is she?" he asked without preamble. He did not care if the elderly woman thought him as insane as St. John.

"If you speak of Cordelia, she left a few minutes ago. A legionary brought her a message, and she told me that she would be back as soon as possible. It seemed she had a very important matter to deal with Do sit and have a cup of tea, Mr. Williams." Miss Redding gestured to another chair as if they had gathered in a grand drawing room.

"Did she say where she was going?" he asked the elderly woman.

"I think she said she was going to the dairy." She frowned. "But that is impossible."

"Why?" He shook his head. "Never mind. Tell me. Did she say where the dairy is?"

"No. But you should ask Miss Beamish. She is sure to know. She is such an intelligent young woman."

He did not voice the groan that started deep within his clenched gut. For a moment, he considered waiting until Pris returned rather than face Miss Beamish. But only for a moment. Every instinct warned him something was not right. There were other people who could help him. Until he discovered what Pris had witnessed when chasing the young woman, he should stay far away from Beamish's daughter.

"If Cordelia returns," he said, "tell her to wait here until I get back."

"I will," she hesitated, then said, "This is an odd place. Be careful, Mr. Williams."

"I shall." As he turned to leave, he knew it was a lie. He would hazard anything to protect his beloved wife and their child. Anything.

Chapter Seventeen

NEVILLE HAD NEVER imagined a mere twenty minutes could seem like forever. The servant who had let him into Miss Beamish's house had told him the *magistra* was occupied, but she would be with him in about twenty minutes. As he paced the open courtyard, his only thoughts were of where Pris might be. He had asked so many people about where the dairy was located. But no one knew, and a couple had said that he had been sent on a wild-goose chase because the dairy had not been built yet. If that was so, why had Pris been told to go there? Realizing he had no other choice, he had come to the grand house where Miss Beamish lived.

Each time he heard someone approach, he paused and waited. Each time the person kept on going as if he were invisible.

Then one stopped. He whirled as he heard, "What are you doing *here?*"

Miss Parker walked toward him. She lowered the stola off her dark hair and scanned the courtyard and the open hallways surrounding it. "Have you lost your mind? You could endanger everyone by coming here so soon after . . ." She swallowed hard, but continued in little more than a whisper, "She is asking questions about where I have been going, and I will not let you be the cause of Ash—of his death."

"Calm down," Neville said as softly. "I am here because I need the *magistra's* help."

She put her hands on his arms and gave him a gentle shove toward the street door. "Go! Nothing is worth what she will ask in return for any assistance she gives you."

"Cordelia is."

"Cordelia?" She pressed her hands to her abruptly colorless cheeks. "What has happened to her?"

"Nothing, I hope, but she has disappeared."

"How? When?"

He told her what he had learned and what he had not. "Nobody seems to know where the dairy is."

"Because as far as I know, it does not exist."

"That is what several people told me, but why would Cordelia be given a message to meet me there?"

Miss Parker moaned and grasped his arm as she swayed. He caught her before she could collapse to the mosaics. "She would not be the first to vanish from Novum Arce."

"Who else?"

"There are only rumors, but I believe at least some of them are true. I know of a woman who was going to become the Imperator's wife, but then one day she was gone. No one saw her leave, and the Imperator was almost inconsolable until . . ."

"Until what?"

"The *magistra* offered him comfort."

His mouth twisted. Was there any man in Novum Arce Miss Beamish had not taken as a lover? He was not going to be distracted by tales of Miss Beamish's conquests. Not when he needed to find Pris.

"Is there another building someone might mistake for a dairy?"

She started to shrug then paused. "If someone wanted to keep milk cold now, the only place would be the icehouse."

"Where is that?"

She began to give him directions, then grabbed his arm, pulling him out of the courtyard and into a nearby room. When he asked her what was wrong, she put her fingers to her lips and shook her head. She closed the door most of the way before pressing against the wall. She motioned for him to do the same, but he stood where he could see out the narrow slit between the door and the wall.

A shadow crossed the courtyard. Livius followed it into the open area. then stopped. Minutes passed. Neville motioned to Miss Parker to remain where she was. They could not leave the room without the legionary seeing them.

Then Miss Beamish appeared. She walked to the soldier and asked, "Is it done?"

A satisfied smile curved his lips. "All done."

"Perfect timing, I must say."

"That is what I aimed for, *domina mea.*"

Curiosity tempted Neville to follow them as they left the courtyard, but he drew Miss Parker forward to ask where the two were going. The abigail put her eye to the narrow opening. He heard another door close as Miss Parker stepped back.

"To the *magistra's* private chambers."

"Good." He opened the door wider. "I will let you know when I am sure that Cordelia is safe."

"Thank you." She grasped his arm again. "Be careful, Mr. Williams. You don't know who arranged for her to go there, but they may have known that you would follow. It could be a trap."

"I know." He added nothing more as he stepped out of the room and left the house.

Neville followed Miss Parker's directions, though he doubted Pris was still waiting there. He hoped she had left when she realized he was not there.

The icehouse was not hard to find. He yanked the door open and winced at the chill and dampness that clung to the interior brick walls. Walking in, he looked around the small space. Pris must have left already. He hoped the whole day would not be spent with him trailing behind her as she went from place to place.

As he turned to leave, something on the floor caught his eye. He went over and saw a strip of fabric sticking out of the door. He tugged on it, but it held fast. Why was soft wool caught in the icehouse door?

He started to lift the latch then halted when he saw a bar had been set into place. He understood the caution because some icehouses had deep wells within them. Shouldering the thick bar out of the way, he yanked the door open. The fabric fell to the ground, drawing his gaze with it to a crumpled form.

Pris!

She did not move. When he dropped to his knees and touched her icy cheek, he bent his ear toward her lips. He held his breath as he listened for hers. For too long, he heard nothing, and then a faint warmth brushed his cheek.

She was still alive!

But barely.

He pulled off his cloak and spread it on the floor, taking care not to step into the inner room. He would not give the beast who had shut her in there the opportunity to do the same to both of them. Wrapping her in the cloak, he lifted her into his arms. She was stiff and cold against his chest, her hair frozen into rigid lines that crackled with ice as he drew the cloak up over her head.

Someone had tried to kill his wife and their child. And he had to get her warmed up before that person succeeded.

PAIN GNAWED ON Priscilla's limbs. Bizarre sounds came from the darkness surrounding her. Moans. Her moans.

"Neville, where are you? Help me!" she tried to whisper but his name became another moan as agony shot up her right leg. "No," she tried to cry, but no sound emerged.

Broad fingers settled on her cheek. Warm fingers. Only when they touched her did she realize how terribly cold she was. Had someone left a window open? Didn't they know it was as cold as a January morn?

But it was spring.

Wasn't it?

She was unsure of anything except how much she hurt.

Everywhere.

"Wake up, Cordelia." Why was Neville talking to her aunt? "Show us you are alive, sweetheart." No, he would never address Aunt Cordelia as sweetheart.

Of course, I'm alive!

Neville repeated, "Wake up, Cordelia." His voice became more urgent.

Why had he not heard her answer? She had shouted it, hadn't she? Or had the words only sounded in her frozen brain? Why did he keep saying the same things over and over to her aunt? *She* needed his help.

Too many questions. No answers.

Just cold.

She craved heat. She was cold. Desperately cold. Then she found a bit of warmth. It was her vexation with Neville. Let it warm her up. She needed to be warm.

"Go ahead," came another voice. A man's voice. Though familiar, she could not put a face with the name.

"I cannot," Neville replied. "I have never struck a woman in my life. To hurt her more now is—"

"This is no time to act like a gentlemen! Bah!"

Fire burst across her cheek as someone slapped it. Hard.

Stop! she tried to cry out. All she heard was a dull croak.

She was hit again. She recoiled, turning her face away.

"Enough!" Neville snarled. "Do not strike her again!"

Fingertips tilted her face back toward his voice. She wanted to speak his name, but her lips refused to move.

"Open your eyes. For the love of God, open your eyes." She heard anguish in his request.

She tried. In shock, she discovered her lashes were held down with stones as big as the ones in the wall around Novum Arce. That was where she was! Sir Thomas's distorted utopia. No wonder Neville was using her aunt's name.

But why had stones been attached to her eyelashes?

Help me!

Sharp pain erupted along her leg again. "No!" she screamed. She tried to bat away the person hurting her, but her arms were as unresponsive as her eyes.

When her hair was brushed back gently, she was able to open her eyes at last. Light struck them, blinding her. A shadow moved between her and the glare. She tried to speak, but her lips quivered with the ice eating at her bones.

"Thank God! You're awake."

She wanted to ask Neville what was wrong with her, but she could not speak. No part of her worked as it should. Neville was there, so she had to be safe.

From what? What had happened to her?

Her thoughts were swallowed by a maw of pain. When she shrieked, she heard Neville ask, "Must you do that?"

"Her feet are nearly frozen," the man said. "If we don't massage feeling back into them, she will lose them."

Asher Snow, she realized. *Roxanne's beau.*

"But she is in such pain!"

The footman snapped, "Would you prefer her to suffer the agony of amputation? If we don't get real feeling back into her limbs, we may lose her."

She blinked, then looked up to Neville's face which was shadowed in what must be lantern light. He looked as if he were suffering as much as she was. She wanted to comfort him, but she could not speak. She tried, but excruciating waves smothered her again.

Neville cursed as Pris's face contorted with torment. He lightly stroked her face and discovered how cold it still felt. Yet her skin had lost the clammy feeling it had when he found her unconscious in the icehouse.

Snow straightened and pulled the covers over Pris's feet. "Warmth is returning to her toes, so she probably will not lose them. Her fingers are already regaining their color. She is a fortunate woman."

Like Pris's, the footman's face was bleached to the shade of the muslin sheets. Snow had been shocked when Neville had brought an unconscious Pris into the granary. The three men had jumped to follow orders, bringing what meager supplies they had and arranging the blankets on the floor.

"Thank you," Neville said to the footman then looked at the others. "Thanks, all of you. She is going to have to stay here until I can come up with a way to get us out of Novum Arce."

"She needs to be well enough to travel," Harrison the coachman said, rubbing his hands together anxiously. "That might take some time."

"Right now, as long as nobody discovers she is alive or that your prison has been found, we have enough time to let her heal. Gathering what we will need to escape will take some time, especially now that we don't have her to steal supplies from the storerooms."

While the men went to finish their interrupted meal, Neville sat by Pris's makeshift bed. Questions plagued him, boiling through his mind along with schemes to obtain his vengeance against the one who had left her to die in the icehouse.

"Who would do this to her?" asked Davis as the lad brought Neville a boiled egg and some bread.

"I intend to find out." He suspected Miss Beamish and her lapdog, Livius, had been involved. He could not forget the soldier's smile when he had told her the task she had given him was "all done."

"What about Miss Redding? Is she safe?"

"As long as she stays in the room behind the office." He would check with the old woman later, reminding her how important it was for her to remain unseen. He knew better than to accuse Beamish's daughter because Miss Redding continued to believe that Miss Beamish would have kept them safe if she had known they were in Novum Arce.

A groan came from the bed. He leaned forward to see Pris's eyes were half opened slits.

"Nev—?"

He halted her by saying, "Yes, it is I. Leonard Williams." He hoped Davis had not heard her breathless whisper. "I am right here."

"Good."

He smiled for the first time since he found her. "Yes, it is very good. You are safe now."

"Safe with you . . ."

As she faded into sleep again, he sighed. He sat on the stone floor and did not move while he waited for her to wake again. He stayed there when Miss Parker knocked their code on the door. She had brought their supper after not being able to locate Neville. When she had found the door unlocked, she had hurried inside and closed it again behind her.

The abigail was horrified to discover what had happened to her friend and offered to help however she could, even though the *magistra* seemed to be keeping a close eye on her. She left quickly, and the men turned down the lantern to leave them in deep shadow.

Not even when the first glow of dawn slid slender fingers around the door and across the floor did Neville surrender to sleep.

PRISCILLA WOKE slowly. Her whole body ached, except for the bottoms of her feet which itched. She tried to ignore the tingling, but it was impossible. As she shifted her leg, she moaned.

"Awake?"

She turned her head to see Neville stretching and yawning broadly. "What are you doing here?"

"Waiting for you to come back to life," he whispered. He glanced to his right, and she saw Asher, Harrison, and Davis asleep on the floor so she understood why he was keeping his voice low. "Why did you go there?"

"There? Where?" She struggled to sit. His arm around her waist helped. She bit her lip to silence her groan.

"Don't you remember? I found you in the icehouse."

"Oh, my!" Memory flooded her head, flinging her back into the terror of the moment she feared she would freeze to death. When his arms surrounded her, offering comfort, she turned her head into his shoulder and sobbed.

He held her until she regained control of herself. He did not chide her to be strong. He did not act embarrassed by the display of raw emotion. He held her, which was what she needed.

When her weeping eased, he whispered, "What happened? Why were you in the icehouse?"

"I came looking for you."

"Me?"

"I was told you were waiting there for me, and I could not wait to tell you what I witnessed on the fell when I chased after . . ." She looked at the others then wiped her wet eyes. "After her."

"That can wait. Tell me what happened in the icehouse."

She did, haltingly, as shivers raced up and down her spine. He tucked the blanket more tightly around her. then got another to cover her as she finished with, "When I went to leave, the door slammed, and

I could not get it open."

"Because it was barred."

Priscilla stared at him in disbelief. "You are jesting!"

"I would never jest over such a matter."

"But how? Why?"

"That is something I intend to find out while you stay here and get better."

"Here?"

His voice became bleaker. "Whoever did this thinks you are dead. It is better we let them think that than to have them try again and be successful next time."

Chapter Eighteen

IT TOOK ALMOST a week before Priscilla could walk without feeling as if a thousand heated needles stabbed her feet. She was grateful to her fellow prisoners in the granary for their help with massaging her feet and hands two or three times a day. They offered her what privacy they could and always gave her and Neville a chance to talk alone when he brought food. That was less often than Priscilla would have liked. Often when the knocked signal came on the door, Roxanne was on the other side. After finding the right key on her second try, the abigail visited as often as she dared. She shared news from outside, including that the search for Cordelia Kenton had been halted when no sign of the missing *actuarius* was found. Before the office had been searched, Roxanne had helped Miss Redding sneak into an unused room in Bellona's house where she could keep a close eye on her. It had been a daring move, but sometimes the best place to hide something or someone was right beneath everyone's nose.

Neville was able to come to the granary only every couple of days, and he could not linger long. The century's training schedule had been increased, though the longer hours did not seem to be making much difference to most of the soldiers who were pretty much ignored by their leaders.

She and Neville got enough time by themselves in one corner of the granary, so she could place his hand over her abdomen and let him feel the stirrings of their child. The glow of joy on his face filled her heart.

But only for a moment because both of them knew the time was growing short before the fuse was lit in Novum Arce. The French spies might already be among them, arranging for an invasion of England. Their joking words about Sir Thomas's plans to build a bridge across the Channel and give Napoleon's troops easy access to English shores did not seem so amusing now.

As Priscilla healed, being kept imprisoned became intolerable. She listened to the men discuss how they would offer their resignations to Lord Beamish, a topic they seemed to find endlessly fascinating. Perhaps because otherwise they would have to face another day of being locked in the granary with no idea when they would be free. Her admiration for them rose with the passing of each hour. They had been incarcerated in the dark for longer than she had, but they continued to believe they would escape and return to Lord Beamish's estate soon enough to tell the baron they no longer wished for a position there.

The signal sounded on the door, and Asher opened the lantern slightly to give Priscilla enough light to answer it without tripping on the uneven stones. Roxanne had already stopped by with their daily food, so it must be Neville! The pain in her feet vanished as her heart soared in anticipation of his touch, his kiss, his loving voice reminding her that soon they would be reunited away from Novum Arce.

Her breath burst out of her in a gasp when she saw who stood in the thick twilight beyond the door. A battered and bloody Roxanne, whose clothing was ripped, was held by men in legionary uniforms. There must have been more than twenty by the door. The only one she recognized was Livius, who regarded her with an arrogantly vicious grin.

Behind her, she heard the three men jump to their feet, but they wisely stayed where they were when Livius barked an order as he entered the granary. He yanked the key out of the lock, tossed it into the air, and caught it with a cruel laugh.

Priscilla wanted to back away, but she rushed forward to catch Roxanne when the abigail was shoved roughly into the granary. They both dropped to the floor.

"I am sorry," Roxanne said with a sob. "They said they would come and kill all of you if I did not own up to my part in feeding you." She pressed her face into Priscilla's hair and whispered, "They asked me no questions about *him,* so I think he is safe. For now."

A pulse of hope bounced through Priscilla but was muted when Livius seized her arm and jerked her to her feet.

"You are hard to kill. I thought you were dead when I left you in the icehouse, but somehow you escaped death." He laughed. "Not this time."

She did not retort, though he waited and waited. Finally, his patience ran out, and he snapped an order for them to be brought out of the granary. He gave the men cloaks like those his men wore. When they hesitated, he warned if they did not don them, he would have Priscilla and Roxanne slain right there.

Priscilla put her arm around Roxanne as they and the other servants were herded into the center of the legionaries. Livius's simple plan became clear. Nobody would be able to see them in the thickening darkness if the tall soldiers surrounded them. She guessed if someone chanced to catch sight of them, no one would admit it.

They were marched to the gate and through it without stopping. Priscilla needed Asher and Harrison's help to climb the fell. Her sandals caught in the small stones, and she would have fallen if the two men had not held onto her arms and gently guided her up the hillside.

She was not surprised when the soldiers marched them to the stone circle. It was empty when the soldiers pushed them inside, then lined up to contain them in a wall of flesh and stone. Not even Livius stepped within the circle, and she wondered if some superstitious fear halted them. The captives were handed a lantern and told to put it on the center stone.

As time passed and the moon rose to wash out the low light from the lantern, Priscilla and Roxanne sat on the damp grass in the center of the circle while Asher, Harrison, and Davis paced. Priscilla drew up her knees and wrapped her arms around her legs. The sensation of waiting for something or someone was palpable.

Water cascaded loudly from somewhere higher on the fell where the gorse could not gain hold on the raw stone. A lamb called for its mother. Faint noises rose from Novum Arce, none of them identifiable.

What did the men have planned? If they had planned to simply kill them, she and the others would be dead by now. She suspected the fake legionaries' scheme had something to do with the stone circle. She pressed her fingers to her lips to silence her moan of despair as she looked at the center stone. The ancient Celts were said to have sacrificed humans to their gods. Did Mithras, the god the legionaries revered, demand human blood as well? She had no idea. Even if he had not when Rome ruled Britannia, the twisted ways of Novum Arce may have altered Mithras into a god who expected such slaughter.

Her hand settled over her abdomen. Somehow, she had to find a way to protect her darling child. Looking down the fell toward the faint lights of Novum Arce, she wondered where Neville was. How could she call to him for help? If she shouted, she would be beaten and perhaps murdered immediately. Hoping he could sense her heart reaching out to him, she prayed that he would soon reach her and rescue them.

Roxanne shifted uneasily beside her. The blood had dried on her face and hands.

"How are you?" asked Priscilla in little more than a whisper.

"If we survive this, I will heal. No bones are broken."

"What happened? Were you seen entering or leaving the granary?"

"No. We were betrayed by someone I should have been able to trust."

"Who?"

"Miss Redding."

"She betrayed you?" Shock riveted Priscilla.

The old woman had seemed grateful for the care Priscilla made sure she had in the bedroom at the back of the office. She had thanked Priscilla over and over and had expressed her happiness that she had been freed from the granary. Miss Redding had been the last person Priscilla would have guessed would try to hurt those who had helped her.

Roxanne sighed. "Not intentionally. She believes the miss is trying to help us." She glanced around, but none of the soldiers seemed to care about their whispering. "She saw the miss and hurried to assure her that she and the others were well, thanks to the miss . . . and to me. The whole house of cards came tumbling down."

Words failed Priscilla. Why hadn't one of them taken the time to persuade Miss Redding she was mistaken in her loyalties? It never seemed the right time to reveal that Bellona had left her and the three men to starve to death. Asher and the others came to sit beside them, but no one spoke. There was nothing left to say as they awaited whatever the fates had planned for them. When the footman put his arm around Roxanne's shoulders and she leaned her head on his shoulder, tears rose in Priscilla's eyes. Would Neville ever hold her again?

A low murmur rushed around the circle. Their guards craned their necks to peer through the darkness.

Something was about to happen.

Priscilla got to her feet, as did the others. Without speaking, they moved to stand back-to-back, so at least one of them would be facing whoever was coming.

Bellona pushed past a legionary to step into the circle. As the soldiers bowed toward her, Neville's story about what he had watched in the cave beneath the Temple of Mithras and Priscilla's own experience when she had followed Bellona up the fell confirmed the young woman had taken complete control of Novum Arce.

She walked directly to Priscilla. Gasps erupted from all around when she reached under her stola and pulled out small pistol. She pointed it at Priscilla's heart as she demanded, "Where is he?"

"He? Who?" Her stalling sounded silly, especially when she stared at the gun. Beside her, Roxanne began to cry. "Novum Arce is filled with men."

"Is acting want-witted the final game you wish to play, Lady Priscilla?"

"No." Priscilla heard Roxanne choke and wanted to apologize for not telling her the truth sooner. She wondered how long Bellona had known the truth and why she had chosen to reveal it now. She did not ask. She must let Bellona control the conversation until Priscilla could gauge exactly what Bellona wanted from her. There must be something, or she would have ordered Priscilla killed as soon as Livius and his troops opened the granary door. "As we are tossing aside fake names, should I address you as Bella Beamish now?"

"Names are not important." Her tone was cool, but Priscilla sensed her curiosity was real. "Why did you come here?"

"We were abducted and brought here, if you recall."

"No! I mean why did you come to The Rose and Thistle Inn?"

Knowing that she must continue the charade Neville had begun while talking to Lord Beamish in Stonehall-on-Sea, she replied, "As ironic as it may sound now, we were looking for *you*. Your father is heart-sick over your disappearance, and he asked us to find you."

Bella's explosion of derisive laughter rang along the hill. "That old fool! I never expected he would believe that silly note I left behind in the carriage. Though I have no idea why he would care. He never wanted me when I was younger. Now he considers me a pawn to cement his position with the government. How many times did he tell me if I did not marry as he wished, I would never marry? Well, he no longer controls me, and I can do what *I* want to do." Her eyes narrowed. "Which leads me back to my original question: Where is Lord Hathaway?"

Priscilla steeled herself so she would not flinch and reveal she had continued to hope Bella had failed to recognize Neville. "I doubt you will believe me when I say I don't know where Neville is, but it is the truth."

"He would not have left without you. He is, I understand, your husband." Her eyes glittered in the faint light. "I must say, Lady Priscilla, you are a lucky woman." She glanced down at the gun she held. "Or at least, you have been until now. For it seems you have pushed your luck one too many times."

She had to say something, anything to keep Bella from firing the gun. "Why are you curious where Neville is?"

"I need him."

"For . . . ?"

Bella laughed tersely. "No need to be a shrewish wife, Lady Priscilla. I have no interest in your husband as a paramour, though it was amusing to watch him squirm when I pretended I did. Rather, I need his lack of scruples and quick mind as I plan the last details of my army's offense."

"You are going to go to war with spears and shields?" She hooked a thumb toward where Livius was listening. He scowled when she continued. "They can barely keep from falling over their own feet."

"And I thought you were supposed to be smart. You are as foolish as everyone else. Those stupes down in Novum Arce are not *my* army. They belong to Sir Thomas, who wants to remake the world into his beloved Pax Romana. These men here are a part of the skilled army waiting for me to give the command."

"To do what?"

"Get vengeance."

"With the help of the French?" She laughed as coldly as Bella had. "Others have attempted to betray England to Napoleon and failed. I know because Neville and I stopped some of them. You will be stopped, too. The British people will not assist anyone trying to hand over our country to our enemy."

"French?" A slow smile spread across Bella's face. "So it *was* you who followed me the night I last met M. LeChat. I suspected as much, which is why I tried to get you out of the way."

"By leaving me to freeze to death in the icehouse?"

She shrugged. "If Livius had done his job right, your death would have been swift at the bottom of the well. In the meantime, I had Lord Hathaway watched. I should have had my own household under better surveillance." She frowned at Roxanne who now stood within the shelter of her betrothed's arms.

"Who is M. LeChat? That cannot be his real name."

"He has another name, of course." She glanced around the stone circle. "He has helped with arranging for the proper people to be brought to Novum Arce to fulfill my aims."

"When you spoke of people being chosen, *you* were the one doing the choosing."

"Or my agents who knew my preferences. Strong men with few morals are my first choice. You would not have been brought here, Lady Priscilla, if you had not intruded when my agents went to collect your husband."

"If you think Neville would ever help you hand England over to Napoleon—"

"You think you know everything!" Bella shrieked, startling everyone, her servants and soldiers alike. "You know nothing. I have no interest in assisting Napoleon's foolish dreams of ruling the world. He is as misguided as Sir Thomas and the Hanovers, who have crushed any attempts to dislodge them from another man's rightful place on the British throne. Like three successive Kings George and one foolish Regent, Napoleon will be defeated one day. All tyrants are eventually overthrown while the true kings will regain their thrones."

Priscilla struggled to understand the young woman's ranting. True kings? Her eyes widened in incredulity. No, Bella could not be planning such an absurd scheme. Then, Priscilla recalled how both Lord Beamish and Bella had spoken of her mother's Scottish relatives who lived north of the border. As far north as Culloden where English regiments crushed the Jacobite uprising?

Not quite believing her own words, Priscilla asked, "Are you talking about when Charles Stuart, the Young Pretender, tried to oust King George II?"

"We prefer to call him Bonnie Prince Charlie, because he was such a fair-faced man."

"Perhaps so, but he was also a fool. At Culloden, he refused to listen to his generals who had guided him to other victories. He abandoned the Highlands to save his own skin. What kind of leader is that?"

Bella sniffed, sounding for a moment like Aunt Cordelia when presented with an opinion she thought unworthy of discussion. "That is what the Hanoverians would have you believe. *They* were the ones who butchered families and tore them from the soil where their ancestors had lived for generations." She flung out one hand as she kept the gun aimed at Priscilla. "Now the army I have raised and have had trained at Novum Arce will finish what those brave men could not."

"What is this?" asked a tall man as he pushed past the legionaries to enter the circle.

Priscilla's half-formed hope that Neville had found them vanished at the man's French accent. M. LeChat! She heard Asher curse vividly, and Davis and Harrison fired hateful glares at the Frenchman.

M. LeChat strode to Bella and repeated his question.

She gave him a seductive smile. "Some unfinished business you need not bother yourself with."

"I need to bother myself with anything that could subvert my—our plans."

"*My* plans," Bella said coldly. "You work for me, M. LeChat. Don't forget that."

Did Bella really believe that? Priscilla saw the Frenchman's amusement. A game within a game. That was what he was playing, manipulating Bella and letting her think he wanted to help her while he served his true masters in Paris.

"I don't have time to waste. If you intend to shoot her," M. LeChat said, casting an indifferent glance toward Priscilla, "then do so."

"I think not." The deep voice came out of the darkness.

"Neville!" Priscilla screamed.

Bella looked around wildly, and Priscilla leaped forward to drive her fist down on the young woman's wrist. Bella screeched in pain, and the gun dropped to the ground. Asher scooped it up, driving its butt into the side of M. LeChat's head. The Frenchmen fell, face first into the center stone. He slid to the ground, unmoving. At the same time, Asher pushed Roxanne between him and the other two servants.

"Kill them!" Bella yelled.

"Obey that order at the cost of your own lives," Neville said as he stepped into the circle. "Put down your weapons now. *All* your weapons. You will not get another warning."

"Who are you to give orders to *my* men?" Bella demanded.

"The same person who gives orders to my men," he replied calmly when the grass rustled behind the legionaries guarding the stone circle.

Two or three men surrounded each of Bella's soldiers, and light glistened on bare steel as guns were held to their heads. Some of the newcomers were dressed as legionaries as well, but others wore ordinary clothing. Priscilla smiled when she saw Duncan pointing a pistol at Livius's head. He must have brought the other men with him to Novum Arce. He was grinning like Isaac when her son did something naughty that turned out to be the right thing in the end.

"I gave you an order," Neville said, his gaze sweeping the circle. "And I told you that I would not repeat it."

Bella's legionaries carefully placed their weapons, both modern and Roman, at their feet. Bella started to scream out an order, but halted when another man stepped into the light from the lantern.

"How could you do this to *me?*" demanded Lord Beamish as he strode to his daughter. "I thought I taught you better than this." He slapped her across the face.

Priscilla was not the only one who gasped out in shock at the baron's brutal treatment of his daughter.

Bella ignored all of them, save her father. She raised her chin and eyed him as if he were beneath her contempt. "What you taught me? All you ever taught me was to grab power where I could. To wield it without mercy. To think only of what I want and never care about anyone else, even someone as close to me as my own child."

"You have a child? How will you ever make a good marriage now?"

She stamped her foot. "See? All you ever think of are your own goals. I don't have a child. I would not be so careless as to get pregnant." She ignored her father's shock at her unladylike language. "I meant that *you* care nothing for me other than as a tool to get what you wanted. What else was I supposed to learn from your antics, *Father*?" She made the name sound like a curse. Turning to Neville, she added, "Demanding hush-money from his fellow lords must be a crime, isn't it? You are a peer. Bring charges against him in the House of Lords."

Lord Beamish began shouting at his daughter, and Bella screeched at him until their words were lost in the mixture.

Neville paid them no mind as he turned to give orders to his men who had gathered the fake legionaries together. "Tie their hands so you can herd them back to Novum Arce like the beasts they are." He grabbed two handfuls of Livius's tunic and stared into the man's eyes, saying in a deceptively even voice, "You have a single choice if you don't want to be tried for the attempted murder of my wife."

Livius swallowed so loudly that it could be heard over the shouts from the center of the stone circle. "What must I do?"

"Something you probably have never done in your whole life. You must be honest about Bella Beamish's plans. If I learn you have wavered from the truth even an iota when you are questioned, I will swear out a warrant for your arrest for trying to kill Lady Priscilla." He shook the man who seemed to shrink in front of him. "Have I made myself clear?"

"Yes . . . yes, my lord." He hung his head, thoroughly defeated.

In shock, Asher asked, "Are you just going to hand them over to the justice of the peace after what they have done to us?" He held up Bella's gun. "Step aside, and I will give him the death he would have gladly given us."

Priscilla stepped forward and put her hand on his arm. "They will not go unpunished, but shooting him would make us no better than they are."

"Listen to her," Roxanne begged. "Asher, you are not a murderer.

Don't let these people make you one."

The gun trembled in his hand, and Priscilla saw the uncertainty in his eyes as he lowered it. "But they—"

"Have lost," Priscilla said. She looked at the two Beamishes who were still quarreling at the top of their lungs. "Miss Beamish has abandoned her allies the same way Bonnie Prince Charlie left his." She glanced at the unconscious man in the middle of the stone circle. "However, I believe it will be discovered that M. LeChat used her to obtain information that he has probably sent back to his superiors in France."

"I will take care of him," said a redheaded man she had seen in Novum Arce. "I will make sure he is taken to London where he can be tried as a spy."

"Thank you, Jack." Neville smiled as he turned from watching the men who had been derided as incompetent by Miss Beamish's men finish tying the fake legionaries together. "It would seem at least one Bow Street Runner was willing to take on the task of finding Miss Beamish, even though Beamish has yet to acknowledge him. I noticed him ignoring you."

"No loss," said the red-haired man with a chuckle.

"I hope you were not planning on being paid."

"I will let my superiors worry about that." He laughed again. "Or should I say ours? I suspect we ultimately work for the same man."

"Quite possible." Even now, Neville was clearly loath to name the person who had sent him north. "Jack Fuller, this is my wife, Lady Priscilla Hathaway. Although I'm sure you have already figured it out."

He put his fingers up to his forehead as if he were about to tip a cap to her. "My lady."

"Mr. Fuller is a Bow Street Runner?" She looked from Neville to the other man in shock. "Why didn't you tell me that there was a Bow Street Runner in Novum Arce?"

"I didn't know until he told me a few hours ago," Neville admitted with a laugh. "He concealed himself well by pretending to be inept with a spear and shield."

"No pretending was necessary," Mr. Fuller grumbled. He motioned, and four men came forward to help him bind the unconscious Frenchman.

Priscilla turned to the Beamish servants. Young Davis's eyes were nearly popping from his skull, and Harrison was helping Mr. Fuller truss up M. LeChat. But Asher still scowled.

"We are alive," Priscilla said. "The yearning for vengeance is what started this in the first place. Let's be satisfied we are alive."

"Listen to her, Asher." Roxanne gently held onto his arm. "The Hathaways have done everything to save us when they could have fled from Novum Arce instead."

The footman sighed. "But they lied to us."

"For their safety and ours."

"True." He held the gun out to Neville, who took it. "I *am* grateful for what you have done."

Roxanne framed his face with her scraped fingers and whispered, "Of course we are. I hope we would have been brave enough to do for them what they did for us. Miss Beamish was right about one thing. Names no longer matter."

He nodded then offered his hand to Neville. "I am sorry, my lord."

"You have nothing to be sorry for." Neville shook Asher's hand then took Priscilla's. "There is one more thing we need to do before we leave."

"Deal with Lord Beamish and his daughter?" she asked.

"Duncan has volunteered to arrange for them to be held until the proper authorities can be alerted."

"He *is* a good friend."

Neville chuckled. "I will owe him big time after this." He looked at where Duncan, with the help of three more of the men he had brought with him, was trying to herd the baron and Miss Beamish down the hill. "They will be someone else's problem now. Our problem is below." He looked down at the settlement. "We must make sure what happened here can never happen again."

SIR THOMAS SAT on his throne beneath the twin banners with the imperial eagle and the bull of the VI Legion, but no one else was in the great hall of the *principia*. Stars glittered through the windows, but the only light within came from the few sconces lit on the walls and a pair of torches flanking the throne.

He stared off into the distance, ignoring Priscilla and Neville as they walked along its impressive length. Roxanne was on her way to collect Miss Redding. The rest of the men who had come to their rescue, including Duncan, were overseeing their prisoners. Livius and his men were being shut up in the granary while Lord Beamish and his daughter would be kept under guard at her expansive house.

Novum Arce had appeared deserted when they returned. Priscilla guessed some of the residents were hiding, waiting to see what happened, but when she and Neville had come down the fell, she had seen a long line of people escaping while they had the chance. No one remained in Sir Thomas's house, so she and Neville had come to the *principia*, expecting to see his most loyal retainers gathered here.

But Sir Thomas was alone.

The room had never seemed so long. Priscilla was exhausted and she had to push herself to take each step. Neville must have noticed because he offered his arm. Grateful, she put her hand on it, letting him guide her down the length of the hall. She stumbled when the ripped toe of her sandal caught on a slightly raised mosaic tile, and his hand held hers tightly against his arm.

As they neared, Sir Thomas did not turn his head. "There are no audiences tonight. You may schedule one with my secretary on the morrow."

"Impossible," Priscilla said quietly.

"Then come to my secretary's office the next day or whenever you wish to make an appointment."

"Impossible," she repeated. "Your secretary has left Novum Arce."

That got Sir Thomas's attention. He shifted on his throne to face them. Did he really believe the cold stare he had perfected in his role as the Imperator would intimidate them now?

"Lying is a sign of a weak mind," Sir Thomas said as if speaking to an insolent child.

"Quite to the contrary." Neville put one foot on the lowest step to the dais. A smile played along his lips. "I have found the act of creating and telling a lie with enough sincerity for it to be believed requires a quick, supple mind."

"Neville," she cautioned. Sir Thomas could not see the truth that his utopia was crumbling around him, destroyed by Bella Beamish who had pulled out its brittle underpinnings.

Sir Thomas frowned. "Neville? I thought your name was Leonard."

"No, my name is Neville Hathaway."

"Hathaway?" He squinted at Neville as if trying to see him more clearly. "The actor?"

"I was many years ago. I am honored you remember."

"Do not flatter yourself. I don't remember you because you were a skilled thespian. Rather, you were in a performance I saw the night I met my beloved late wife. Everything about that night remains clear in my mind." Sir Thomas dismissed him with an indifferent wave of his hand.

"Whether your name is Leonard Williams or Neville Hathaway, it does not matter to me. I asked you once to begone and return on the morrow if your need to speak to me is urgent and genuine. Why won't you heed your Imperator?"

"Because the play is finished, the audience is departing, and the actors have left the stage save for you." Neville climbed the steps to stand by Sir Thomas who slowly came to his feet. "It is over."

"Guards!" Sir Thomas shouted. "Guards!"

Priscilla walked up and stopped on Sir Thomas's other side. Gently, she said, "They will not come. Your soldiers have either sworn off their vow to serve you or are imprisoned because they were foolish enough to obey Miss Beamish's orders."

"What? Why?" He looked from her to Neville, clearly baffled. "Why would my legionaries follow Bellona?"

"Because they are not *your* legionaries," she answered before Neville could. Trying to keep her voice calm and kind, she went on, "Maybe they were at one time, but you could not offer them the rewards Miss Beamish could. Here, they had no true enemy but ennui. With her, they believed they might have the power to topple a king."

"And some," Neville added, "were never your legionaries at all. They were volunteers to the Scottish cause Miss Beamish holds dear. She helped them sneak in here so they could use your training field for their practices and your storerooms to keep their weapons hidden."

"That is nonsense."

"Sadly, it is not. It is the truth." Priscilla felt sorry for the man who had never imagined his utopia would be perverted in such a way.

"She was using you." Neville's voice became less stern. "While you dreamed of recreating Pax Romana, she was plotting to overthrow our king and put a descendant of Bonnie Prince Charlie on the English and Scottish thrones."

"I do not believe it. Bellona is completely dedicated to Novum Arce."

"She is only completely dedicated to herself and her cause, which was doomed before it began." Neville stepped down from beside the throne and assisted Priscilla to the floor before he said, "I know you hoped for something perfect here, but Novum Arce is done. A lot of its people are gone, spreading the word of what really has been happening here, from the kidnappings to the coercion to marry."

"They would not dare!" cried the furious man. "No one will believe their lies. And your lies!"

"They believed yours," Priscilla said quietly. "Good-bye, Sir Thomas."

Neither she nor Neville looked back as Sir Thomas raged. They had gone only a few steps when someone came through the main door.

"Aunt Tetty, what are you doing here?" Priscilla cried, not wanting the old woman to take the brunt of Sir Thomas's anger. "It is—"

"Fine, my dear." Aunt Tetty patted Priscilla's shoulder, then marched past them at a speed that belied her age. She halted in front of where Sir Thomas was still cursing them in the foulest language Priscilla had ever heard, even when she had been in the lowest sections of the London slums.

"Enough, Thomas!" scolded the old woman. "I will not have you speak so in the presence of a lady."

Priscilla gasped when Sir Thomas paused in the middle of a word. She expected him to snarl something at Aunt Tetty, but he subsided, sitting on the throne again and bowing his head in what looked like shame.

Neville frowned. "Who are you, Aunt Tetty? Really?"

"I have worked in the St. John household since I was a child. First, in the stillroom and later as a nursery maid and finally as the governess." She looked at Sir Thomas who had not moved, save for tears that dripped on his knees. "Though I am sorry to say so now, Novum Arce was my idea."

"Yours?" asked Priscilla at the same time Neville did.

"I thought it would be a good way for him to stop squandering his money gambling." She flung out her hands. "Rather than fill up the pockets of cheating gamesters, he could build something beautiful. And it was beautiful when it began. People who struggled to feed their families had work and warm, dry homes. With Thomas's funds, we never had to worry about deprivation."

"The wall—"

"Was intended to keep out thieves. It was never meant to keep people in. At the beginning, we could come and go as we pleased. It was Thomas's vision that people would be part of Novum Arce because they wanted to be. But that changed after Miss Beamish stayed here several days then left. It was many months before she returned. I had not thought to see her again because I could not imagine a young woman like her living here."

"You knew Miss Beamish *before* she was brought here?" Priscilla asked.

"I did because she visited Thomas's estate. Knowing Lord Beamish as he did, Thomas believed Miss Beamish was neglected and unhappy. He wanted to give her everything, and he played along when she set up what was supposed to look like an abduction."

"She arranged that as well?" Neville gave a terse laugh. "She was a busy girl."

"Quite so. Somehow, she convinced Thomas to kidnap others for the community, selecting women whom she thought would be compliant and men who would . . ." A faint pink rose up the old woman's face. "Men she would find attractive."

"We know the stable boy at The Rose and Thistle was one of her agents."

"Among others. I doubt we will ever guess how far her web reached, but it was her cruel disregard for her servants that convinced me that her plans had nothing to do with Thomas's. I am sorry you were caught up in her game, Cordelia."

"Actually my name is Priscilla Hathaway, and this is my husband Neville. We—"

She was cut off when Sir Thomas shouted, "Now I understand. You helped them destroy Novum Arce!" He leaped off the throne dais and toward Aunt Tetty. His hands were outstretched like talons to close around her throat.

Priscilla pulled the old woman away as Neville stepped forward and drove a single fist into Sir Thomas's chin. The man halted and stared at them in disbelief. Folding, he collapsed to the floor where he groaned once and was silent.

"Go," Aunt Tetty urged.

"Only if you come with us," Neville said, shaking his reddened knuckles.

"I should stay and help—"

"Come with us," Priscilla said gently. "If you stay here, he will kill you." She put her hand on her abdomen. "In addition, Lord Hathaway and I will soon find ourselves in need of the services of a good nursery maid and governess."

Aunt Tetty stared at her for a moment then nodded heartily as a smile spread across her face.

Neville offered his arms to both the old woman and Priscilla. Together, they walked out of the *principia* and Novum Arce. None of them looked back.

Epilogue

GAZING AROUND the table in the dining room at Tarn's Edge, Priscilla listened as Duncan related—*again*—the efforts he had expended to find out where she and Neville had been taken after they disappeared from the inn. The children and Burke listened as intently as if they had not heard the story twice already. Aunt Cordelia acted bored, but her aunt was thrilled to hear how brave her husband had been.

Priscilla wondered if Duncan had any idea that Neville intended to speak to the highly placed person who had sent him to Novum Arce. She had no doubt that there would soon be a change in Duncan's status. A very nice change that would please him and her aunt. But nothing could be said until everything was officially announced. She hoped it would be soon.

"May I, my lady?" A white-gloved hand hovered near her plate.

"Thank you, Snow," Priscilla said with a smile for the former footman who also, at least temporarily, served as the butler at Tarn's Edge.

As Aunt Tetty had, Lord Beamish's servants eagerly accepted Neville's offer of employment at the rundown estate. Harrison had gone south to return Lord Beamish's carriage and was expected back any day. The Oldfields were happily planning to move into the first cottage to be rebuilt on the estate, and Mr. Oldfield looked forward to taking up the job his forebearers had held: the estate's gamekeeper. While Mrs. Oldfield still cooked, she was training her daughter to be her successor. Roxanne had been named as housekeeper. Young Davis was already proving his worth by keeping both a dirt-covered Beowulf and an equally filthy Isaac out of the house until they both were clean.

It was not as happy an ending for Lord Beamish and his daughter. The truth of his attempts to obtain power in Whitehall and hers to steal King George's throne and hand it over to a pretender had made them both pariahs. No door opened to them, and even their names were no longer spoken aloud among the *ton*. There were whispers, however, that Beamish's estate might be forfeited to the throne if charges of treason were brought. It would be a small price to pay to avoid the gallows, but Priscilla guessed they would be allowed to live out their lives in the house which had become their prison where the only company they had was each other. Most of their allies had been swiftly sentenced and were on a ship bound for the distant penal colony in the far southern Pacific.

Neville had been correct when he said that what happened at Novum Arce could not be allowed to happen again. With the conspirators scattered across the planet and Sir Thomas abandoning his dream and returning to his gambling now that he did not have Aunt Tetty to keep him from wasting what was left of his family's fortune, it would not.

As soon as the dishes were cleared from the meat course, Daphne said, "We have an announcement to make." She put her hand on Burke's. "Do you want to tell them?"

"No, you tell them. I told my mother."

Neville arched a brow at Priscilla, and she covered a laugh with a cough.

"Burke and I have decided where we will hold our wedding ceremony," her older daughter said. "It will be here at Tarn's Edge."

As her sister and brother cheered, Neville muttered, "We don't have much time to build a chapel."

"Burke," Priscilla said, paying her husband no mind because he would go to any lengths to get the chapel rebuilt for Daphne's wedding, "is your mother agreeable with this decision?"

"It seems she has friends in Lakeland she wants to visit. However, I believe the truth is that Lord Candless keeps his pack of foxhounds near here, and my mother loves to ride to the hunt. She hopes to combine the wedding with a little sport."

"It is settled." Daphne smiled. "We could not wait to tell you."

As the conversation began around the table again, Priscilla said, "I have an announcement as well. Or I should say Neville and I have an announcement. In addition to welcoming Burke and Beowulf into our family, we will be welcoming one more."

Aunt Cordelia scowled. "Sweet heavens, Priscilla, what other stray pup have you brought home now?" Her eyes narrowed as she looked at Neville. "You don't need any other curs cluttering up your home."

"That is no way," chided Neville, "to speak of your next great-niece or nephew."

"You are having a baby?" cried Leah.

"A baby?" Isaac jumped to his feet in excitement. "Whose baby are you bringing home?"

"Don't be silly, Isaac." Daphne tugged him back down into his seat. "She means she is having a baby. She and Neville."

Leah giggled. "He will really be Papa Neville now."

Neville rolled his eyes, and the children laughed more loudly.

"Children!" Aunt Cordelia's voice snapped like a buggy whip across the table, leaving silence in its wake. "Enough of this vulgar talk. Priscilla, such topics are not for the table."

"Yes, Aunt Cordelia," Priscilla replied dutifully. Again, she glanced around the room where the people she loved most had gathered.

And she understood why Sir Thomas had been wrong from the very beginning. Building a new world was not the way to create a utopia. Living in perfection was savoring the love and joy one found among family and friends.

The End

About the Author

Jo Ann Ferguson has been creating characters and stories for as long as she can remember. She sold her first book in 1987. Since then, she has sold over 100 titles and has become a bestselling and award-winning author. She writes romance, mystery, and paranormal under a variety of pen names. Her books have been translated into nearly a dozen languages and are sold on every continent except Antarctica. You can reach her at her website: joannferguson.com or by email:

jo@joannferguson.com